Readers love
Murder and Mayhem
by RHYS FORD

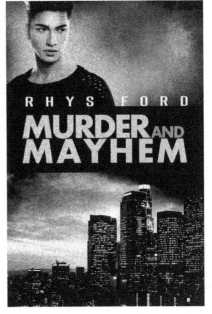

"Once again Rhys Ford takes readers on a wild, adrenaline filled ride in her newest romantic suspense offering, Murder and Mayhem."
—Fiction Vixen

"I am definitely looking forward to more in this series. Ex-thief and righteous cop make a fantastic detective duo."
—Reading Reality

"With such imagery and twisted plot threads, I couldn't walk away from this book. I wanted to solve the mystery, but I didn't want it to end, either."
—GGR Reviews

"There is no question that Rhys Ford goes full throttle with the first in a brand new series called *Murder and Mayhem*."
—Under the Covers Book Blog

By Rhys Ford

Clockwork Tangerine
With Poppy Dennison: Creature Feature 2
Dim Sum Asylum
Grand Adventures (Dreamspinner Anthology)
There's This Guy

COLE MCGINNIS MYSTERIES
Dirty Kiss
Dirty Secret
Dirty Laundry
Dirty Deeds
Down and Dirty
Dirty Heart
Dirty Bites

HALF MOON BAY
Fish Stick Fridays
Hanging the Stars

HELLSINGER
Fish and Ghosts
Duck Duck Ghost

MURDER AND MAYHEM
Murder and Mayhem
Tramps and Thieves

SINNERS SERIES
Sinner's Gin
Whiskey and Wry
The Devil's Brew
Tequila Mockingbird
Sloe Ride
Absinthe of Malice

Published by DREAMSPINNER PRESS
www.dreamspinnerpress.com

RHYS FORD

TRAMPS AND THIEVES

DREAMSPINNER
PRESS

Published by
<head /><small>DREAMSPINNER PRESS</small>

5032 Capital Circle SW, Suite 2, PMB# 279, Tallahassee, FL 32305-7886 USA
www.dreamspinnerpress.com

Tramps and Thieves
© 2017 Rhys Ford.

Cover Art
© 2017 Reece Notley.
reece@vitaenoir.com
Cover content is for illustrative purposes only and any person depicted on the cover is a model.

ISBN: 978-1-64080-037-3
Digital ISBN: 978-1-64080-038-0
Library of Congress Control Number: 2017910304
Published September 2017
v. 1.0

Printed in the United States of America

This paper meets the requirements of
ANSI/NISO Z39.48-1992 (Permanence of Paper).

This book is dedicated to Sadonna Swann, who foolishly placed her trust in me by letting me turn her into a character for this novel. Oh, you silly thing. Hope you can walk in those heels.

Also, a shout-out to the San Diego Crewe, who has to put up with me grousing about how to find new ways to kill people.

Acknowledgments

MUCH LOVE to the Five, the sisters of my soul: Lea, Penn, Tamm, and Jenn. Also to my other sisters who help me maintain my sanity, Ren, Mary, Lisa, and of course the precious Ree.

A huge heartfelt thank-you to Elizabeth, Lynn, Grace, Naomi, lyric, and everyone at Dreamspinner Press for all of their hard work and faith. I don't have a page large enough to name everyone, but please know, I am so very grateful to all of you.

Lastly, a major huzzah to everyone who has let me drag them around Los Angeles while I suck up the feeling of its streets, neighborhoods, and everything else.

One

ROOK WORKED his fingers out, reveling in the stretch of fabric across the backs of his hands. His nerves tingled beneath his gloves, palms itching in anticipation. It'd been too long since his last job. Hell, years since he'd coaxed a lock open or tumbled a safe, and his teeth ached from the excitement.

After sex—and Rook could make a good argument that sex still ranked second—stealing was the closest thing to reaching nirvana as someone could get. Or at least it had been before Detective Dante Montoya entered his life.

There could be no thoughts of the sexy, handsome Mexican-Cuban detective. Dante Montoya was a distraction on the best of days but deadly when trying to negotiate through a job. The last two months of Rook's life were more an emotional roller coaster than steady climb. His world teetering just out of control with Dante's uncle coming to work with him, his shop, Potter's Field, reopening after being shot up by the cops, and the sudden, but not unwelcome presence of one sloe-eyed, smoked-honey-voiced cop in his bed was enough to make any man crazy, but toss in the devastating gutting of his diamond-stash nest egg, and Rook was about ready to pull his hair out from the stress.

Besides, he had a job to do.

He missed the jobs. Missed the rifling through other people's things and picking out what he wanted. It was the ultimate hunt, a slithering into the dark spaces behind people's lives and digging his hands into the things they wanted to keep secret.

There'd always been something sexual about piercing someone's security, then seducing a house or business to lay itself open for him, ripe and plump for the taking. Walls needed coaxing, a bit of flirtation and slyness before they whispered their acquiescence.

The house he was in needed no such seducing. Not really. He'd taken four weeks to prepare for the job, training hard to regain the flexibility he'd let go after his retirement. The overstretched limberness needed to slide into tight spaces wasn't something he'd planned on worrying about when he plotted out his new life.

1

A twinge along his right thigh was a quick reminder of how far he'd let himself go. His muscle mass and core strength hadn't changed, he'd seen to that, but his flexibility had gone to shit. Four weeks of careful stretches and insane yoga classes got him close to where he'd been before he'd thrown it all away, but Rook wondered if close was going to be good enough.

The two-story house was a modern glut of glass, polished off-gray wood planks, and sleek white walls, a stark assault of bleached squares and rectangles perched solidly on a broad cliff face, its enormous greens spotted with small clusters of gardens and odd statues. Its mostly glass western-facing walls promised a stunning view, probably as breathtaking as its price. Like many of the houses on the hills, it was bristling with attitude, an aloof structure protected from the general population by high walls and spiky plants menacingly clustered and too thick to walk through. Sitting on the edge of a cliff meant no back wall was needed, or so some idiot probably thought, but it was nice to see the city below without the blur of a transparent Plexiglas barrier used on most of the surrounding hillside homes.

To Rook, the house resembled random sugar cubes some god dropped from the sky when making its morning cup of coffee and was possibly the ugliest place he'd ever seen.

A single step into the house and he'd be crossing back into his old life. Rook didn't know if the risk was worth it. Everything could crash and burn, leaving him picking up the pieces of… what, he didn't know… but *something*. His stomach clenched with both anticipation and dread, and he longed to pick the locks on the far door, then empty out whatever the owner of the house stashed inside his hidey-holes. His nerves jangled, keening for him to make up his mind to go back to his old life or turn around and go on with the one he'd found.

If only the empty Ark of the Covenant prop in his West Hollywood warehouse didn't mock him. He needed that kind of security in case everything went to shit. There wasn't anyone he could count on to bail him out of life's messes. He couldn't be certain of anyone, not just *yet*. Maybe even never, and Rook *needed* to know he had a safety net he could count on.

Since there was only one thing Rook knew more about than pop culture and movies—stealing—he was going to have to return to his roots. A few hits and his nest egg would be replaced with no one the wiser, including Montoya. This one, however—this one was for free—his own personal fuck-you and welcome back to every whisper behind his back and turned-up nose.

"God, they weren't lying. Just a standard piece of shit." He studied the door, tamping down a wave of goose bumps across his chest and shoulders. "Feels like I'm digging up a dinosaur."

The lock on the door off the back patio was a laughable excuse for protection, a simplistic top-of-the-line latch some security company picked up at a high-end home improvement store. Rook debated simply kicking it in just for the sheer pleasure of watching it pop open, but damaging someone's property tended to piss them off, and nothing fueled a victim's drive for justice like rage. The gloves on his hands were a familiar skin, a thin, featureless, and expensive latex and microfiber hybrid he got from an elderly Chinese woman in Singapore.

He had to take a moment to subdue the tingle in his belly when he unfurled his packet of tools. It'd been a bit since he'd touched them in any way other than the occasional halfhearted pass at the various pieces he'd bought to keep his hand in. It felt different working on the real thing. As much of a piece of shit as the lock was, it kept him out.

And if there was one thing Rook hated, it was being kept out of something he was curious about.

He'd wanted to play with it more, play it out to get the full, long stroke of cracking the house open, but he didn't have the time, and no matter how slow he went, it wouldn't be long enough to satisfy the itch under his skin he got when trying to break into a place he really shouldn't be. A slender curve of metal and a pick would be enough to get him through the door. He paused, sniffing the ice-cold air beyond.

"Jesus, I'm getting hard just standing here." Sex was a definite second to breaking and entering, or at least the foreplay of it was.

The ache in Rook's lower back, a pleasant pull of muscles he'd kept limber, ghosted a memory through his brain, echoes of a hot mouth pressed into his skin, silken Cuban whispers promising all manner of delicious, wicked things Rook had to look forward to later that day. His body tightened in response, remembering the glide of slightly callused palms over his back and thighs before supple thumbs dug into his ass, kneading his cheeks in a gentle massage with a sharp bite and a quick slap at the end meant to push Rook out of bed.

"Okay, maybe sex before Montoya. Glad I can still fucking walk," he muttered as he paused at the measly lock, shaking off the feel of his lover's body on his. "Let's get this done and see what our boy Harold's got stashed away."

It'd been forever since he'd worked on something as simple as the mechanism and security system his mark had installed on the mansion's back entrance, but Rook took his time, enjoying the teasing open of the device, letting the initial rush of breaking in wash over him.

It was nearly exactly like sex. A few strokes of metal on metal, a hint of metallic kiss he could taste on his tongue when a tumbler gave way, then a rush of warmth over his skin. Rook sank into the silken velvet of the melancholy happiness filling him, closing his eyes when it grew too much for him to absorb.

"Fuck, I missed this," Rook whispered, stroking the edge of the lock. "Why the *hell* did I give this up?"

"Are you there, Rook?" Alex's voice crackled in his ear. The two-way turned his cousin's melodic baritone into a gruff, cigar-roughened bass drilling into Rook's brain. The jawbone headset was a sleek piece of tech he'd have loved back in the day, fitting neatly into Rook's ear canal and barely noticeable until Alex boomed through it like a squat Viking chasing after a rabbit on a fat white pony. "Were you talking to yourself?"

"Well, sure I've got to talk to myself, 'cause I've got an idiot on the other side of this mic," Rook teased back. Sighing as the moment passed, he stood up, ready to disengage the house's main security system. "What's up?"

"A cop car just passed right by me. Suppose they come back?" His cousin sounded worried, but Alex always sounded worried if he drifted too close to the line of criminal activity. He was the kind of guy who'd turn in a dollar he found at the beach and pay a parking ticket left on his windshield but written for the car behind his. "Really, Rook. Are you listening to me? What do I tell them?"

"Alex, you're a blond twenty-ish guy in glasses who looks like he's one hieroglyph away from discovering where the Stargate is buried and sitting in a sports car worth more than the average cop's house." Easing the door open, Rook stepped into the house and took a deep inhale of its air-conditioned air. "Believe me, cuz, when I tell you, the only reason they'd stop to talk to you is to check to see if you're lost."

"Are you sure?" Rook heard the strain in Alex's voice. "Suppose—"

"Yeah, I'm sure. Besides, if they were really curious, they'd run your plates." He chuckled into the headset. "And then wonder how the hell a cop's husband can afford that car. Now just sit tight. You're the getaway driver, not a cricket in a top hat sitting on my shoulder."

"But—"

"Alex, I love ya, man, but I've got to get to work," he reminded his cousin. Cracking his knuckles, he grinned wide enough to make his cheeks ache. The walls were singing, promising him a payoff rich enough to fill the dent in his bruised ego. "Get off the line, wait for me to ping you, and make sure you're dolled up and wearing your prettiest dress out there, because in about fifteen minutes, I'm going to need you to dance us out of here."

Los Angeles's late-afternoon sun burnished the scatter of furniture in what seemed like the fifteenth living space Rook found in the frigidly designed house. The glass-and-white-wall motif carried on to the interior, pops of color coming from oversized leather furniture and some of the ugliest contemporary art Rook'd ever seen.

"Not enough time to sneer at shit, Stevens." Rook did a mental check on the minutes he'd given himself to get into his target rooms, hating he didn't have enough leeway to peruse the canvases lining the room's long wall. "Probably crap pieces he bought at those art sales on the side of the road."

He knew his victim well enough to know Harold was more bluster than brains. Flashy and gaudy was how the pompous ass judged something's worth. The sterile house and its overly clean lines were less of a fashion statement and more of an homage to a Swedish box store, but there were cracks in its antiseptic appearance, small dollops of flotsam and jetsam scattered about.

"That's right. Party on Friday. Bunch of people to impress with wine and hipster food." Rook jogged his memory. "Housekeeper's off until Monday. You're out playing golf, but shit, you could have picked up a bit, Harold."

An empty champagne flute lay on its side behind a planter, a scallop of fuck-me-hard red lipstick on its rim, and a foot away, the shimmer of a gold cuff link winked from a corner of a plush white area rug. Dried, cracked blocks of cheese kept picked-over mummified salumi company on a wet bar near the stairs leading to what Rook hoped were the bedrooms, but what concerned him more was the unmistakable, odiferous evidence of a dog deposited under the steps.

"Shit, does he have a dog?" Nothing Rook gleaned from Harold's life mentioned a dog or a pet of any kind. He cocked his head, listening for a bark or scrambling nails on the sleek floor, but he heard nothing. "Okay, so maybe dog went with. Either way, just... don't step in its shit."

There were urban legends, a guy who knew a guy who'd been nailed because of a cat hair and feline DNA, and if Rook was going to ruin his perfect no-arrest record, it wasn't going to be over a damned piece of fluff.

The floating marble stairs were deep, curved in a bend meant to fuel dramatic entrances and possibly inspire spontaneous sexual encounters if the one on the bottom was willing to risk banging their head on the ebony stone planks. Rook moved quietly and quickly, crossing the upper landing in a few long strides with his target just down the hall.

The recon of the building placed a master suite taking up half of the upper floor and facing the cliff, with entire banks of floor-to-ceiling windows meant to showcase a million-dollar view of West Los Angeles and the rest of the city. He'd seen the city view from the backyard, and it looked much like... a city. The same city he lived in. The one where he could grab an order of carne asada fries at three in the morning after going a round of mini-golf in Sherman Oaks. It was where he'd done some of his best work, lifted some incredible hauls, and had some of the best sex in his life.

Still was having some of the best sex in his life, his brain whispered, because Montoya had no intention of leaving.

Even though everyone else had.

"No time for that shit." Shaking off the melancholy tickle, he pulled up short in front of the bedroom door, a broad, glossy black barrier, locked according to the snippets of information he'd gotten from anyone he'd spoken to about the property and Harold's habits.

It swung away from him, jarring slightly open when his fingers touched it, gliding back on silent hinges without a whisper of sound.

"Fuck."

Unlocked doors made him nervous. They tightened the gums around his teeth and poured a dribble of cold silver down his spinal cord. *This* door was an anomaly, one his lizard brain leaped to rationalize in a scramble ranging from a forgetful Harold to another burglar beating him to the punch.

A bit of afternoon sun crept around the cracked-open bedroom door, the six-inch gap allowing enough light into the shadowed hall to run a bright line down the outside frame. There were sounds coming from inside the room. Slushy noises Rook couldn't quite place. They sounded—he cocked his head to listen—like a fish tank filter or even a white noise machine left to run during the day. The scratching rumble wasn't alarming, just unfamiliar. It could be anything, really. Just not something he knew about. Still, the house... unsettled him. Something was off, a wrongness lingering in the air, and Rook took a step back, his gloved fingers hovering a few inches away from the door.

The sunlight cut out, swallowed by a rushing shadow pouring past the doorframe. Rook caught a flash of pale skin and dark clothes swaddling flailing limbs. He dodged the first blow by chance. Startled by the movement, he'd pulled back, ready to protect himself when a heavy object struck his raised arm. The blow reverberated through his forearm, the downward force pulling at his shoulder. Years of tumbling along the carnie circuit kicked in Rook's muscle memory, and he rolled with the blow, following through with its momentum, letting it carry him down and forward into the shadow's gut.

The grunt he got was a satisfying one, but his attacker was heavier than he looked and Rook only gained a few inches of space into the room. His hip struck the doorframe, throwing him off-kilter, and the floor's slickness made his footing treacherous. He couldn't see what hit him, not with the whitewash coming through the bedroom's wall of windows.

The figure was a silhouette in a balaclava against the light, but his arm went up again, straining to lift the heavy oddly shaped object he held in his right hand. Unwilling to get struck again, Rook lunged, trying to grapple at his attacker's waist, hoping to catch his opponent's arms and tangle his limbs to keep him immobile. Rook struck hard, shoving them both back to get clear of the door.

Close-in fighting was something Rook'd cut his teeth on. The carnival circuit was a hard one, a physical, violent world with short, hot skirmishes and long, simmering memories. The smack of flesh hitting bone was as familiar to Rook as his own face, and he'd used his clenched fists to brawl his way out of trouble long before he learned how to coax open a door or charm the people around him.

Propelling his body with a push of his legs, Rook slammed into his attacker, going on the offensive in the hope of getting some control of the conflict. He needed to get into a more open space than the hallway with its dangerously tight landing and open stairs. With his back toward the steps, it wouldn't take more than a few pushes to get him to the edge, and then the dog shit under them would be the least of his worries. He landed a punch to his attacker's ribs and followed by a knee up, hoping he could keep the man off-balance enough to either drop what he was carrying or at least not have enough momentum for a solid hit.

He struck hard and fast, pinpointing his punches to where he could get in past the man's chaotic windmilling arms. Ribs were a good landing spot, but Rook liked under the belly button, jabbing his clenched fists into the soft roll of flesh to distract, then bringing up a punch to the face. He got one good hit on the intruder's covered jaw, but Rook knew the knitted cap pulled down over most of his face took away a lot of the impact. In the fluctuating shadows, he couldn't make out more than a slice of eyes and pale skin surrounded by a field of thick black yarn, but a push of hot air along Rook's wrist told him the intruder was struggling.

The damned bedroom floor proved to be Rook's undoing. Since it was made of the same glossy dark stone as the stairs, Rook didn't see the glisten of moisture until it was too late. He struck the edge of a thin puddle and twisted in midair when his foot shot out from underneath him. Having to choose between continuing the fight or minimizing his fall, his instincts took control over his brain and Rook turned, hoping to take the impact with the side of his body and protect his joints while his attacker flailed about with the cylindrical weight. Unfortunately while his muscle memory was intent on saving Rook's ass, it left the side of his head wide open, and the intruder's desperate swing scored a direct hit.

The pain was a swift blast of white stars and ache. His head shot back from the blow, and the impact was hard enough to push Rook's jaw to the side. He tried to absorb some of the hit by giving in to its arc, but with his body turning in the opposite direction, the most Rook could do was soften the blow. The intruder lost control of his weapon, and it flew off, hitting something in the room with an oddly wet splat.

Rook landed hard, tangled around himself and gasping from the echoing throb along his temple. Panicked, his brain ground out commands, urging Rook to get to his feet, to gain some ground before his attacker could strike again, but his head hurt too much, and his eyes couldn't seem to find anything to focus on. Blood coated his lips, but Rook couldn't find where he'd bitten himself or even if he cared enough to do more than jab at the inside of his mouth with his tongue.

Self-preservation forced him to turn over, and he blinked, trying to orient himself in the room. His hands were wet, and the walls spun about a bit, but Rook pushed himself up. Clenching his fists, he squared himself off, readying to continue the fight. Shuffling around on the balls of his feet, Rook scanned the room, keeping his arms up and loose, but the room was empty, silent except for his own heavy breathing.

"Son of a *bitch*," he spat, disgusted enough to take a few steps to follow his attacker, but the jab of pain across his eyes brought Rook up short. Pressing the heel of his hand into the middle of his forehead, he willed the throb to subside as he took stock of his options. He'd taken too long to get up, and the bastard chose to run instead of sticking around. "Fucker's probably already out the front door. Goddamn it."

Rook took a moment to catch his breath, and he dabbed at the blood on his lips with his tongue, disgusted by the taste of metal in his mouth, and for some reason, he couldn't get the smell of it out of his nose. Wiping at his face with the back of his hand, Rook was surprised to see only a light tacky smear of dark red on the beige latex.

"What the fuck?" Blinking, Rook let his eyes adjust to the bright light numbing the room's features, hoping to clear the stars across his vision along with the headache burrowing its claws into his temples. His hand came away clean when he ran it over the spot where he'd been struck on the head, but the bloody aroma hounded him. "Where the hell am I bleed…."

A clatter of tiny nails on the marble floor drew Rook's attention, and he turned around, catching the full brutal wash of sunlight streaming through the western-facing windows. It took a moment, but a small orange puffball of a dog was the first thing Rook pulled out of the receding shadows as his vision adjusted. It beamed up at him, panting with a toothy smile. Then Rook spotted the naked dead man in the middle of the room—a dead man with an oddly familiar avian statue lying across his hairy, bloated stomach.

In life, Harold Archibald Barnsworth Martin had been a blustery force of ego and condescension, puffed up on an importance fueled by money and an infantile temperament. In death, he was a stiff plank of white flesh mottled with dried blood, his manhood a shriveled spaetzle of flesh tucked up under his purpling stomach.

The Pomeranian danced around Rook's legs as he bent over to retrieve the Bluetooth link he'd dropped in the fight. Giving the dog a reassuring scratch, he tucked the speaker into his ear, hoping it retained its connection. Tapping it on, he winced through some crackle, then heard Alex shout a hello over the line.

"Alex, I'm going to need you to call the cops," Rook said as he picked up the dog and cradled it to his side. It squirmed while he carefully approached Harold's body. He didn't have a lot of hope the man was still alive, and when he saw the caved-in remains of Harold's head, he knew the asshole he'd come to prank was never going to spit insults at him from across a dining room table ever again.

The object he'd come to steal balanced precariously on Harold's stomach for another moment before gravity took over, sliding its chunky black form down the fleshy curve to come to a rest against Harold's rigid, tucked-in arm. A squared-off ugly bird made of resin and resentment, the Maltese Falcon stared up at Rook, an unblinking, judgmental witness to Harold's death.

"What's going on, Rook?" Alex broke through the dog's whining to be let down. "Why am I calling the cops?"

"Because someone's murdered our asshole cousin," he muttered, edging back away from Harold's still form. "And it looks like he was killed with my damned bird."

Two

LOS ANGELES glittered amber and blue behind him, the skyline fanning out around the surrounding low-lying hills. The springtime night was cool, a slight bite to the air with a promise of frosty morning lingering on the edge of the horizon. Tucked into the canyons and rises, the upper reaches of Hollywood were far from the loud brashness of its boulevards and the garish desperation of its more well-known neighborhoods. Still, the city strained to be heard in the hills.

Just past dusk, the night held a hint of water in it, chased with a metallic taint from the canyon's gritty dust. Another sniff brought in the rasp of sage and pine, a sweet, smoky aroma tickling his nose. The city was an amber-and-ebony serpentine sprawl around the hills, its golden palette dotted with sparkling gemstones of traffic lights and neon signs. And despite the peaceful lull around him, Los Angeles refused to be still.

The unmarked car's rolled-down windows let the city in, taking a bit of the edge off of Montoya's restlessness. A whisper of early-evening traffic from the distant streets fed Los Angeles's constant murmur, a tumble of rolling whooshes with an occasional horn popping an aggrieved warning. Somewhere below, lost in the city's bowels, a siren chased through the streets, an unseen ambulance warbling its mournful cries.

A long, meandering drive through the hills was just what he needed, an odd Zen Dante could only find when surrounded by the scent of gun oil, abused police equipment, and the dubious remains of Hank's lunch tucked under the front seat of their department-issued vehicle.

"Shit, I got mustard on my pants," Camden grumbled, breaking the mood. "Wife just fricking washed these pants, and now there's mustard on them. She's going to kill me."

"So you wash them before she sees it." Dante sat up straighter, the car seat squeaking under him. Hank rumbled something soft and guilty as he drove, and Dante glanced at his partner, amused at the blush creeping over his face. "You do know how to wash your own clothes, right, Camden?"

"I may or may not have been banned from the laundry room," the redhead confessed. "In my defense, I was trying to help. Who the hell puts things that can't go into the dryer in the hamper? Hampers are where you put the clothes you can just toss in and walk away. You don't put fifty-dollar bras that fall apart if you look at them wrong in a hamper. It's just not right! What happened to the good old days when you could trust your own clothes?"

"You, Camden, are a menace. I'm surprised Debra even thought you were marriage material."

As partners went, Hank Camden was one of the best. Chipped off of Scottish and Viking stock, he was a lanky man with ruddy features, copper-bright hair, and freckled under his weekend-lawn-mowing tan. Amiable and gregarious, he easily coaxed old ladies and children when taking eyewitness accounts and made friends with even the most hardened criminals, often leaving them behind bars with a hearty laugh and a promise to play a round of hoops once they got out. But behind the Foghorn Leghorn charm was a steel-trap mind and a cunning detective with a solve rate most cops could only dream of.

Dante'd been lucky with Hank, far luckier than he'd been with his first partner, but then, he couldn't have gotten worse than a bitter cancer-ridden senior detective bent on taking down a cat burglar named Rook Stevens, no matter what the cost. Vince was drummed out and died not long after he'd been caught falsifying evidence, and Dante's career barely survived Vince's fall from grace.

The thing he liked about being partnered with Hank Camden was the ease of their relationship. On paper, they shouldn't have worked. While Dante was a gay Cuban-Mexican kid from Laredo, Hank was from an upper-middle-class suburban family, heavily educated and married to a woman he loved deeply enough to have several children with. Camden was an awkward freckled cop with an easy grin and an even easier manner.

He was also one of the sharpest cops Dante Montoya had ever met.

In the years since Vince's death, Rook'd gone straight—as hard as that was for Dante to believe at first—and Hank'd proven to be a solid partner, accepting of Dante's sexuality even though he wasn't so sure of Dante's taste in men.

Their friendship deepened during the long days spent cooped up in a police car sifting through Los Angeles's millions for the ugly few who'd taken up killing as a pastime. He'd been a steadying force while Dante struggled with his conflicted emotions over Rook, a former thief Dante'd spent a good chunk of his early career trying to arrest. The fallout of that failed investigation nearly cost Dante his career, so when Stevens surfaced again, Dante'd been chomping at the bit to take the slippery thief down.

He'd fallen in love with the damned thief instead.

Sometimes Dante wasn't sure about his taste in men either, but there was something about the lean, muscular former thief that stroked every hot spot in Dante's body. From his odd green-blue heterochromia, to his striking, strong features, Rook'd dug into Dante's heart and made himself at home, all the while protesting their relationship. Rook's sarcastic drawl and sharp wit were tempered by his generous heart, and despite his best efforts at hiding his true feelings, Rook cared about the people around him.

Hank steered the car out of a turn and onto another winding street. "God, I wish someone in this city would just draw a fucking straight line on the map once in a while. You better pray the GPS is steering us straight, or some damned Minotaur's going to eat us. We're off shift in what? Half an hour? Going to take us that long to get back to the station."

"Your knowledge of mythology amazes me." Dante chuckled. "I didn't think they did ancient Greek porn. Learn something new every day."

"Hey, I was a lit major for a year and a half before I decided I liked shooting people." Hank glanced at Dante. "We're going to be coming out at that taco shop… the bright pink one. You want to stop and grab something to eat before we head back to the station? Or maybe Cuban. You're half Cuban. How come we never eat Cuban food?"

Dante's phone chimed in before Dante could answer, and the partners exchanged looks. It'd been a long day, over ten hours of chasing down dead-end leads which culminated in a long drive up into the hills to speak to a well-aged former Playboy bunny with a raspy drawl and roaming hands. They'd been technically off shift half an hour ago, but none of that meant anything to anyone back at the station. As long as the car was out, they were considered live catch for any crime-baited hook.

"Captain?" Camden asked softly. "Nah, can't be the captain. Can't imagine you tagging Book's number with 'The Devil's Brew.'"

"No, it's Rook," Dante said, digging his phone out of his jacket pocket. "Hey, bab—"

His lover ran on high-octane, a spit of words and temperament Dante often struggled to keep up with. Most of their time together was spent trying to slow Rook down, but this time, he wasn't having any of Dante's calm.

A hurried stream of words and emotion tore through the line. Then a sharp voice cut into Rook's stream-of-consciousness babble.

"Wait, don't hang up. I didn't catch all of that," Dante snapped. "You're where? I'm coming to get you. Wait… listen to me, *cuervo*, cooperate but wait for me. What station are you at?"

"Um, hold on." Rook's murmur grew distinct, then strengthened when he rattled off an address in West Los Angeles. "Did you get that?"

"Yeah, I know that station. Did a stint there. Now do me a favor, take a deep breath, and repeat what you just told me." He motioned for Hank to pull over. The story didn't get any prettier in its second telling, and Dante rubbed at the growing throb forming along his forehead. "Okay, yeah. *Dios, cuervo*, it's like… try not to let that smart mouth of yours get you into trouble, and I'll get right over there. Love you—and he's hung up. Son of a bitch…. Camden, pull over. Rook's stepped into some shit. I can drop you off at the station—"

"Hell no. Where you go, I'll go." Hank threw the sedan into park in a red zone, ignoring the filthy look he got from a woman in a pink tracksuit walking a swarm of hairless dogs on a handful of sparkling leashes. "What the hell is going on with Stevens?"

"Nothing good." Dante pulled a face. "Better I drive anyway. That way you can sweet talk someone down at Dispatch to get more info than what Rook's got. Damned idiot's neck-deep in dead bodies again."

"*DIOS, CUERVO*, what have you gotten yourself into?" Dante Montoya pulled up to the curb, edging the unmarked gray sedan in behind a pair of black-and-whites lined up along the front of the station.

"Dunno, but it looks like your boy's in it deep," Hank muttered. "I'm getting stonewalled by everyone I know at the station. 'Course, if it's got Rook Stevens's name on it, most sane cops wouldn't touch it with a ten-foot pole. You, however—"

"Make one joke about me, Stevens, and my pole," Dante growled, "and you'll be walking back to the station on two broken legs and a fat upper lip. Let's see what's going on inside."

The West Los Angeles station was a solid square of cinder block and dull paint sitting on a prime piece of real estate off of the 405 and Santa Monica Boulevard. The station's parking lot gate was left half-open, giving Dante a peek into a lot where a small cluster of men milled about, and the building's entrance was easy enough to find, a bright red square punching through the drab façade, and if there was any doubt about Rook being inside, Dante nodded toward a sleek black McLaren being lowered off of a flatbed tow truck onto the station's main parking lot.

They were in a neighborhood Dante could only have imagined when he was younger, one he'd become more familiar with during his time behind the badge. Much more upscale than the middle-class bungalow he shared with his uncle Manny, many of the homes were tucked behind landscaping and with low white plaster walls running around their property edges. A few hard-looking palms interrupted many of the front lawns' carpets of too bright grass, and the other end of the street ran to businesses focused more on organic foods and reusable grocery totes than coupons and cheap vegetables.

Dead was still dead, though. No matter how quickly the community could get their potholes filled in. For all of the differences in Los Angeles's diverse neighborhoods, Dante found people were basically the same, but it seemed as if the richer the house, the quieter the simmering, so when something blew, it blew up big. Distance between houses meant no one heard the violence brewing behind the family's walls. It took having the ugly seep out between the cracks in a family's foundation for someone to notice, for someone to call for help, but oftentimes, help arrived much too late.

"Rich people bleed in their silence, and the poor bleed so much no one notices," his uncle Manny once told him. "But no matter what, we all cry and die the same, *mijo*. That's why you're here. To wipe our tears and honor our dead."

In this case, they were outside of his district, and Rook's call had been short, to the point, and troubling. Other than knowing there was a house with a dead body in it, Montoya and Camden were walking into another cop's station blind, but knowing Rook, they were probably going to find themselves in the middle of a shit storm without an umbrella.

"Camden, any word on who was on-scene?" He couldn't see the tow truck driver, but the McLaren was getting a lot of attention from the station's uniforms, small dribbles of blue-garbed cops wandering outside to take a look at the sports car. Hank shook his head, and Dante sighed. "Hate not knowing whose toes we're going to be walking on before we go in."

"Sorry, but I've got nothing. Sherry down in Dispatch says things inside's pretty chaotic. Since West Los Angeles caught it, we won't have conflict of interest, so the captain'll be happy about that." Hank nodded at the black McLaren 570GT blocked in by a sea of uniformed police. "We're definitely not in Kansas anymore. This district's got some serious money. What'd Rook tell you over the phone?"

"Remember I told you the dead guy's his cousin and not one he likes," Dante informed his partner. "One Harold Martin, formerly of Bel Air and now a temporary resident of the Los Angeles County Morgue. I didn't get a lot out of Rook other than that and to meet him down here if I could. Swear to God, he's going to make me go gray before I'm forty. The McLaren over there belongs to Alex, another cousin. That does not bode well. If he's got Alex mixed up in something, then that's going to make things really sticky. Bad enough Rook's a menace. Archie's not going to like him dragging the good seed down the rabbit hole with him."

"Okay, so?" Hank tapped an away code into their console, informing Dispatch they were going to be out of the car. "How many damned cousins does your boyfriend got? It's like a clown car over on his genealogy chart."

"Don't know. Stevens isn't exactly the Sunday-go-to-dinner kind of guy, so I've never had a full head count. You met Alex. Slender blond guy with the glasses, cute. Your wife thought he was adorable. He was at the barbeque Manny threw at the house a couple of weeks back. He's with Castillo from North Hollywood."

"So Grandpa Martin's favorite grandsons have a type." Hank rolled his eyes at Dante's confusion. "Cops. They're gay guys who hook up with cops. Sheesh, Montoya, connect the dots here. What about the dead guy? Did you know him?"

"Harold? Might have met him once or twice, but honestly, the family's not too happy about Rook showing up and landing in Archie's lap, so he doesn't see them much. The one who owns the McLaren's cool. Got a comic book shop, so he and Rook really hit it off. Nice guy. Law-abiding, which is a damned nice thing to have where Rook's concerned." Dante shook his head at the thought of Rook having an accomplice in trouble lurking in his family tree. "Castillo and Alex are good people. So are his folks, but the rest of them are... they're the kind of people who are nice to you only because they don't know where you're going to be useful later on, so they're hedging their bets. One of them actually asked me to fix their driver's parking tickets."

"So they're assholes."

"Sounds about right. Look, I've got to find Stevens." Dante opened the car door. "Why don't you sniff around and see what you can find out. Go

16

kick the McLaren's tires and see if you can get anything out of that bunch. Maybe one of them was on-scene. Only thing Rook told me was he might be in a shit storm of trouble but wasn't sure. And you know him, that could be anything from an elephant followed him home to he accidentally started a revolution."

"That's what happens when you fall in love with an ex cat burglar, Montoya. Especially when he's Rook Stevens," Hank teased. "Might as well accept you've signed up for a lifetime of trouble."

"Don't remind me," he sighed. "But damn, he's worth all the trouble he brings with him."

Hank snorted. "He better be because this is the second or third time you're picking him up from a police station."

"Okay, let's go see what my favorite asshole's gotten himself into," Dante muttered, steeling himself not to sign a cross over his chest as he strode past the front of the property. "With any luck, we'll be in and out before anyone at the top knows Hank and I are here."

THERE WERE more uniformed cops and LAPD cars spread out over the street than he'd seen at some drive-by shootings. The front lobby was empty of everything but plants, squat leather-covered chairs, and an occasional table, and he'd had to flash his badge to get the attention of the rookie temporarily stationed at the front desk while the on-duty officer ogled Alex's car through a window. The station itself felt and smelled odd, a mixture of a floral air freshener and a bite of something acrid. It took a moment for Dante to realize he was missing the scent of coffee and the rattle of cop voices rumbling in a low indistinct babble underneath the station's daily grind.

"Sir? Detective Montoya?" The kid at the desk looked like he was about twelve despite his starched uniform, and his voice cracked into a squeak when Dante turned toward him. "Um, Detective Vicks said to let you go on back. The bullpen's down the hall and to the right. If you have any questions, just ask someone."

"Thanks, kid." Dante winced when he heard himself, clipping the visiting officer's badge the kid gave him to his jacket. He remembered first pulling on his uniform and strapping his gun to his side, an oddly sickening-giddy feeling he'd outgrown without realizing it. "Um, appreciate the help."

The young cop was right. The bull pen was easy to find. West Hollywood was a hell of a lot smaller than his own station and, considering the communities it covered, more than a little bit worn around the edges. The computers on the various desks were mostly new, but the carpet was a short plush blue he'd seen in the outer hills offices before it was torn up and replaced with more durable, pleasing colors. The overall tone of the people he passed was quiet, and no one stopped him when he walked by.

A couple of quick turns and he found himself in a smallish room with windows set up high on the wall, the streetlamps outside pushing in a bit of orange glow to combat the sea of fluorescents washing the bull pen with a glaring brightness. The detective desks were definitely old-school, heavy khaki metal monsters softened by flotsam of family photos and the occasional struggling plant. A set of doors lined up on the southernmost wall led to interview rooms if Montoya guessed correctly.

There seemed to be a gaggle of cops around one of the squad desks, forming a wall of blue uniforms and stern expressions, a firm indicator of serious discussion. As Dante crossed the room, a few of the cops wandered off, and Dante was left with a clear view of the man who'd brought him to his knees.

Rook Stevens was a complicated mess of sensuality, charm, and contrariness, a tall, slender, muscular man with vulpine features, a full mouth, mismatched blue-green eyes, and a nose for trouble. Leaning against a desk, he stared out one of the interview room's doors, his mind clearly on other things. The distracted air gave Rook a sense of vulnerability, a tenderness Dante normally only saw when they were in bed, exhausted from intense lovemaking. Cuddling Rook was something done only after breaking down his walls, a slightly prickly high fence of distracting behaviors and lacy half lies.

His lover hadn't gotten around to cutting his hair, but Dante found himself liking the heavy shag of caramel brown framing Rook's face, the glaring overheads picking up glints of deep auburn and sienna running through Rook's thick mane. A bit of worry tugged at Rook's expression, and his gaze kept returning toward the wall's bank of doors. He'd deny being concerned, having spent his life bricking his heart up behind a thick wall, but Dante knew better… now. For all of his aloofness and distance, Rook loved as deeply as he loved cautiously, doling out bits of his soul in the little things he did and said.

And judging by the bite of his teeth on his lower lip, Rook was working on an intense fret.

There was a moment when Dante was sure Rook saw him. He could see it in the tensing of Rook's long legs and trim hips. Most lovers would relax when seeing the man who'd brought them to a screaming peak that morning, but not Rook. There was always an instinctive battle of fight-or-flight for Rook, deeply ingrained almost-fears he'd trusted to keep him alive during the turmoil of his early years.

The badge at Dante's belt gave him a path in through the cops, but it was tough going. There was a challenge in their faces, hardening further when he approached Rook. He wasn't from their house, and despite the gold shield the LAPD gave him, Dante knew he was on the outside looking in.

Nodding at a barrel-chested older cop named Robertson, according to the tag on his uniform, Dante reached for Rook, tugging at his shirtsleeve, then held his hand out to the grizzled uniformed officer. "Hey, name's Montoya."

"Yeah, I know you. You're Camden's partner, out of Central, right? I knew Giada. Good cop. Pity he went sour." He grunted, taking Dante's hand for a quick, firm shake. "Mark Vicks pulled this one. Surprised to see you here."

"Stevens and I are…." There was nothing loving in Rook's expression, and for the first time since Dante'd fallen in with the ex-thief, he stood on shaky ground. They'd never talked about what they were to each other, and despite the couple of months they'd been circling each other's lives, Rook'd proved to be slippery and impossible to nail down on the one thing Dante needed answers to the most: what the hell they were to each other. Choosing his words carefully, Dante continued, "We're involved. Shot me a phone call and asked me to come down."

"Really? 'Cause he didn't have one on him. A phone, I mean." Robertson frowned. "Patted him down myself."

A glance at Rook only got Dante an eye roll from the thief, and he suppressed another sigh. "Look, Robertson, is there someplace he and I can talk?"

"Vicks said to keep him here, but no reason why you two can't use one of the empty interview rooms. They're still questioning the other guy on the scene with Stevens, so it'll be a while. But leave the door open so if shit goes south, we can get in." The cop frowned at Dante, a florid blush of red flagging his cheeks. "Don't get any ideas about slipping off, Stevens. I know about all of your shit."

"Does it look like I'm waltzing off?" Rook snapped back, and Dante finally let loose his sigh, practically hearing the clink of handcuffs locking down on his lover's wrists.

"We'll be right here," he promised Robertson. "I just want to see how he's doing."

Shoving Rook was never an idea, but the urge to fist his hand into the back of Rook's shirt and drag him into the room was tempting. The stubborn in Rook's personality hardened his gaze, and Dante was left with no illusion he meant business. Normally charming and engaging, there wasn't any sign of the carefree, amiable mask Rook wore on a daily basis. No, the man pacing off the interview room in long strides was the Rook Dante only saw when Rook was feeling cornered, and alarm nibbled at Dante's stomach, worry something'd pushed Rook a few inches too far and his lover was contemplating taking a run.

There was a bit of swelling on Rook's lip, and he moved gingerly, touching his side when he turned. Dante eyed Robinson through the door's window, measuring up the other cop. The hiccup in Rook's grace was noticeable, and he was torn between jumping down the entire bull pen's throats or asking Rook if he was faking an injury for sympathy. The conflict between anger and suspicion must have shown on his face, because Rook's pacing stopped and his eyes narrowed.

"Stop looking at me like that," Rook snarled under his breath, his eyes pinned to the door. Robertson stood framed by the opening, his attention clearly on what was going on in the interview room. "You're acting like I'm going to pack up and leave."

"Are you?" He hated asking that question, hated it down to his guts, but Rook lived his life in rolls of confidence and fear, a brash, cocky trickster who'd spent too many years with one foot out the door and one step ahead of the law. "I'm going to say no, but I don't know. You're not talking to me, and that's not going to help with what's going on. What's going on in that busy head of yours, *cuervo*? First thing that pops into your head, you tell me."

It was eerie sometimes watching Rook's eyes. He'd once spent a few moments covering half of Rook's face to see what he'd look like with either blue or green eyes, but Dante hadn't gotten further than a second or two before they both dissolved into laughter. Now with Rook's hair falling across his face, Dante caught the rich cunning in Rook's hazel-gold eye, his dark lashes tossing long shadows over his sharp cheek. The blue was softer, Dante realized, a disarming blush of sky and optimism in an otherwise saturnine face.

"Talk to me, Rook," Dante whispered, sitting on the heavy table in the middle of the room.

There were three chairs pushed up against the wall, metal and plastic origami constructs he knew from experience were too hard to sit on for very long, and from Rook's tightly wound body, he had little hope of coaxing Rook to settle down. Leaning forward on Rook's next pass, Dante hooked his finger into Rook's waistband and pulled, hoping his lover would let himself be led in.

Dante didn't know what surprised him more, Rook letting himself be dragged into the *V* of Dante's legs or Rook resting his forehead against Dante's temple and draping his long arms over Dante's shoulders.

"I'm not sure if I should kiss you or kill you." Rook's breath was hot, spiced with cinnamon and a hint of tea. "I hate you're a cop, but right fucking now, I'm damned glad you're wearing that badge."

Their kiss was as hot and slow as a Los Angeles summer night, a scalding, slightly damp erotic whisper loaded with promises only Rook could keep. There was a nibble, teeth sharp on Dante's lower lip, then Rook ground his hips into the growing heft in Dante's crotch, heating up the already warm air between them. Rook's hands wandered up Dante's thighs, squeezing at the muscles he'd worked on that morning in the gym, and his skin tightened under his pants, remembering the feel of Rook's ass against his hip bone when they'd woken up, limbs tangled together and sticky from the night before.

"I'm not going to run, Montoya," Rook promised, his words edged and dark. "Told you that before."

"Sometimes I need the reassurance, *querido*, especially when you look at me like you're wondering if you have enough cash to hide in the shadows for a few years," Dante replied, sliding his hand under Rook's shirt, his thumb along the ridge of Rook's belly button. "Now tell me what happened. Are you hurt?"

"I'll tell you what happened, Montoya," a voice boomed from the open door. There was no mistaking the cop standing there. Authority and thinly controlled ego spat fire from the broad-shouldered man's voice, and his lip curled into a sneer as his hard eyes raked over Rook and Dante. "What's happened is your little boyfriend here broke in and murdered his cousin, Harold Martin, and I'm going to be the cop who finally took Rook Stevens down."

Three

"GUESS VICKS is done with Alex." Rook eyed the man in the doorway. "Lucky me. He's come back for seconds."

Detective Sean Vicks was a bear of a man, thick necked and worn hard around the edges. His eyes were granite narrow slits in a rough-hewn, craggy face, his heavy nose battered with bumps, and a thin white scar ran down his left cheek, one end puckered tight into a tiny star. His shoulder holster creaked when he crossed his massive arms over his chest, the seams and rolled-up sleeves of his button-up dress shirt straining at the muscles bulging beneath cheap, wrinkled ivory fabric. Standing in the doorway of the interview room, his shadow, cast by the bull pen's bright lights, swept over them, and Rook felt Dante's fingers dig into his hip, drawing him closer.

"Cute," Rook muttered, tugging at Dante's wrist. "Let me go. You don't need to protect me from the big bad. I've been chewing through cops since before you were one."

"You ever think I'm holding you back so you *don't* chew through him?" Dante chuckled but loosened his hold. "He probably wants to ask you some questions before letting you go."

The station was a loud mess of noise and stunk of fear. Even in the detectives' area, there was a shred of something desperate in the air, the lingering feel of biting into a piece of foil and rubbing it between aching teeth. The smell of burnt coffee and sweat hung in the corners of the room, its pale gray walls streaked with gouges and sneaker sole marks along the bottoms near the floor. The room gave Rook the shivers, feeling the walls pressing in on him with every breath he took, and he couldn't keep his eyes off of the inset one-way mirror, their shadowy movements fooling him into seeing someone through the reflective glass.

"You're Montoya? Out of Central, right?" Vicks's hooded gaze was hard, flicking between them. "I'd heard you'd hooked up with the guy who pretty much killed your partner."

The fluorescents picked up the silver in Vicks's close-cropped brown hair, and his voice rolled into the room before him. His arms stayed at his side, a tacit refusal to offer a hand to Rook's lover. The discourtesy didn't sit well with Rook, especially since Vicks'd already tried to shove him in a corner about finding Harold.

"Yes, I am out of Central, Detective." Montoya's voice went flat, and the heat in his tone deepened his accent. "What killed Vince was cancer. Stevens had nothing to do with it."

Vicks snorted. "Adorable you call your boyfriend by his last name."

"Not to be rude and interrupt the pissing contest, but I'd like to get home soon," Rook cut in between them. "I stay here much longer, I'm going to have to register to vote in this damned district."

"Sure, let's get back to the case. I want to talk to you about your cousin's account of the afternoon." The detective's smile bordered on reptilian, shaking a bit of confidence from Rook's spine. "He seems to remember things a little bit differently than you do. You can stay if you want, Montoya, but I'm going to need Stevens here to clarify a few bits before there's any talk about him leaving."

Alex folded. Rook could see it on Vicks's face. He was fond of his slightly older, or maybe younger cousin—his mom's inability to remember Rook's birth year notwithstanding—but Alex was, in his heart of hearts, so law-abiding he made Rook's teeth hurt.

"What'd he tell you? That we were there to return a pair of bowling shoes or something?" Rook pulled one of the chairs over, then straddled it, facing the door and Vicks. "Don't think I said anything to you other than I went into Harold's house and found him dead on the floor."

"I'd believe you, but unless you fell down the stairs or one of my guys popped you in the face, that cut lip of yours says something different. See, here's what I'm thinking." Vicks stepped all the way into the room, then closed the door behind him. "I think you don't like losing, Stevens, and dear old cousin Harold got your goat. Not something you're willing to just let slide, not if you—a well-known thief and a con—was conned out of something he really, really wanted."

Pulling free of Dante took some doing. Not because the cop wouldn't let him go, but rather Rook felt *safe* with the feel of his lover's heat on him. Montoya was a distraction. He didn't have time to sort out the confusion brewing inside of him, not with having to spin some damage control over what Alex told the cops. Rook knew he wasn't going to be able to think if he could feel Dante, because it took every ounce of his willpower to step away and stand on his own.

He hated having Dante as a weakness, someone Vicks or any number of people could use against him. In the past, he'd have distanced himself as quickly as he could as soon as he felt even a tingle of affection, shoring up his defenses and protecting himself, but this time, it was different. This time, there would be no letting go—even if Montoya was willing to let him walk away.

Something Rook knew was never going to happen so long as either one of them could still breathe.

"Does he need a lawyer?" Dante stood, matching Vicks stare for stare. "Because that can happen."

The lawyer thing was a surprise, especially coming from a cop... even his own cop, and Rook leaned back, gripping the top of the chair's back, watching the two detectives have a silent battle of wills. He'd put his money on Dante any day. Dante wouldn't give in to any of the other cop's pressure, standing firmly at Rook's side, as odd as it might seem, where Vicks was a bully, a familiar construct of ego and brute force, one Rook knew all too well from growing up on the circuit. The problem he saw with Vicks was if they didn't find someone else for the cynical cop to focus on, he wouldn't stop hounding Rook until something gave.

In a lot of ways, Vicks reminded Rook of Dante's old partner, and *that* took Death knocking on the asshole's door before he finally stopped chewing on Rook's tail.

"How about if we pull that rabbit out of our asses after Vicks tells me what Alex said?" The look Dante gave him promised a hell of a lot of talking as soon as they got someplace where no one would overhear them. "I'm interested in finding out why I wanted Harold dead."

"See, this is where it gets tricky, because your cousin's a bit vague on a few details, and he can't verify seeing this ski-mask-wearing intruder you claim attacked you. And I say claim because your supposed injuries could be self-inflicted, or you could have even had Alex hit you," Vicks replied, hitching a hip on the edge of the table Dante vacated. "You're barely scratched and there's hardly any bruising. So the story about you fighting someone off is a bit weak."

"I don't think Alex even knows how to make a fist, much less punch someone," Rook scoffed. "I told you, the guy caught me with a hook and I slipped on the wet floor. He didn't go out the front or Alex would have seen him. The hillside's easy enough to slip down, or he could have cut across the lawn next door."

"Maybe. Or just maybe you're lying," Vicks mocked. "Your cousin alleges he doesn't know why you needed to see Harold, but the bit about you being concerned about him doesn't ring true. Alex also informed me the three of you aren't close. In fact, he's of the opinion you and Harold have a bit of a rivalry going."

"Rivalry about what? Not like we're going after the same woman." Rook nodded toward Dante. "I've already got the best Los Angeles has to offer."

"More cute. The two of you are going to make me too sick to choke down my TV dinner when I get home." The detective sneered. "Actually, there's your grandfather and the pile of cash he's probably sitting on. My theory is you're pulling probably the longest con of your life. You roll into LA, set it up so it looks like you've gone straight, and then con the old man out of everything he's got."

"Hole in that theory," Dante rumbled. "He's actually Archibald Martin's grandson."

"Old man make you spit on a swab?" The detective chuckled when Rook squared his shoulders. "Yeah, I didn't think so. You're not the type of guy who'd do that. Even if you were the old man's grandkid. Smacks too much of someone tagging you, and if there's one thing guys like you hate, it's being tracked."

"If you saw Archie, you'd know I didn't need to get a Q-Tip shoved into my mouth to see I was his grandson. And once again, Harold was dead before I got there," Rook pointed out. "If you got a good look at him, you'd see that. You don't need to be an expert on dead bodies to know he was *very* much dead."

"Funny how you think that, because we're not so certain he was *very* much dead when you showed up. Coroner's not gotten to him yet, but I did hear something kind of interesting from that neck of the woods," Vicks replied. "Prelim says Harold was knifed in the gut sometime this morning. Looks like someone got him about fifteen or so times. But the funny thing about poor cousin Harold, that isn't what killed him."

"Someone gets stabbed that many times and you're telling me that didn't kill him?" Rook refused to meet Dante's puzzled gaze and shut down the panic brewing in his belly. As far as he knew, Harold was dead, but a whisper of doubt slithered past his confidence. "Okay, I bite. What killed Harold?"

"Cousin Harold was down for the count, and according to the fine people down at the morgue, he was probably going to die or had died from bleeding out of his wounds." Vicks's grin deepened, curling up to leave a tiny evil light in his eyes. "But it looks like someone came back to finish the job and caved his brains in with one ugly black resin falcon, a statue that looks remarkably like the one Harold's mother tells me the two of you argued over this past Sunday. So tell me, Stevens, you still going to call that lawyer now, or are you and I going to have a long conversation about how you literally took care of sharing a massive inheritance and got revenge with bashing Harold's head in one bird?"

IF EVER there was a man Dante wanted to wrap up in blanket and tuck into bed, it was Rook Stevens.

Dante also wanted to shake some sense into the man and then either fuck him senseless or tie him to a chair but mostly tuck him into bed until all of the shit storm Rook stirred up passed over them. And no matter where Rook went, there was sure to be a storm.

The car ride over to Archie's home had been long and silent. If it'd been any other man, Dante would have said his boyfriend was sulking, but Rook didn't sulk. He plotted, conned, and finagled, but sulking wasn't a part of Rook's makeup. The silence between them was a charged quiet, and Dante could practically hear Rook's brain churning away next to him.

Driving up to Rook's grandfather's place still made the poor little Laredo kid in Dante wince. The rambling castle, imported brick by brick from the British Isles, stood in the middle of Los Angeles's gamboling low hills, a jutting gray edifice to the Martin ego. Ivy artfully climbed up its turrets, and instead of a moat, an enormous water fountain—about the same square footage as Dante's modest bungalow—dominated the front drive. Massive arched windows sparkled from their casings along the front wall, their stained-glass panes adding a prismatic shimmer to the slate and verdant structure.

Rosa opened the door nearly as soon as they pulled up, her elegant, beautiful face somber with worry. She let her fingers trail over Rook's arms when he passed by, the long-legged former thief stopping only long enough to leave a brief kiss on the Hispanic woman's cheek before he stalked down the main foyer.

"Hello, Rosa." Dante closed the front door behind him. "Where's the old man?"

"In the yellow room," she replied, then chuckled, probably spotting the confused look on his face. "Down the hall and to the left, right after the pink grandfather clock. The door's open. You'll probably hear Mr. Archie yelling. He hasn't stopped yelling since Alex got here with James."

As far as Dante was concerned, whoever decorated the inside of the Martin castle needed to have their eyes checked. While most of the furniture in the rooms ran to classic pieces, the halls were a gauntlet of questionable taste and possible evidence someone took a handful of psychedelics that never wore off. There weren't any empty flat surfaces, with every table bristling with odd knickknacks ranging from very expensive vases to animals made of jute and painted seashells. The grandfather clock was less pink and more flaming orchid, its garish face resplendent with gold lettering and cloisonné birds. Rosa was right. The door was open, but the yelling being done inside was sharp and edged, a familiar enough rasp of smoky tones Dante'd loved to hear murmur his name.

"Do you believe this shit?" Rook's long legs took him easily across Archie's living room. "Asshole thinks I killed Harold. I didn't even hate the asshole enough to... okay, yeah, so I broke in, but fucker *took* my damned statue. No one steals from me and fucking walks off."

Or, Dante mused, he thought it was one of Archie's living rooms. It could have been a sitting room or, hell, a closet for all Dante knew, since most of the rooms were too big to ever be called cozy. He'd lost track of where he was in the Martin patriarch's house a long time ago, half wondering if there wasn't a Minotaur wandering about somewhere. It didn't matter where Rosa, Archie's long-suffering housekeeper, put them, no room in the shipped-over-from-Ireland castle was big enough for a Martin's ego, much less two of them.

Thankfully, the third Martin in the room was Alex, a relatively calm and rational example of the bloodline's explosive temperament. Standing next to a wet bar hidden inside an ebony armoire, Alex gave Dante high hopes the conversation wouldn't resolve into pitchforks and torches. Unfortunately, Alex balanced his Zen attitude by falling in love with a strong-willed Latino detective who apparently knew Vicks well enough to form a long-lasting, hardened hatred. James Castillo, a dark-haired sarcastic detective from North Hollywood, saluted Dante with a bottle of beer from his place on a delicate-looking white-legged couch.

"Rook, Harold's dead," Alex pointed out. The family peacemaker, Alex would eventually soften some of Rook's blunter edges, but he wasn't holding out for a miracle. "The statue isn't important."

"I know that," Rook growled back, shoving his hands into the pockets of his jeans. "Shit, thanks for buying us clothes, James, if I didn't say that before. I'm just... so damned mad, and for some stupid reason, I'm fucking pissed off as hell at Harold for ending up dead."

"Sit down, Montoya, and watch your boy wear a hole in my expensive carpet." A few feet away from James, Archie sat in a purple velvet wing chair, its empty twin flanking the other side of the room's river-stone fireplace, and he motioned for Dante to join him. The old man's face was pale, his leathery skin puckered in around his pursed mouth. Grief lingered in his expression, but worry for his other grandsons left a weariness in his eyes. "Alex, bring the man a beer when you come back. And one for me too."

"Has he filled you in on what they were doing at Harold's house?" Dante muttered beneath another round of Rook's ranting. "He didn't say anything in the car."

"No, so far, it's only about Harold stealing something from him and a little bit about Alex being a shitty liar," James replied in his soft Angeleno-Mexican rumble. "I'm fine with him being a shitty liar. Keeps things honest between us. Between the two of us, Montoya, I think I got the better deal."

"I lie just fine," Alex protested, juggling a couple of cream sodas and a craft beer Archie claimed he stocked for Rook. "No alcohol for you, Grandpa. Nurse said nothing past nine 'cause of your meds."

"I oughta fire that damned nurse," Archie grumbled, beetling his thick eyebrows together. "She's sucking the life out of me. A man should be able to have a beer if he wants one."

"Sure, have a beer. Have five. Chug it down with your meds. Just make sure you leave everything to me and Alex, because according to that damned cop down there, it's why I murdered Harold the dickwad." Rook stopped his pacing, meeting his grandfather's bi-colored gaze with a glare. "I don't want the house. Alex can have it. How about the cars? Maybe the collection of stuffed flying monkeys in the dining room? Or the herd of porcelain llamas in the library?"

"You're not too big for me to put over my knee and spank," Archie threatened softly, shaking his cane at his grandson. "And I'm leaving the damned monkeys to my lawyer, Lynn. She's had her eye on them for years now. Now shut up about the damned beer. I'll drink the soda. God knows what's going to happen to your scrawny ass once I'm gone. Going to have to bring Montoya up to snuff or he'll be bailing you out every other week."

"I'd just leave him in there," James muttered to Dante. "He'd get into less trouble in jail."

"Yeah, fuck you, Castillo," Rook shot back with a cocky smile. "I'll drag Dante to a desert island in the middle of the ocean before I ever go to jail."

"Shut up about going to jail and get this damned thing open for me, you little bastard. We need to talk about what you found at Harold's, and no sugarcoating it. I'm old, not weak. I can grieve after we find the bastard who killed that boy," Archie grumbled at Rook. "What the hell was wrong with bottle caps and a church key?"

Dante only had to look at Archie to see what his lover would look like in sixty years or so. Proud, with elegant, hawk-like features, Archibald Martin suffered no fools, but a bit of softness lurked beneath his hard, crusty surface. There were differences, some not so subtle, but their mismatched eyes were cunning with a hint of sly, and their faces ran to stubborn more than Dante liked. But where Archie bullied and ordered people around, Rook danced them over to where he needed them to be, silver-tongued but aloof enough to make someone want to please him. Watching the pair of them fight bordered on ludicrous at times, especially when Archie pushed Rook too far and they then had to walk themselves back from a crumbling cliff.

There was no mistaking the love they had for one another. That much was clear. Even in the small things Rook did, like twisting off the top of his grandfather's drink, there were signs of affection if someone only knew where to look.

"You want a glass?" Rook held the plastic bottle out for his grandfather to take, but the man's leathery blue-veined hand shook slightly when he reached for it. "Maybe a tumbler. One of those rubberized one? With some ice?"

"Yeah, that's good. I want it cold. Go do that, or get Alex to do it." Archie nodded to his other grandson. "Kid, I want to hear Rook tell me why the cops found him standing over another damned body. And Harold's, for fuck's sake. Why Harold? Boy was tits-on-a-fish useless and a little mean, but he didn't do anything other than annoy people. Didn't have enough brains to really piss anyone off."

"Pissed Rook off," Alex pointed out.

"You, babe, are not helping," James replied with a grin. "That's called a motive, something we're trying to avoid right now."

James met Dante's glance with a helpless shrug, sitting up on the couch to make room for Alex. They'd both come from work, holsters tucked under leather jackets and their jeans dusted with Los Angeles's filth. James's cowboy boots were worn down, broken in from years of use, and there was something scrawled on his right heel, a flash of black marker Dante caught when he crossed his leg.

"Something on your foot, man," Dante said, nodding at James's foot. "What did you walk in?"

"Not in. Into." James made a face, angling his foot so Dante could see Alex's name scribbled on his heel. "And that would be a Martin. Long story. I'll explain later."

"Will the two of you shut up?" Archie grumbled. "Rook's going to start explaining what the hell he was doing at Harold's house. Or so help me—"

"Give it up, old man," Rook countered. "If it weren't for me and Alex, you'd be stuck here with only Rosa to talk to. And that's only if you're lucky she doesn't park you in the library and take your cane away from you."

"Just… talk, *cuervo*," Dante took a welcome sip of his beer. "I need to know what I'm going to be dealing with where Vicks's concerned. Did you see him smile when you played the lawyer card? He wants a fight, and he wants it with you."

"What *did* that cop say, Montoya? I already had the suits on their way as soon as this one called me, but none of them got back to me with anything other than it was being handled and they had to bully Rook into letting them photograph where he was hit." Archie slapped at the chair's thick arm. "If that cop—Vicks—if he's using this to brownnose someone, I'll nail his badge to his ass and hang it over my damned fireplace for decoration."

"*Tío*, I don't think this house could take any more decoration." Dante grimaced. "Lawyers showed up before Vicks could read Rook his rights, but he'd already started to turn the screws while we were in the interview room. Vicks doesn't like playing by the book. Wasn't hard to see that."

"He's not right in the head, but that station doesn't have a lot of options. Hard to keep detectives there. Place can be a shithole," James said, his eyes narrowed and sharp. Moving to make room for Alex, he shook his head. "Never liked that asshole to begin with, but you don't fuck with a man's rights."

"Had a lot of dominance games going. Shoving into personal space and smirking. He made sure we felt like we were pinned in. Classic psychological terrorism. Probably beats his kids or dog," Rook murmured, resuming his pacing for a few strides, then stopped in front of his grandfather. "I didn't kill Harold. Sure, he was a dick, but—I didn't kill him. Vicks told me Harold was still alive when I first came in… then walked that back with Dante in the room. Harold looked dead when I got to him, Archie, like cold dead, but now I can't be fucking sure of that."

"No one thinks you killed him. I'm not going to say I liked Harold—nobody did—but you'd never murder him. No one in the family would, and if anyone was going to, it'd be a Martin." Archie's reassurance was gruff and tinted with anger. "That cop tries to put this on you, we'll bury him."

"Rook, what the hell were you doing there?" Dante asked, trying to get the conversation back on track. "And Vicks said something about the bird statue?"

"Remember when I told you I scored a Maltese Falcon at auction? Not one from the earlier films. It was one from a '75 spoof called *The Black Bird*." Rook's eyes took on a familiar fanatical gleam, and his voice dropped a register, pouring a seductive velvet into his voice. "They made a cast from one of the originals and threw out a few resin copies. You can tell by the serial number on—"

"*Cuervo*, as much as I love you, can't have you going off on something right now," Dante cut him off. "Less about the bird and more about how it's connected to Harold. Didn't you say he bought it? Or you lost it?" He leaned over to Archie. "Vicks said someone struck Harold with the statue and that's what killed him, but I don't trust anything that ass says. What he… told us, there's no way he'd have survived that attack, even if he'd been alive when Rook was there."

"See, the bird's important." Rook stopped in midstride. "Used to belong to a guy who… mentored Hawkins—"

"Who's Hawkins?" James hissed at Alex. "Jesus, this is worse than a telenovela."

"Cat burglar," Alex whispered loudly back, "one of Aunt Beatrice's old boyfriends. Rook's Fagin—"

"You two," Archie grumbled. "Hush. Finish up, boy, before I pass out from boredom."

"I won the bird from one of Natterly's estate auctions. Harold bid against me, because Davis Natterly let it slip I'd wanted it. He's tight with Harold and his mom, which I didn't find out until afterwards, or I'd have said something like—keep your mouth shut around Harold." The gleam in Rook's eyes was back, but this time, it was fueled with a righteous anger. "After the auction, Harold sniped it. Handed over his credit card, said he was buying it for me as a present to show no hard feelings, and yanked the bird out from under me. As far as Davis was concerned, he was doing Harold a solid by letting him get it for me."

"He should lose his license," Alex grumbled. "I don't care how much of a favor he thought he was doing."

"Yeah. Davis and I had a few words, but we're kind of stuck with each other. He and his brother score some really good estate listings, and I need the merchandise, so reporting him isn't going to do me any good," Rook admitted. "Anyway, once I found out Harold jacked the statue, I demanded it back. That's what he was preening about a couple of weeks ago at dinner. He had the falcon and wouldn't stop poking at me. So… I told him to fuck off and that I'd just take it."

Dante rubbed a hand across his face, then sighed. "Okay, so you told your cousin you were going to break into his house?"

"And take back what was mine. Fuck him. What's a few doors? I had all the codes, but it was good to see if I could do it." His lover nodded, then looked around the room at their shocked faces. "What? I was going to leave the fucker a check. But I didn't kill him. Vicks's got a couple of theories he's kicking around. Said I knifed Harold, then brought Alex back so I could find Harold's body."

"Assuming then you found out Harold was alive, so you then finished killing him with the one thing you were going to steal from him?" Dante picked at the label of his beer, reasoning out Vicks's case. "Forensics would have to match up the timeline, and then he'd have to break your alibi. We won't know where you were until we get the morgue's report."

"Mr. Archie," Rosa called out from the doorway. The concern on her face when they drove up turned to worry, a deep line wrinkling the skin between her eyebrows. "One of the lawyers is on the phone. He said they've just arrested Ms. Sadonna. The detective on the case thinks she hired Rook to kill Harold for her."

"God, the idiots I hire. Why the fuck would they think that?" Archie's face flushed red, and a vein pulsed on his forehead. "Why the ever-loving hell would Rook even have anything to do with Harold's wife? She's a tart, and the boy doesn't even like women."

"Um, I did have something to do with her." Shooting Dante a sheepish look, Rook rocked back on his heels. "Because Sadonna's the one who gave me the security codes so I could break into their house."

Four

SHADOWS DRAPED over Potter's Field's main showroom as the dark was kept at bay by the slender strips of LEDs running along the bottom of the shop's glass cases. Sparkles of faint blue kicked back from the dozens of reflective memorabilia displayed throughout the enormous space, glittering pieces of childhoods forged from books and screens. The shop itself held only a small fraction of his whole inventory, cheaper pieces people would spot in a window and reminiscence on Saturdays spent eating sugary cereal in front of a flickering TV. Rook's wealth lay in the high-ticket items kept off-site, pieces in a vast collection he scrounged and haggled for at auctions or estate sales. It was the hunt that kept him going, giving him the rush Rook needed to scratch the itch he had inside of him.

He'd come a long way since the days of running short cons and hawking coin tosses for stuffed animals on the fairgrounds. As much as he missed the thrill of cracking open a door and slipping through the shadows, Rook *liked* knowing he'd built something on his own. Potter's Field was something he'd imagined up and made a success, using connections and every bit of pop culture trivia he'd soaked up while working the big tops and rides.

Rook knew every bit and bob the shop had to offer. His hands touched each one, no matter how big or small. After the loss of his Chewbacca statue to a hail of police bullets, he'd been the one to set the six-foot-tall soft sculpture of UrSol into its place, debating with himself furiously about if the Mystic should be put safely behind glass or left bare to the world, allowing people near the artistic marvel.

He'd opted to leave the Mystic bare but cordoned off by black velvet ropes, trusting the store's customers to look, take pictures and selfies, but not to touch.

"And if that isn't an allegory for me, I don't know what the fuck is," Rook muttered to himself. "Or is that a metaphor? Shit, now I have to go look it up. I hate not knowing crap."

"You know more than I do. About a lot of things," Dante said, leaning against the doorframe connecting the store to the lift leading to Rook's apartment. "A hell of a lot of things, *cuervo*. I'd say you make me feel stupid, but that says more about my ignorance than your intelligence."

He loved Dante Montoya for a lot of reasons. His hot body, the way the Latino made him ache to be touched, the conversations they had about everything under the sun and sometimes a few outside of the galaxy, but the main reason he adored having Montoya in his life was the man pulled no punches and was always willing to defend Rook against anything, including himself.

Until he met Dante, he hadn't trusted anyone to fight *for* him. Archie and Alex said they were willing to go in on a battle, standing shoulder to shoulder with him, but it took a husky-voiced, amber-eyed detective who forced his way past Rook's walls for Rook to actually believe anyone would care for him.

Dante Montoya made him *feel*—made him *love*—and that was something Rook hoped he'd never forget.

"I love you, but that was something Harold liked to poke at me about." The store's ambient light tugged on Dante's handsome face, stroking the plump of his lips with a faint azure tint. "I never went to school, and he went... shit, to everything. He gives... gave... me shit about how I said things, like foyer. Called me ignorant. I learned by reading. How the fuck was I supposed to know it was pronounced *fo-yay* from a damned book? He'd mock me all the time, just to get a rise out of me. Sure, I hate looking... *stupid*, but not enough to kill him...."

He should have felt stronger standing in the middle of something he'd built, but the whispering doubts were still there, the tiny slivers of sharp rebuke lurking in his mind, reminding him he'd come to a sorry end like everyone else he knew. There were regrets, large ones, and questions like should he have turned in the stash he'd saved for a rainy day? Was Montoya worth that sacrifice? Was he expecting Montoya to keep him around? It wore at him, picking at his confidence until he was riddled with holes and the only thing he had to fill them were the memories of when he'd failed.

Dante touching his face, work-roughened fingers skimming over his chin and then a swipe across his lips, brought Rook back from the edge of his worrying. Smiling, his lover caught him up, hooking a strong arm around Rook's waist to pull him into a hug.

"First off, baby, I will never get tired of hearing you say you love me," Dante whispered into Rook's mouth as he brushed a kiss over his lips. They stung slightly, chapped from chewing on them, a worry-tell he'd worked hard to break, but now, on the straight and narrow, those things didn't matter anymore. "Secondly, you are one of the smartest men I know. You scare me with everything you know. The random things you store in your head amazes me."

He should have pulled away. He kept meaning to. Every time Dante held him, a part of Rook said to step back, to not be held in, but he stayed. He always stayed, and the soft light in Dante's eyes told him he knew of the wars raging inside of Rook's mind.

Instead Rook deflected. "You're just sucking up to me because you owe me twenty bucks from the last poker game."

"The damned game was rigged. I just haven't figured out how you did it." He playfully tugged on Rook's lower lip, pinching at the plump, then laughing when Rook bit his finger lightly. "Your cousin was... an asshole. You threatened him because you're someone he couldn't bully. Even when he was being the worst he could be, there was always something you were that he'd never be, a man who could stand on his own two feet, and when you get knocked down, no one can stop you from getting back up again."

"But still, not murder."

"No, not murder. Not you," Dante agreed. "But why.... Did I meet her? What's her name?"

"Sadonna Swann. Like Madonna but with an *S*." Rook grinned. "She says that all the time. She's a tease, but I *like* her, and she can give as good as she gets. I don't know if you ever met her. She and Harold didn't exactly run in the same circles. Okay, mostly she thought dinner at Archie's was like trying to sit down with a table of starving hyenas."

"She's not wrong," he pointed out.

"No, not by much." Rook had to give Dante that. The infrequent Sunday dinners at Archie's were a knife-in-the-back kind of event where the good china was scraped by expensive silver and the wine flowed as freely as the veiled insults. "She's blonde, curvy. Pretty, old-school glam. Like a modern Mae West. A little bit older than you. You'd know her if you saw her. Really kicks ass on stage, especially in meaty things like *Streetcar*. She was great in that. But she got famous doing movies. She was in that this-isn't-Swamp-Thing-but-totally-Swamp-Thing movie I made you watch a couple of weeks ago. The one with the nutria. Strictly B-movie stuff but solid work."

"Wait, the one whose dress kept getting wet and torn?" Dante cocked his head, humming for a second, then asked, "The one Manny said is restarting her career?"

"Yeah, don't let an actress hear you say that. They'll tell you they're just looking for the right project." If doubt chewed on him, guilt over Sadonna was making a meal of his guts. Pulling free of Dante's embrace left Rook hollow inside, but he needed some breathing room, space to work out the jumbled emotions in his head.

A few steps took Rook over to the spot where he'd found Danielle, murdered by his assistant and once trusted friend, Charlene. Both women were now dead, caught up in a violence he'd been ill-prepared to deal with. Charlene's betrayal and her willingness to kill anyone in her way had been a shock to Rook's core. All in pursuit of the gems and gold coins Rook'd stashed away as a nest egg in case things went sideways.

Charlene died a few feet away, her life seeping out of her in the back entrance's corridor. The store held too much death, and still, a hell of a lot of dreams. A part of him wanted to rip everything up by the roots and go elsewhere, but it'd taken him too damned long to find his home, and now too many people, including Dante's uncle Manny, depended on him to be there, needing to feed their families and continue on with their lives. Running away would solve his problems but fuck up a lot of people in the process.

There'd been a time when Rook wouldn't have cared what happened to the people around him. He'd cut more than one string, buried more than a few shallow friendships to keep himself safe. Now it was so damned different. Now when trouble hit, Rook found himself standing to protect the people he'd have left in the dust only a year ago.

Dante's presence in his life, in his bed, meant he had to shed any connection to the days he'd spent freeing the rich from the burden of their wealth. He didn't like having a conscience. Hated the tingle of wrong in the back of his throat and brain. There hadn't been a rebuke in his thoughts—ever—not until he'd let Dante Montoya in, and now it was as if he were caught in a bumper car ride every time he ran up against something even remotely illegal.

Or... unjust.

"I know what you're thinking, *cuervo*. I see you looking over there," Dante said, leaning against one of the glass cases. "You're not responsible for Danielle's death or Charlene's either. Only Charlene's to blame for that. She dragged you into it. And this thing with Harold? It's not on you. I wish you hadn't been the one to find the body, but that's something you're going to have to deal with."

"Can't help it. It's just… I went for years without this much death." It was a hard admission, but the murder and violence was taking a toll on him. "It's one thing to… break into places, but killing someone? I mean, I've seen dead bodies before. Most carnies don't… they don't go to doctors, and it's not like I haven't found someone in their trailer. It's how life is there. And shit, it's a hard life. People hurt each other—even kill each other—but this, right after Charlene and everything she did? I don't know how to deal with it."

"Charlene… all of that? That was betrayal. I'm not saying she deserved what happened, but if you knock on Death's door, chances are, he's going to answer." Crossing his arms over his chest, Dante gave Rook a slight heart-pounding smile. "I'm glad you survived it, and I'm thankful we came out of that, but if you've gotten yourself into the middle of something now, we'll deal with that too, *querido*. This time, though, you tell me everything that's going on. Okay?"

"Yeah, okay," Rook agreed. "Mostly I'm pissed off about Sadonna getting arrested, because now I'm wondering what the hell is going on. Not going to lie to you, I was kicking around the idea of breaking into the house to get the statue, but she's the one who came to me with the codes. Harold pissed her off about something, and she wanted to get back at him. I was the easiest way she could do that."

"Did you tell Vicks that?"

"No, but Alex did. He knew I was going in, because Sadonna slipped me the alarm codes. It's probably why Vicks tagged her." He chewed on the idea for a bit, turning it over in his head. "I fucking shut down, Dante. I sat down in that seat and everything just… I stonewalled."

"Why didn't you just tell Vicks the truth?" The reproach was a soft one, but there was a bit of steel in Dante's words, a gentle reminder Rook strayed from the straight-and-narrow path he'd put himself on. "If Sadonna gave you the codes, he should know about that. It would clear you."

"Habit," he confessed. "I'm not saying it's right, but damn, those habits are hard to break. Because shit, Dante, he sat me down, and all my brain just started screaming to shut him down, dodge it, and get the hell out." As much as he'd wanted to shed those instincts, they hit hard and fast.

The smell of a cop house, with its bitterness and unwashed dregs, evoked a flight response Rook couldn't seem to fight. "Now Harold's dead, the two of us are in Vicks's crosshairs because he's got no where else to look, and I don't know if Archie's going to help her get out. Me and Alex, sure. We're his to the bone, but Sadonna? He might let her twist in the wind, and that doesn't sit right with me."

"I want to know who was there in the room when you got there. If Harold was knifed earlier, then who knocked you down?" Dante shifted, a rivet on his jeans tapping the glass. "Vicks didn't believe you. That tells me he's not going to look hard for the real killer. You're going to have to go back and tell him the whole story, starting with Sadonna suggesting you break in."

"I can't let Sadonna go down for this, Montoya." He shook his head, not liking the feel of guilt weighing his chest down. "It's not right. Someone else wanted Harold dead. Everything was still in the house. The safes weren't touched. Hell, even the damned silver was still lying on the counter, covered in dried food. It wouldn't have taken that long to shove a lot of that into a bag and take off."

"I'm not going to ask why you looked at the safes." Dante chuckled when Rook gave him a withering look. "Let's just say it was to reassure you the motive wasn't burglary. It could be they didn't have time. We won't know anything solid until the morgue comes back with their report."

"There's a lot of should haves I've got going on in my head." Vicks shaking him down was only a glancing blow. The detective acted like he knew more, but from what James intimated, Vicks was known to be a dick. "I can't just sit this one out, Montoya. I've got to do something. Help her out somehow. I feel like this shit's my fault."

"Did she tell you what Harold did to piss her off?" Dante's eyes were hooded, their deep honey color nearly sepia in the faint light. "And don't take this wrong, but could she have played you? Set you up to find him?"

"Maybe? My gut tells me no, but we all know how good my gut's been about women lately." He grimaced. "I do *like* Sadonna. She's old-school Hollywood, you know? A bit bawdy but snarky. She's the kind of woman who walks into a private dick's office, asks him to take her case, then leaves him with nothing but regrets and bittersweet memories. But would she jack me over? I don't think—"

The sound of something striking the store's front glass boomed through the shop's main room, and Rook flinched, curling his arm up over his head. A wave of heat bloomed across the floor, the acrid scent of chemicals or alcohol burning his nose, and before he could blink away the dryness in his eyes from the scorched air, Dante was on him, rolling them both down to the floor.

"What the hell?" The sting of flaming cheap vodka seared Rook's nose, and he fought to get out from under Dante's weight. "Let me go! The shop!"

"Stay down!" Dante shouted into his ear as he rolled to the side. "Get out and call 911. I'm going for the extinguishers!"

Another arc of fire followed, a stream of flames lighting up the shadows along the glass cases, but Rook could only catch a glimpse of the bottle before it struck the floor. The carpet burned under the spreading sea of fire, black smoke billowing up to the store's open ductwork. The front windows crinkled, and another boom shook the shop, slamming Rook's eardrums with a percussive wave. It was getting harder to see, even hard to breathe as waves of smoke filled the space. Crouched against one of the side cases, Rook reached for Dante, alarmed to find his lover wasn't there.

"Montoya!" He scrambled through his brain, trying to remember where the fire extinguishers were. "I don't have my damned phone!" A canister rolled over, striking his foot, and Rook grabbed for it, thinking to toss it back out. "Shit, no. Don't grab. Cover. Fucking shit."

A spiral rack of hoodies was the closest thing to a dampening cloth he had. He swaddled the canister with one of the garments, hoping to suppress as much of its exhaust as possible, stamping the cotton over the tear gas grenade. Coughing, Rook staggered to his feet, amazed to find the front windows were still mostly intact save the one by the door. Dante appeared out of the thickening, stinging fog, his arms wrapped around an extinguisher. He'd pulled his shirt up to cover his nose and mouth, his eyes going wide when he spotted Rook.

"Get out!" His shout was muffled but clear enough for Rook to understand him.

"I need to call! Shit, where's the damned store phone?" Rook covered his mouth with his arm. Battling through the haze, he slid in behind the cash register, grabbing at the landline. They'd gone with a traditional clunky model, keeping with the retro-vintage feel of the shop, and Rook's fingers shook as he tucked the handset under his chin, tangling the curled-up cord around his wrist.

Hitting the emergency buttons, he ducked down, hoping the air closer to the floor stayed clear. An operator picked up immediately, and Rook rattled off the store's address first, repeating it again when she asked him to slow down.

"Potter's Field. Someone tossed Molotovs and tear gas into the windows. I'm on a landline, so I've got to get off the phone. I'm with Detective Dante Montoya from Central. He's got an extinguisher, I think."

"Get out of the building as quickly as you can," the operator ordered. "If you can get clear, do so now. I'm sending in help. Hang up, and once you're outside, see if you can call back on a cell. We'll want to make sure you got out so the fire crew isn't looking for you."

An extinguisher's hiss reassured Rook Dante figured out how to use the damned thing, but the room was quickly becoming a hazard. Taking one last kick at the wrapped canister, Rook got it toward the elevator corridor and through the door as another canister shattered through another of the store's windows. It careened around out of sight, leaving a stream of noxious smoke pouring out from behind a sales counter.

Whoever was outside was determined to draw them out, and Rook wasn't certain that's where he wanted to be.

"Can I bust the windows out?" he screamed over the crackle of the extinguisher, brandishing the rack. The single spire was heavy enough to do some damage, but Rook feared fueling the flames with a rush of air. "Got to get the smoke out!"

"Go! It's not that bad. Knock the broken one out," Dante yelled back. His voice was rough, drawn to a rasp from the smoke. "Just stay clear!"

The fire was small, eating through a piece of industrial carpet laid down to cut back on noise, but the retardant held. The extinguisher was an industrial monster the salesman talked Rook into, and as far as he was concerned, was a hair smaller than an actual damned hydrant, but Dante handled it with ease. Shoulder muscles bulging under his sweat-dampened shirt, Dante hefted the canister up and laid down another stream of spray.

"This better not go to shit." Rook choked on his own spit, coughing out a lungful of smoke. Swinging the rack up, he struck the broken front window with the heavy pedestal, then swore when he lost his grip on the bar. It was enough of a strike to get the base through the window, and he had to duck quickly, covering his face to avoid the errant pieces of glass trickling down from the frame.

The rush of cold air was immediate, and his heart pounded from the fear of the fire catching the torrent and engulfing Dante. Rook's mouth and nose burned, raw from coughing and smoke inhalation, but he went back into the store, intent on pulling Dante out. Grabbing his lover by the arm, he tried shouting, but his voice cracked, a speckled pain pricking down his throat.

"Come on!" Rook tugged, trying to drag the heavier man out. "Go out the back. Guy in front could have a gun!"

"Yeah. Okay, fire's done." As if Rook hadn't been trying to move him out into the clear air, Dante scooped his arm around Rook's waist, dragging him toward the back. The swaddled canister was still smoking as they went by, and Dante stumbled over it, working the jackets loose. "Keep going, *cuervo*. Right out the back."

The canisters' plumes were lessening, but it was getting harder to see. Rook blinked, shocked to find his eyes were swelling and he couldn't breathe through his nose. A hot panic took his nerves, shaking his senses, and he began coughing, unsure if he was pulling in air or simply holding in trapped smoke. He heard Dante hitting the back door open, its heavy weight striking the building's side.

Hollywood's night air hit them with an icy slap, and Rook's lungs seized up, caught in the need for oxygen. The coughing began anew, huge racking spasms twisting his spine and cramping his belly. Swallowing didn't help. His throat was dry, too dry, and felt as if he'd gulped down a handful of caltrops for dinner. Sirens cut through the neighborhood's low rattle, and from the sounds coming from the front walk, people were beginning to gather at the edges of the block, witnessing yet another spectacle at Rook's expense.

"*Fuck.*" The shakes finally hit, and a dread tightened Rook's gums, his tongue sticking to the roof of his mouth. "Could have lost you, Montoya. Fucking *hell.*"

"Hey, I got you," Dante murmured into his hair, stroking Rook's back. "Shop's going to be fine. Just some carpet and a couple of windows. Shit's been worse, *cuervo*. You're fine."

"Sure I am," he coughed into Dante's chest. "So how come someone's now trying to kill me?"

Five

"OH GOD, *mijo*." Manny walked through the wide breach in Potter's Field's front wall, avoiding the workmen trying to remove one of the door's steel frames. "What *happened*?"

"Someone tried to kill Rook." Dante shoved a push broom across the now bare floor, clearing away a scatter of glass fragments. Glancing up at his mother's younger brother, he snarled, "*Again*."

It'd been a hard night, fraught right up until the moment he dragged his lover upstairs to the former dance studio Rook'd converted into an apartment, scrubbed the hell and tear gas remnants off their bodies, then tumbled naked into bed. Then the nightmares hit, long drawn-out terrors Rook couldn't seem to wake from. Nodding off, he jerked out of dozing, damp with sweat and wild-eyed, reaching for Dante nearly every other hour until his body couldn't seem to hold out any longer and Rook finally surrendered to an uneasy sleep.

Dante left a sleeping Rook in bed, but he hadn't stayed there. Five minutes after Dante woke up, Rook was on his feet and out the door, disheveled and needing to stretch his legs. He'd taken enough time to brush his teeth, pull on a pair of tattered jeans, and give Dante a kiss hot enough to take his breath away. Muttering he'd come back with coffee, Rook grabbed his keys and ghosted out.

Two hours ago.

Hollywood seeped in through the broken windows and propped-open front door. The midmorning sun baked the four-lane boulevard, warming the street's web of tarry patches until their scorched licorice stink permeated the breeze. Bits of street traffic flashed past the intact windows, the thump of a bassline coming from a chunky lowered Toyota rattling Dante's teeth when it rolled by. There were a few appreciative mutters at the burly men fitting plywood sheets into a cleared-out window frame, and Dante grinned when his uncle pursed his mouth to give a tuneless, soft whistle when one bent over to pick up a power tool from the sidewalk.

Last night, Rook'd covered the glass cases while Dante spoke to the cops, then stood, staring at the broken remains of his storefront. To Dante, the curated merchandise seemed to be intact, but at some point, his lover's gaze had gone flat and sullen, much like his mood, until the units dispersed. Then he'd reached out for Dante's hand and held on tight as Dante led him upstairs.

"Let me put my bag down, and then you can tell me what's going on." Manny eyed one of the workmen, a warm smile flickering across his expressive mouth. "And he… or you… should have called me. This is my job, you know. I'm supposed to be handling all of these things for him. Leave the broom. The day staff will be here soon. They can help clean up until we're ready to open. Is everything here? Were we robbed?"

"Place looks like a war zone, but I think it's okay. Firebug guys said it was probably someone who didn't know what they were doing. Probably meant to vandalize or rob the place, maybe smash through the windows, using the fire as a cover. Problem was, the bottles they used were heavy and had way too much accelerant in them. So in the end, not a robbery, just… a shit storm, and I don't know where Rook's gone." Dante gave a skeptical glance at broken panes he'd hastily boarded up at two in the morning after the uniforms he'd called in finally left. "They're not going to install new windows, *tío*. These guys are only securing the—"

"I know what they're doing. You leave that and make sure I have some coffee." His uncle nodded toward the door leading to the shop's office and storage areas. "I am going to find a sheet. Then you're going to catch me up on what happened last night with you and your *cuervo*."

"What's the sheet for?" Dante rearranged a tarp over the odd soft-form sculpture Rook put in place of his decimated Chewbacca. "Everything that needs covering is taken care of."

"Oh, *mijo*. The sheet isn't for covering things. It's to spray paint and make a sign to hang on the boards outside." Manny barked a laugh. "Now go on and get the coffee going. I'll be along as soon as I can get someone in to watch the store while they finish up here."

THE COFFEE maker had burbled its final gasp by the time Manny joined him in the office. His uncle bustled in, juggling his messenger bag and a large plastic tote weighted down with what looked like white fabric. Dante reached for the heavy bag, grunted at its heft, then maneuvered it into one of the two odd chairs Manny bought for his private domain.

What was once a bit of floor space for the store, a quick frame-out and drywall made an employees' lounge and office at the end of a corridor leading to the back door and storerooms. Newly built, the place still smelled a little bit of paint, and everything glistened with bits of chrome among the comfortable padded chairs in the lounge. Manny'd objected to a space, but Rook was stubborn. If he was going to hire Manny as the store's manager, the older man would need an office, and the employees Manny hired would need a place to take breaks.

Manny's objections were drowned out in a bit of Rook's cockiness, but Dante knew his uncle was secretly delighted, especially when Rook told him to decorate the spaces however he wanted as long as there was a coffee machine, a fridge, and a couple of couches.

Since the steel monster in the lounge looked like it was built to torture secrets out of an Alderaan diplomat and produced about as much coffee as information they'd pulled from the princess, Dante bullied a pot of strong coffee from the old-school electric percolator Manny set up on an old Victorian-era sideboard behind his desk.

It was a fairly nice-sized office, with windows running along the top of the outer-facing wall, and decorated by a gleeful Manny in a style Dante could only call early garage sale remnants and bingo-playing *abuelita* castoffs. A heavily embellished cherrywood executive desk shared the space with a red leather chesterfield sofa, two swing chairs, and the sideboard. A faux Tiffany standing lamp dominated a corner by the door, and Manny sighed when Dante pointed out it was missing a crystal from the cascade of teardrops dangling from its stained-glass shade, and when Rook rolled out an enormous, slightly faded Persian rug he and Manny found at a swap meet, they'd both rolled their eyes at him after he dragged his toe over a cigarette scorch at its edge.

And if he wasn't quite sure he'd lost his place as Manny's favorite, Dante knew for certain Rook shoved him aside, tucked the marred edge of the rug under the chesterfield, then blushed when Manny hugged him and murmured in Spanish that he loved him.

There'd been significant changes in his uncle in the few weeks since he'd began working for Rook. He was still nearly a mirror image of Dante's mother, a relatively short, soft-around-the-middle Mexican man from Laredo, but there was a spring to Manny's step, an eagerness to go out into the world every morning. His broad, ready smiles were now a touch more sincere, and more than once, Dante'd come in from the back of the building from Rook's place to find his uncle holding court among a group of rapt tourists and staff with his opinion on an old movie Dante never heard of.

Dante could no longer deny it. The evidence was right in front of his face. His slightly round former drag queen, breast cancer conqueror of an uncle... *glowed.*

"You're looking at me funny, *mijo.*" Manny eyed him suspiciously, hanging his bag on the hat rack by the door. "What happened?"

"Nothing." He leaned forward to stand up and get coffee, but his uncle waved him back down, passing the couch toward the sideboard. Bone-tired, Dante slumped into the sofa, grateful for the comfort. "I was just thinking how you look happy. Almost like you've got a boyfriend or something."

"Please, the last thing I need is a boyfriend. I've got too much to do now. That sort of thing is going to have to wait. I wouldn't say no, but I'm not going to dig around for someone to say yes." Manny came back with a couple of coffee mugs, nudging Dante's foot to move him over. "Get settled and take one."

"Why am I moving?" Grumbling wouldn't solve anything. His uncle wanted to sit on that side of the couch, so of course he'd move, but not without a little grousing as he went. The sofa squeaked under him as he shuffled over, then reached across to take one of the mugs. "This one mine?"

"Yes, it is bitter and dark like your soul." Tucking his legs under, Manny teased, switching to the Spanish they'd both grown up speaking. "Now, tell me, what happened? Who is trying to kill our little crow?"

"It's more than that, Uncle. Our little crow's gone back to his old tricks." Dante took a deep breath. "And it all starts off with that dead cousin I told you about."

Manny listened. Silently. Intently. And leaving Dante with little doubt he had his uncle's full attention. He'd started with the call and the cops, then drifted into his worry about Rook's storm of nightmares.

"I don't know what to do, Manny. That cop, Vicks, has me worried. He's mean, spiteful, and I know that gleam in his eye, the smugness on his face. He wants to hurt Rook for something, but I can't tell you what," Dante confessed softly, setting his empty coffee cup on the floor. "Yesterday was a minefield. Getting that call from Rook, him telling me he'd broken into a house—his cousin's house—and then finding the man dead? It was already too much, but to come home, after all of that, to this happening? How much more can he take? Can *we* take?"

"Are you worried he's done with you? With living a normal life?" His uncle leaned in, placing his soft hand on Dante's thigh. "Because he loves you, son. I've seen him look at you, talk to you. He is very much in love with you."

"But does he love me more than he fears being trapped?" His question stung as it left him, its barbs ripping his throat as he yanked his words free. "Because right now, Uncle, I worry he's going to run. Not because he doesn't love me. But because he can't help but run. It's all he's ever known."

THE FIRST time Rook'd seen Sadonna Swann, he was fourteen, heartbreakingly scared, and on the run. A job he'd been pulling went south, and he'd been left twisting in the wind by the supposed adults on the heist with him. With an ocean of cops on his ass, ducking into a sci-fi double feature when a theater employee went back in from a smoke break was a surefire way to save his own skin.

He'd already known he was different. The skimpily clad women working the sideshows did nothing for him, even when they rubbed up against his admittedly a bit too skinny teenaged frame, but the strong men and the male crew working setup made parts of his body tingle where they hadn't tingled before. Talking to his mother, Beanie, was out, mostly because she'd been AWOL for over six months by then, and everyone he'd had around him was scattered to different carnivals, an inevitable destiny for people who worked for an embezzling con artist with more greed than business sense.

Left to drift, he'd taken up with the first show who'd have him, an unfamiliar circuit with a few of the sketchiest carnies he'd ever known. He'd already done a few jobs in California and found he loved the spice it brought to his blood, but this time it was different. This time he'd been thrown under the bus by the people who were responsible for extracting him, and even if Rook knew how to get back to the field where the carnival set up, he wasn't sure he wanted to.

The cool dimness was a welcome relief after the bone-melting San Antonio heat, and he'd climbed up to the top row of the theater, slouching down to avoid notice. He was alone, lost, and in a city he didn't know, traveling with a road crew he didn't like. With his heart pounding an erratic, scary beat in his ears, Rook'd tucked himself up into a ball and breathed a sigh of relief when the lights dimmed and the movie began to play.

Sadonna—like Madonna but with an *S*—Swann oozed sex. And not just any kind of sex but molten hot, burn your tongue on her wit and cocky smile sex. For all of his apathy toward women, when Sadonna Swann burst onto the screen wearing a dark blue military-style trench over a cleavage-revealing white shirt and a pair of hip-hugging black pants tucked into brown riding boots, Rook wondered if he was falling in love. It could have been her chewing through the scene with a snarl and a wink or even the double tap-tap of her laser pistols as she blew alien brains all over the screen in a fourth-wall-breaking splatter on the camera, but no matter what it was about the slightly crass flaxen bombshell, he'd lost a piece of his heart that day.

And when he'd discovered she was married to his asshole cousin, Harold, he'd briefly mourned his one-sided love affair with the only woman who'd made him rethink if he really liked dick as much as he had before he'd seen her.

"I didn't kill him," Sadonna rasped, her trembling fingers raking back her trademark thick blonde mane. "Sure, sometimes I wanted him dead, but I didn't kill him. You've got to believe me, Rook."

For an aging sex kitten, she normally didn't look a day over thirty, but the murder wore her down, and the jail's harsh lighting didn't do her strained features any favors. Her wrists were swollen and red from the cuffs the cops slapped on her during her arrest, probably on too tight and too long judging by how she rubbed at them as she talked. They'd either taken her clothes or she'd been arrested wearing a tight gray T-shirt and black sweats. Her lush body was a promise of heat and sensuality, but her beautiful face with its sad, tired sea-green eyes whispered tragedy and regret.

Sadonna Swann was everything Charlene, his former assistant, had wanted to be. Successful enough to be recognized, but not so popular as to shut her life down every time she stepped out the door. Her acting range was tighter than most headliners, but there was something about Sadonna's retro bombshell body and classic beauty that drew the eye. Getting older in Hollywood was the kiss of death, but she'd managed well enough, embracing her past roles and playing up any parts she could pry out of stingy directors' cold, clammy hands.

"I didn't think you did. This is insane, babe." Rook looked around, uneasy at the thick Plexiglas wall separating them and the armed behemoths holding court behind him. "I didn't think they'd lock you up. Figured Vicks would do to you what he did to me: catch, threaten, and release."

The detention center was fairly decent, although Rook didn't have much experience in them. He'd not actually made it behind formal bars. Other than a stray hour or two at a police station's holding cell, he'd never truly lost his freedom. There'd always been a way to slide away from the noose tightening around his neck or someone he could socially engineer to release him before he earned an overnight stay.

Sadonna hadn't been so lucky. Archie's refusal to sic his lawyers on the LAPD stymied Sadonna's release, and her own lawyer, a decent man who dealt more with entertainment contracts than criminal charges, hadn't delivered Sadonna a golden ticket out the front door. She needed assholes and bulldogs, but instead she'd brought a pigeon to the bargaining table to do battle with the court, and he'd been chopped up and served as stew nearly from the moment he'd come through the door.

"That asshole!" Anger curled her lip, throwing a bit of ugly into her words. "That's someone I'd like to see hit by a bus—"

"Hold those kinds of thoughts until we get you out of here. Or do you want to have all of your mail forwarded to Century?" Rook tapped at the glass, and the guard standing near the door cleared his throat with a menacing rumble. "I've got Archie's lawyers to take a stab at getting you out of here."

"God, he must love the fuck out of you, kid." She eyed him. "Because that man would sooner watch me rot on a hot tin roof than help me out. He's still mad I didn't give him any great-grandkids, but there was no fucking way in hell I was going to start shooting out babies. Especially not with Harold."

"I'm not even sure why you married Harold in the first place." Rook grinned at her pained grimace.

"It seemed like a good idea at the time." Sadonna wrinkled her nose. "I might have been a little bit drunk. And we were in Vegas at a wrap party. Next thing I know, I'm married and he's puking in the bathtub at the MGM. Then we stayed married, because well, Archie told him to. And if Archibald Martin told Harold to jump, Harold would climb the tallest building he could find and pitch himself off of it."

"Well, Archie was pissy about the lawyers, but I reminded him it looks shitty to just let you rot, especially since I'm the one who probably put you here." He wasn't good at handling the guilt nibbling at him, and looking at Sadonna through a thick pane of Plexiglas wasn't helping his stomach settle down either. He had a plan, one he'd thought on as he walked through Hollywood and read the names on the stars beneath his feet. "And he does like you. It's why he wanted you to have kids with Harold. Thinning out the Martin bloodline is a dream of his. It keeps him up some nights."

"Maybe you and I should have a kid, then." She fluttered her eyelashes at him, guffawing when he instinctively recoiled. "Yeah, I didn't think so."

"Mostly because I don't want a kid, not because... shit, don't pull me into that game." He tsked. "Last time I talked to the head suit, they're going to get you bail, and Archie's either going to post it or I will. Either way, you're getting out."

"And go where?" Her sculpted brow arched up, the beauty mark on her cheek lifting when she quirked her mouth. "They've frozen my assets, remember? I'm a flight risk, and I sure as hell can't go home. And don't tell me Archie's going to take me in. You and I both know he'd sooner see me selling pencils on a street corner than let me into that house."

"Actually, that's exactly where you're going. Lurch the Lawyer said it would show the family supports you and help with your case. I don't know about Harold's parents, but after Archie got some sleep and bacon, he eventually agreed with me that you didn't kill the idiot. Hold on." His phone burbled in his jacket pocket, and a quick check made him grin. "They've got you bail, and Archie said he'd pop for it."

"So now he's dying and wants into Heaven?" She leaned her head back, rolling her shoulders until they touched the chair's firm metal back. "Sorry. I'm just... I don't know how to process any of this. It was a *joke*. Harold was supposed to be playing golf not... lying there dead."

"Yeah, I know. Vicks is going to keep hammering at you. I know his type. Only way you're ever going to be free of him is if someone confesses to killing Harold."

"Or if I leave the country," Sadonna muttered darkly, then rubbed at her wrists again. "I'm kidding. I'm not going to go anywhere. Not until this is resolved, but living with Archie, I might have more peace if I stay here in jail."

"No can do, babe. I need you out here." Rook stood up when a guard approached Sadonna, murmuring she was scheduled for release. "Because I'm going to prove you didn't do it. And I'm going to ask Dante to help."

Six

FROM THE moment Dante Montoya saw Rook Stevens through a one-way glass window in one of Central's interview rooms, he'd known the cat burglar was trouble, the kind of bad-boy trouble anyone in their right mind would have tossed into a bin and walked away. Problem was, too many people had done just that, and now Dante was dealing with being crazy in love with a man who'd lived on scraps of affection and rotted dreams.

There were times when it hurt Dante to look at Rook. His heart couldn't take the rush of conflicted emotions, and torn between wanting to shake some sense into his lover or swaddle him and drag him under the covers to spend the rest of the day in bed, Dante knew he could do neither. Rook fought being controlled, raged at being hemmed in, and even stiffened when hugged. A little piece of Dante died every time he watched as someone Rook cared for touched him, his heart breaking in that moment between touch and relaxation when Rook's fears urged him to run.

Rook'd stopped running, but the instincts remained, a wild soul caged by the invisible threads connecting him to the people he'd learned to love, and now he was pacing the length of the loft's living space, eating up the wooden floor in long strides.

Spanning the length of the post-Art-Deco building, the loft apartment's polished wooden floors and high ceilings were a reminder of its time as a dance studio, its three golden brick outer walls lined with nine-foot-tall mullioned crank-levered windows Rook'd fitted blackout curtains over to combat Los Angeles's unrelenting sun and the neon signs lining the streets. The living room was big enough to swallow up three eight-foot couches and a large-screen television hidden in a free-standing credenza. Old movie posters and kitsch decorated the main space, splashes of color on the mellow brick. A galley kitchen, built-in cold room for vintage costumes, and enormous bathroom ran down the left side of the space, while a long wall of ten-foot-tall black lacquer bookcases cut off the rear third of the loft, creating a room for Rook's soft king-sized bed and antique Asian chests.

It was a long space, perfect for Rook to move around in, and he took advantage of every inch, slowly bouncing from spot to spot in the nearly spartan living room until Dante snagged him by the waistband on his fourth or fifth pass.

"*Cuervo*, come here." He dragged Rook down, folding him into an embrace. "You're making me dizzy, and you said you wanted to talk, so let's talk."

Rook didn't fight him, but the rigid stiffness dug into Dante's ego, scooping out a piece of his pride with a savage bite. It was only a moment, maybe two, but it was enough, and Dante held on tight, refusing to let Rook go. One exhaled breath and Rook gave in, his joints and muscles relaxing, spilling him into a sprawl over Dante's lap.

Burying his face into Rook's hair, Dante simply held his lover, taking him all in.

He'd changed. Dante saw it in the little things, minute shifts in Rook's behaviors. Some Rook explained when Dante asked, while others he filed away as signs of Rook unfurling, growing into someone who wasn't constantly looking over their shoulder or waiting for the other shoe to drop.

There was time spent cooking, or rather in Rook's case, attempting to cook. Sips of wine, usually followed by a grimace, were shared between them, oftentimes ending with Rook's glass being dumped into the pasta sauce because he didn't like reds. They took walks in the evening, sometimes catching a movie at an old drive-in while stretched out in the back of Dante's truck. Swap meets and fresh-air markets tickled Rook's fancy, and he plunged eagerly into bins and junk tents, ferreting out odd treasures Dante couldn't make heads or tails out of.

There were gaps in Rook's knowledge, a slice of life in between rarified objects d'art and street smarts, and Dante slowly discovered Rook's challenging of the norm came from curiosity about things he'd never experienced growing up on the sideshow and carnival circuit.

His new soap was scented with cinnamon, curry, and sugar, an extravagance he reveled in now he could carry a scent. There were parts of Rook's life he was beginning to shed, slivers of ash flaking from who he was, caught in a wind of change. He'd sublimated odd bits of his life, things Dante never would have considered until he'd fallen in love with a reformed cat burglar. Odors drew dogs and tickled a human's senses, a dangerous event when sneaking past security. The richness of life was open to Rook—everything from onions and garlic to vivid colors creeping into his wardrobe.

Rook laughed more, made noises and unspooled a bit of the tension he wore around his spine and chest. There was a bit more teasing than in the beginning, something Dante welcomed as a change to the almost edged-steel banter they'd flung at each other before. The differences were subtle, a casual intimacy building between them. Nothing delighted Dante more than Rook stealing a tortilla chip from his nachos or handing Dante a cup of coffee—two sugars, black—in the morning before they headed their separate ways.

But the biggest, most incredible change of all was Rook giving his heart to a cop.

They lay with Rook's back to Dante's chest, and he cradled Rook against him, sliding a hand over his heart. Rook's beat fluttered, racing as quick as his thoughts, then after one shuddering breath, began to slow. Then Dante waited, letting Rook choose his words and moment.

"You're probably pissed as shit at me." A hint of defiance rolled under Rook's smooth tone. "Didn't mean to leave you with that crap downstairs. I really left Manny a message not to come in. Figured I'd take care of it when I came back."

"Not a problem. Gave me something to do, and well, you know Manny. He likes bossing people around." Dante kissed the back of Rook's head. "He's really damned proud of that sign he made on the sheet. I don't get it, but he's damned proud."

"I can't believe you're even related to him. That sheet's perfect. He even got the *I assure you we're open* perfect."

"You're going to make me watch another movie, aren't you?"

"I'm *so* going to make you watch another movie. Dude, you're *literally* Dante! You're not even supposed to—never mind. We'll catch you up." Rook leaned his head back, twisting slightly in Dante's arms so he could see his face. "Really not pissed? 'Cause I'd be pissed."

"I'm a humble and noble man," he teased, not surprised when Rook snorted. "Now tell me why you left like a bat out of hell this morning."

"I fucked up. This morning. Leaving you instead of talking shit out." Rook's expression closed, and Dante watched while his lover fought a brief internal battle. Then his mismatched eyes brightened again. "I'm sorry about that. Just needed to walk some stuff out in my head because… hell, I can't shake the feeling that I screwed Sadonna over, Montoya. Then I got caught up in some tangled shit about women, and... I figured out I don't fucking trust women, babe. Especially after Charlene. I just don't trust them."

"To be fair," he replied. "You don't trust *anyone*, Stevens."

"I trust *you*."

"Fair enough," Dante conceded, fighting a silly grin spread over his face. "Talk to me about the trust thing."

"There's a lot of... I don't want to say baggage, because it feels more like fishing lines with those teardrop lead weights on them, but they're hooked into me, dragging me down." Shoving his bony shoulder blades into Dante's chest, Rook made himself comfortable, stretching his long legs out over the couch. "I needed to see Sadonna. Talk to her. Because my gut says I owe her, but then there's a part of me that thinks... maybe she did this. Or had a hand in it. So I begin second-guessing."

"How so?" Shifting slightly, Dante eased Rook into a more comfortable position. "Explain."

"When I was younger and doing... things you don't want to hear about, one of the hard, fast rules was you never walked away from the team you hooked into. Yeah, sometimes it went to shit, but I always stuck by it. And I judge people who bail." Rook's voice got softer. "Beanie... my mom... bailed all the time, and I told myself it didn't matter because I had other people at my back. But Charlene... and a couple of others... shook me, Montoya. I sat there in the back of the cab taking me over to where they were holding Sadonna and it hit me. I felt like I'd set her up. She had my back on getting into the house to get back at Harold. She could have tossed me to the wolves and said she didn't give me the alarm codes, but she didn't. Sure, I got Archie to get her out and post bail, but this crap's still hanging over her."

"And you feel like it's your fault?" Stroking Rook's stomach, Dante mulled over the conversation. "Okay, so now what?"

"Now's when I beg you to help her get loose of the charges." Rook sat up when Dante rumbled an objection. "Wait, hear me out."

"You hear me out first." He held still, letting Rook turn around to face him. "Okay, I can't stick my nose into an investigation. Especially not with someone like Vicks. There's hardly any evidence against her—"

"You know as I do, this isn't the movies. Circumstantial evidence convicts as much as direct does. He's only got her and me to focus on, and he just needs to connect a few dots from Harold's dead body to a motive, even if it's a lie. You think she's going to be able to work if they drag this into court? He's just got to keep digging at her, ask people a few questions and hammer at where she was the night Harold died." Rook's argument was solid, especially if Dante thought back to the sly look on Vicks's face before they left the police station. "I'm not asking you to work on the case. Maybe just... hell, I don't know. I *owe* her, Montoya. I can't put her in a forget-about-it bucket because of what Charlene just did to me. She's family. Kind of. And—"

"You owe her," Dante finished for him. "In that squirrelly brain of yours, you owe her."

"I'm not asking you to do anything illegal," Rook murmured, sliding his hands over Dante's thighs. "Just... *help* her. With anything we can hand over to the lawyers and say, here, look at this."

If it was anyone else, he would have said no. Straight out of the gate. Without any hesitation, but Rook asking for a favor was new. It was kind of a thin olive branch, withered from abuse and neglect by other people, but still, an olive branch he was trusting Dante to take.

"Okay," he replied, holding up his hand when a cocky grin broke over Rook's face. "But hear me out. I'm going to talk to the captain first and see what he says. If Book tells me no, then it's no, and I go dig up the number to that guy Hank's old partner, Bobby, runs around with. He's friends with a Brentwood PI. But if the captain tells me I can do a couple of things for her, you've got to promise you won't stick your nose into it. Because if there's one thing that *cuervo* nose of yours is good for, babe, it's getting you into trouble."

"Deal. Next question, anybody get back to you about the firebombing?" Rook's fingers were on the move, tracing over the lines of muscles under Dante's jeans. He was distracting, a spill of hair throwing shadows over his handsome face when his nails raked over the inside seam. Rook looked up when Dante let out a soft, mournful groan. "Oh, sorry. Talking. Yeah."

"Later. *Dios*, but yes, later." He stole a kiss and a little of Rook's breath, flicking his tongue across Rook's before pulling away. There was a bit more heat in his lover's gaze, his elegant, graceful hands poised and still on Dante's thigh. "As for the Molotovs? Just a few calls checking in with me but nothing hard to go on, other than the asshole probably had no idea what he was doing. They found a broken one on the walk at the side of the shop, so maybe he dropped it or fucked up the toss. So we don't know that it's connected to Harold. Could have just been—"

"If you say burglars, I'm going to be offended." Rook dug his fingertips into a ticklish spot on Dante's thigh, releasing him when Dante gasped. "And no, I don't have any more enemies than I did the last time some assholes shot up my place. Oh wait, those assholes were cops."

"Hey, it wasn't me, *cuervo*. I was just the one to take you down," Dante reminded him, tugging at a lock of Rook's hair. "It could have been someone trying to rob the place and they gassed the front to cover up what they were doing, but it makes no sense to burn the place down."

"They knew we were inside. Or guessed once we started yelling at each other." Crossing his legs underneath him, Rook began tapping his fingers along the couch's back, an odd rhythm Dante was beginning to recognize. "The tear gas was fucked."

"Think you've got someone who wants you gone?" It was a possibility, one Dante couldn't discount. "Competition. Who do you run up against all the time?"

"Are you asking me who I piss off?" Rook grinned at Dante's lifted eyebrow. "Shit, who *don't* I piss off? Vicks is the last cop who got mad at me. Competition for stuff I collect? Shit, there's like fifty or more people who fight with me over things, but if it was a collector, they wouldn't have targeted the shop. Too much merchandise."

"There's a lot of people who are of the mind-set that if they can't have something, no one else can. I have a cousin who'd leave ice cream out after he got a bowl so it'd melt before anyone could have some." Dante rubbed his thumb over Rook's wrinkled nose. The light shifted, turning golden and sparse as the sun dropped below the building lines outside. "As much as I like you giving people the benefit of the doubt—"

"Shit, Montoya," he scoffed. "I'm not. You can't get a good profit if something drops below a certain condition rate. If someone was trying to burn me out to score my inventory, they'd want that stuff intact. What is it? Money, sex, or revenge, right?"

"Usually. We can rule out sex, unless there's someone out there I should know about." That got Dante a sour look and an elbow nudge into his ribs. "So that leaves us money, which you ruled out—"

"Damn it," Rook grumbled under his breath, rubbing at the back of his neck. "Shit, somebody out there might think I killed Harold and is mad about it?"

"Exactly what I'm thinking, *cuervo*." Dante nodded, hating where his mind led him, but he wasn't going to let someone try to destroy Rook, not when they'd just begun to knit their lives together. "Because unless there's something else we don't know about, all we've got left is revenge."

"WAIT, HOLD up." Hank glared at him from across the picnic table. "Let me get this straight. You asked Captain Book if we can dig into your boyfriend's B and E case to prove that his dead cousin's wife didn't kill him?"

"Pretty much," Dante conceded. "But the captain agrees with me. Vicks isn't giving the wife a fair shake, and from what Book's been hearing, that asshole's got it in for Rook. Vicks thinks Rook and the wife—Sadonna—have something dirty going on and I'm some kind of a smokescreen for them."

"That's *bullshit*." Hank's voice carried across the parking lot, drawing attention from several people in line at the Korean-Mexican food truck nearby. "You're asking me to believe Stevens gets into a relationship with you so a few months later he and some movie star he's back-dooring can kill her husband and no one looks at him because they think he's gay?"

"Yep," Dante mumbled around a mouthful of *kalbi* taco, "Pretty much."

"*So* much bullshit," his partner asserted. "Not that I'm one of your boy's fans, but who the hell would fake a relationship with *you*?"

Dante looked up from dredging a french fry into a small tub of kimchee dip. "Really, Camden?"

"That's not what I mean. If I were gay, *I'd* fuck you," Hank protested. "But that's the point. I'm not gay. If he wasn't gay, he wouldn't fuck you. Or you fuck him. Not that I want to talk about either one of you fucking each others' *whatever*. I don't even talk to you about my wife and I having sex, not that we can switch like the two of you—"

"Three words for you, Camden. International Women's Day," he ticked off, chuckling at Hank's confused look. "You, my friend, have a lot to learn about sex if you don't think a couple—any couple—can switch off."

"I'll get a book—"

"You're going to need more than a book," Dante replied. "And yeah, I agree. Rook's not with me for a long con. Sure, there are guys who do that. Vice can tell you stories, but there's no gain for Rook or Sadonna. Harold's money is his, or rather, Archie's, and California's a community property state for the most part. No one except Alex's parents, him, and Rook are rich by their own right in that family. Everyone else is like a tick with its head buried under Archie's skin, sucking him dry."

"So what are we going to do, then?"

"There's no *we* here, Camden." He shook his head, but it was useless. His partner's face flushed, drowning the scatter of freckles over his nose and cheeks. "Come on. I can't officially investigate anything. As it is, Book said if he hears one word about me crossing Vicks's radar, he's going to shut me down. Me, I'm already stained from what Vince did. I don't want that on you."

"You're just slinging the bullshit out like ketchup today," Hank blustered, reaching a long arm across the table to stab Dante in the chest with a stiff finger. "You and I are partners. This affects you. I'm in. I know that asshole Vicks. He's mean and slimy. His captain thinks he's golden because he's got a solve rate, but it's full of holes. Soon as the papers hit the DA's desk, everything falls apart. I've had a couple of informers drift out towards the beach and end up in Vicks's crosshairs. Easy marks for him but vital for me. Tossed them in a cell, and once they got out, they were ghosts. So if you're taking Vicks to the mat, I'm going to be there to tag in."

"You hate wrestling, and Camden, I can ask a lot from you." Dante moved his kimchee dip out of his partner's reach. "But don't make me have to speak at your funeral after your wife kills you for working after hours on a case that's not even yours."

"Montoya, let me say this once and only once." Hank stuck a fry under Dante's nose, waving it furiously. "You're like a brother to me. Hell, I love you more than I love some of my own brothers. The younger ones—the ones I never learned their names because I was already in high school by the time they came around—but still, love you more than them. My wife loves you, but she adores the fuck out of your boyfriend. So let's be clear on this: I will be helping you.

"Now then, I got some vacation time coming, and so do you." Hank smugly coated his fry in Dante's dip, then popped it into his mouth. "The big question is, where do we start?"

"Have I ever told you I loved you, Camden?" Dante swallowed at the lump forming in his throat. It dislodged to his chest, threatening to choke him further, and Hank looked away, suddenly interested in a pair of skateboarders working tricks on a cement pylon.

"Couple of times," Hank replied softly. "I'd like to head this off at the pass before Vicks puts any effort into building a flimsy case on them just to bump to his numbers up, because you know he's that kind of cop. It doesn't matter if someone's guilty or not, he just wants to hand the DA someone's head on a platter. After that, he can walk away."

"Even if Sadonna never sees in the inside of a courtroom, she's going to get tarred and feathered. You know how this city is. She won't be able to grab a Double-Double without paparazzi on her ass."

"Question remains, where do we start digging?"

"Right now?" Dante slid the contested bowl of dip back across the table toward his partner. "I say we start with the merry widow and see where we go from there."

Seven

BERGAN'S CURIOS and China Shop sat on the corner of broken dreams and fanciful hopes. It was a small West Hollywood business tucked in between a pool hall frequented by Filipino wannabe gangsters and a shop of tasteless shoes made for large-footed women and drag queens caught in a never-ending sale of any sequined item. The space ran up and down all three stories of the building, cutting a wedge through the dreary single-window apartments on either side. If there ever was a Bergan, he was long gone before Rook ever crossed the store's threshold. Instead, the shop was manned by a permanently scowling short man who sat perched on a barstool and despite the various hours Rook dropped in to peruse the ever-changing selection, always seemed to be working Bergan's front counter.

Wizened, with a hook nose, the man was more goblin than human, and the baring of his yellowed teeth could possibly have counted as a sneer, but Rook categorized it as simply the man's one and only smile. Never having learned the older man's name, Rook thought of him as Hoggle and came by frequently to dig through the inventory for treasures, sometimes stepping over one of the scrawny, often-stoned young men hired to stock the store's shelves. He'd slept with a couple of the stock guys when he was younger, but they were as transient as the merchandise, oftentimes as nameless as the shop's owner. Apathetic and underpaid, they were a sea of mostly pretty faces who knew nothing about the inventory they handled and pretty much were told to shove something into any empty space, making it next to impossible to shop for a specific thing amid the flotsam and jetsam Los Angeles washed up on Bergan's front stoop.

The shop was a mess, untidy and jumbled, with hardly any light, dirty windows hemmed in by narrow aisles on the outer walls, and a sea of heaped knickknacks in the occasional clearings in the center of each floor.

Rook loved the place nearly as much as he loved Montoya, coffee, and a well-cooked egg.

He was sitting cross-legged on the floor, happily sorting through a pile of mechanical tin toys when a dark shadow fell over him, blocking out what little thin sunlight came through the narrow window behind him. It was large, too large to be any of the slender men shuffling from floor to floor, rearranging the shop's inventory, but sometimes the light played games on Bergen's upper floors, throwing odd, menacing shapes against a wall, only for it to turn out to be something as silly as an inflatable Bozo punching bag. Still, while it'd been a long time since he'd had an icy tickle run up his spine, it was a sensation too familiar for Rook to ignore.

"I am not going to say *hello* like some stupid cheerleader in a horror movie." Dusting his hands off, Rook peered into the shadows.

There was movement, an unsteady shuffling, then the creak of one of the old shelves being jostled, a cascade of ping-ping-pings rolling out of the yellowed dimness surrounding him. Getting to his feet, he bit back the urge to call out, reminding himself he'd just promised not to. Time bent oddly in a curio shop, and Bergan's was no different. Its corners held the whispers caught in mirrors and fortunes told over long-washed-away tea leaves left to steep in silver pots.

He'd fallen into a game of cat and mouse, one Rook knew all too well. The scrape of feet was deliberate, an uneven scour of soles on the shop's slightly dusty floor. He caught sight of a bulky shape moving through the outer shelves, working in toward the landing. The silhouette was too massive to be any of the stock boys, and as far as Rook knew, only the diehards ever made it up to the third floor where most of the lighter inventory was kept since, much like the shop's owner, its creaky lift never made it up to the third floor.

A few steps more and the shape caught the light again, illuminating Vicks's face before he turned to step around a worn velvet chair.

"Huh," the cop grunted, stepping out of the darkness, his brutish scowl pulling free from the shadows. His gaze flicked over Rook, and his cheeks plumped with a thin smile, but the menace in his eyes remained as he padded into the dusty space. "Hello, Stevens. Fancy meeting you here."

There were times when only sarcasm in its rawest base form could satisfy the tickle in the back of Rook's throat, but this didn't seem like one of those times. He didn't like the way Vicks loomed, pressing into the tight space between the toys and the walnut hutch someone filled with cheap porcelain bunnies. Especially when he felt like a rabbit whose briar patch was just invaded by a bear.

"I'd ask how you found me, but that's not as important as why," Rook challenged Vicks, lifting his chin up slightly to meet the man's hard gaze.

It didn't make up the differences in their height, but it was enough to give Vicks pause.

There was no way around the cop, and Rook's phone was in his jacket pocket, the garment flung over the chair Vicks rounded earlier. Tamping down the panic creeping up from his belly, Rook didn't care for the smirk on Vicks's face or the tilt to his head when he caught Rook glancing at the staircase behind him. Fear nipped at Rook's nerves, throwing up whispers of what happened to former cat burglars caught in the dark by a bully with a gun.

He'd taken beatings from cops and carnies both, their fists and batons battering his body until it hurt to breathe, to think, and he'd folded in on himself, praying for someone to stop the pain or for God—a mute and deaf God—to take him into the dark so he could stop feeling the meat on his bones turn to mush. Some of the beatings were Rook's stupidity catching up with him, but other times—frightening, lonely times—he'd simply been in the wrong place at the wrong time. He'd looked at someone wrong or took the last piece of potato in the mess line, and the next thing he knew, he was breathing hard through his mouth and counting his teeth with his tongue.

Vicks had the look of a man who'd use his fists, who'd take his time and layer on the pain until Rook could no longer pull his fingers in tight or bend his knees. He couldn't risk Vicks touching him. Not with the open staircase there. It would be a simple matter of chucking Rook over the unstable rail and watching him plummet to the first floor, bouncing off the banisters on the way down.

"What the fuck do you want, Vicks?" Rook pressed. Bravado was only going to carry him so far, and Rook needed to get out as soon as he could before Vicks let loose the anger he seemed to have bottled up behind an extremely shaky control. "I told you everything I knew, so what? You couldn't hold Sadonna, so you're coming back 'round to me? You've got no reason to be on my ass."

"Well, first off, finding you was easy. I've had a couple of my guys following you ever since I got the call you'd gotten hit." He gave up all pretense of benign aggression and instead moved in for the kill, as it were, pressing into Rook's space with a few strides across the floor. One of the toys met its fate beneath his heavy leather hiking boot, its squished body releasing a dribbling caterwaul before being pushed into the soft wooden floor. "Came to ask you a few questions about what happened to your store."

He had to be losing his touch. There hadn't been a whisper of a tail on him that morning, but it'd been a while since he'd had to worry about such things, years even. And now it was all tumbling back on top of him.

Because he just couldn't walk away.

"Cops came and took my statement. Montoya's too. That's going to cost you about three large." Nodding at the toy's flattened limbs, Rook faked a grimace. Judging by the faint flare of Vicks's nostril, he could still lie with a straight face, convincingly enough to worry a cop. It took away some of the sting at being followed, but not enough to soothe it away. "Hope you brought your credit card."

"You think you're cute, Stevens?" A flush rolled up from Vicks's chest, creeping over his neck, then pinking his ears. "You've got a big mouth on you. Someone should help you close it sometime."

"Not going to be you, dude." The rational part of Rook's brain appeared to be having a brief seizure, unable to stop the flare of rebellion Vicks seemed to bring out in him, and the words were out before he could clamp down on his unruly tongue. "Everything I've got to say is in the incident report. Maybe get someone to read it to you."

"Let's see how big you are without Montoya here to back you up," Vicks growled. "Don't want to talk here? Let's head down to the station, and then we'll see how cocky you are. You walked out before I was done with you. Be happy to take another crack."

"I'd say fuck you," Rook shot back, "but I'd sooner lick a dirty astray a hobo pissed in than put my mouth anywhere near that shriveled tiny mouse fetus you have for a dick."

He came at Rook hard and fast, a blur of rough grit and authority, but Rook was ready for him.

The man's hands were nearly on him before Rook slid away, a simple feint and duck of his shoulders. He wasn't going to overpower the detective. He lacked the strength for that, but he could balance the man's brute force with evasion and a limber body, keeping himself out of Vicks's reach. Vicks's nails snagged on his hair, yanking a few strands out at the roots, but Rook refused to be cornered. Instincts kicked in. Carnie sharp and paranoid, he bent nearly in half to edge under Vicks's outstretched arm. A quick two-tap jab to Vicks's ribs was enough to drive the air out of the man's lungs, forcing the cop to pull his elbows in, giving Rook a clear shot at the stairs, but the shop's contrary nature undid him.

The hit had been a good one, a stab of fingers into soft flesh followed by a quick punch to the same spot. It threw Rook's footing off, having to twist in mid pop, but the floor's gritty surface smoothed out his slide. His sneaker caught on something, one of the toys or an odd joint in the floor, and Rook flailed, recovering, but not before Vicks sidestepped and closed in, blocking Rook once again.

"Fucking son of a bitch!" Vicks lashed out, slapping at the back of Rook's head, but he dodged out of the cop's reach, getting away with a light graze of Vicks's fingers along his ear. "I can have you up on assault—"

"Don't play that game with me, Vicks. No DA in the world is going to think I jumped you. You came after me, remember? People downstairs are going to tell anyone who'd listen that I was here first." Rook paced off some distance from the cop, pushing himself farther away from the stairs. Vicks's arms were long, too long for Rook's liking, and the wickedness in his expression was enough to make a dead man wary. Balancing on the balls of his feet, Rook kept his stance light, shifting around the pile of toys he'd been sifting through. "What do you want from me? And don't give me any crap about the break-in at my store. You could give a rat's ass about that."

"Think those asswipes downstairs are going to protect you? You just struck an investigating officer. I could take you in, and the idiot by the door wouldn't even blink," Vicks said through gritted teeth, rubbing at his side while he paced closer to Rook. Anger sparked a war with reason, the battle clearly being waged on his face while he debated violence. Reason must have won out, because Vicks slowed his advance, shifting his walk to circle around instead of treading over the heap. "Don't forget, you're still a suspect in the case until I say you're not, Stevens. Everything about you interests me. Like how someone hits your store right after you're dragged in for questioning about your cousin's death—a cousin you had issues with and the same cousin whose house you broke into."

There was a certain look in someone's expression, an impenetrable flatness Rook knew there would be no getting around, and the detective definitely had it shellacked all over his face. Vicks had no interest in listening to him or even looking any further than Sadonna for the murder. It would be a bonus if he could somehow tie Rook into it, and the hunger for Rook's arrest rolled off of Vicks, a lust-driven powerful want the cop couldn't hide. He was getting off on the idea of locking Rook down and tossing the key. It made no sense. It was too personal. Too intimate, and for the life of him, Rook couldn't figure it out.

So he did what he always did when he was cornered, verbally jabbing wildly in the hopes of scoring a good enough hit and making it around the cop, then down the stairs.

"Wife invited me. You can't seem to keep that in your head," Rook pointed out softly, glancing toward the stairs. They were loud, their voices carrying through the packed floors, and while Rook didn't think anyone would hear them, it didn't hurt to pray. "Sadonna gave me the security codes so we could prank her husband. Judge thought that was enough to get her bail. Just a matter of time before the lawyers kick her free of the charges."

"See, here's my problem with that, Stevens. *That* was the second story you told me." Vicks sneered at him. "I'm thinking the third might get even more intriguing. Maybe include details about where you hid the knife you used to kill Harold and what you're getting out of the widow for killing him. There's something about you and the wife, something that doesn't add up, but then not a lot of you adds up."

"It's simple. Sadonna's my cousin's wife. Someone killed him."

"Then why the lie? Why not cough her up to begin with?" The cop scraped some of the toys aside with his foot where Rook's stumble had scattered the pile's edges. "I'm going to be your shadow, Stevens, and I'm going to keep hammering at you until you slip up. This time Montoya isn't going to be here to run interference for you. This time you're playing in my sandbox."

"That why you came here to find me instead of at the apartment? Because of Montoya?" Dante was the only weapon Rook had, and he played on Vicks's ego and anger to fuel a fire Rook already suspected burned in the detective's belly. "Dante's got you running scared? So scared you can't just call to ask me what floated up to the top of your brain? Instead you've got a couple of plain-clothes following me when they could be out actually doing something useful."

Another few steps, sliding past the cereal-box toy Vicks smashed, brought Rook a little closer to the stairwell. There were a few pieces he'd wanted from the bucket he'd poured out onto the middle of the floor, but they weren't worth his neck.

"Scared of Montoya? The thing with his partner beat him down, not like he was anything to write home about to begin with. No, he's a paper pusher, and all I can figure out is he blew someone a few times to get that gold badge he's wearing. But now you've got Montoya by the dick, and everyone on the force knows that. Probably why you got off the first time.

He sell out for you back then too? That why his partner got the shaft?" Vicks spat at Rook's feet, the wet floating on the floor's dust. "Won't be long before his captain yanks that badge of his. He's just covering for the jobs you've been pulling, but this time you've fucked up. This time you got caught with blood on your hands, and it's not going to just wash off."

"I'm the one who called the cops, remember?" Rook argued, his mind racing, wondering if he could get down the first flight of stairs before Vicks pushed him. "I found Harold after someone stabbed him. You think I took Alex back there so I could *pretend* to find Harold? If I'd killed him, why the hell would I take Alex there? Why the hell would I tell *anyone*? And *again*, there was someone there in the house."

"There was no other guy. No, I'm guessing you needed someone who'd vouch for you or the wife. Maybe the two of you did it together? Harold's mother said the vic and you went at it during the last dinner party, and imagine my surprise when I found out Sadonna wanted a divorce but everyone I talked to said Harold wasn't keen on letting her go. So yeah, you took Alex back to the scene of the crime specifically to find the body. You made up the story about someone being there and then bet that pretty cousin of yours would hold the line for you, but he couldn't, could he?" Vicks closed the distance again, coming within grappling distance. "Instead, Alex practically gift wrapped you for me, and then you had to scramble. What did you promise the wife so she wouldn't turn on you after you tossed her under the bus? What do you have on her? What did you take out of the house that you don't want me to know about?"

"You're swinging at nothing, Vicks. First, you're saying I'm pulling jobs—which I'm not—and then you're talking about me killing Harold for Sadonna. None of that's real. He doesn't have any money. It's all Archie's. Hell, if what you're saying is true about her wanting a divorce, then she'd probably end up having to pay *him* alimony ...." Rook trailed off, a niggle of doubt working its way into his mind. "So what? You think she decided killing him was easier, less messy, and that she somehow convinced me to do it. There *was* someone else there, Vicks. That's who you should go after. Not me. And sure as hell not Sadonna."

The sound of a shotgun's action being slid into position broke the tense silence left behind Rook's words. A face peeked out from behind Vicks's chest, the wizened and angry owner leveling his weapon at the floor. Clearing his throat loudly, he stomped up to the top step, then braced himself against the rail.

"I'm Detective Mark Vicks. I'm a cop over at West LA," Vicks rumbled. "I'm going to reach for my badge—"

"Should have IDed yourself when you came through the door. You know how us idiots need to have everything spelled out to us before anything bad happens. Reaching for it now isn't going to help. I'm thinking I should have one of the boys call the cops and let them straighten this all out." Sunlight picked out the thin strands of hair scraped over the man's forehead, gilding them to bronze. "You got a warrant?"

The cop's eyes narrowed. "I don't need a warrant to question—"

"Is he being detained?" The short man cut Vicks off. "Is he under arrest? Because from where I'm standing, it's not just my stuff you're stomping all over. If he's not, then you should be going. Unless you want to talk to him, Stevens."

"Not really," Rook offered up. "And just so you know, he *is* a cop."

"Doesn't give him the right to harass you. Not on my property." The man hobbled to the side, shotgun still pointed down. His legs were bowed, knees jutting out in front of him, but his spine was ramrod straight, keeping his shoulders squared. "When you write up your report—because I'm assuming you're going to do that—my name's Harsgard Thorkenberry. My husband's out of Central. He's one of the leads in Internal Affairs. You might run into him once in a while. So unless you've got something else to add, I'd suggest you find the front door, and don't let it hit you on the way out."

For a moment, Rook feared Vicks would challenge the man, but shaking his head, he gave Thorkenberry a sly smile, then glanced back at Rook. "We're not done."

"Anything you've got to say, you can say it to my lawyers," he replied slowly. "Same ones as Sadonna's. You should have their number."

"I'll tell you whose number I got—*hers*." The cop stabbed at the air, pointing a hard finger at Rook. "You want to know why I think you and the wife have something going? Because she's done it in the past... to her own damned husband. He wouldn't give her a divorce because she's his beard. Without her in the picture to cover who he fucks on the side, Harold would lose that cushy do-nothing job he's got over at Grandpa's. Pretty conservative over there. The kind of people who draw the blinds when there's a rainbow outside, or didn't you know that's how dear old Granddad likes to run his businesses. Straight, white, and under his thumb."

"Bullshit, Archie's an asshole, but he doesn't give a shit what color someone is or who they fuck. He's more interested if they can do the job," Rook countered. "And Harold *wasn't* gay. He had nothing to hide."

"See, that's where you're wrong, because apparently, there's proof," Vicks bit back. "A few pictures and a video tape was all it took, and suddenly divorce wasn't off the table over at the Martin household. Then Harold apparently grew some balls and told her to go fuck herself, probably because he saw how Grandpa didn't give two shits when his prodigal spawn turned up a faggot. It just didn't matter anymore, and poor Sadonna was left holding the bag, still married to the albatross around her neck. So no, Stevens, not too far of a stretch at all. Now you've got to ask yourself, who was being played here? Alex for being dragged into this shithole you dug or you for falling for yet another dumb blonde's sob story?"

Eight

"YOU SURE about this, Camden?" Dante wanted to give Hank one last out before they crossed a line neither one of them could back down from. "Book said things might get a little bit sticky with Vicks in the picture. I don't want to drag you down with me if this all goes sideways."

"Are you fucking kidding me, Montoya? Are you asking to be punched in the face? Because I can so punch you in that pretty face of yours without even blinking an eye." No one could give a withering look like a freckled cop raised by a hardscrabble mother with too many mouths to feed, and once again, Hank delivered a cutting glance from the passenger's seat of Rook's SUV. "I told you already, we're doing this. I'm just glad you scored the boyfriend's ride so we're not stuck in your truck or my Cheerio-mobile. How'd you manage that?"

"He bought one of the new Rovers to use when he's on store business, then tossed me the keys." That'd been another argument Dante quickly lost. "Said it's easier to separate mileage and business expenses if he's got one personal vehicle and another for the store."

"You think it's a lie?" Hank scoffed.

"You and I both know that's a lie." Dante pulled around the fountain in the middle of Archie's driveway, easing the SUV behind an unfamiliar red sports car. "The truck's iffy at times, Manny's car is off the table now that he's working at Rook's, and well, that minivan of yours—"

"Not my fault the dog *and* the kid both puked in the far back seat and no one found it until it was cooked in," his partner protested. "I wasn't the one who fed him expired yogurt."

Dante slanted a look over at his partner. "The kid or the dog?"

"The dog," Hank confessed under his breath. "I might have accidentally given the kid the yogurt, but no one told her to share it with the dog."

"Nice." The driveway was damp at the perimeter, and Dante carefully avoided the misting sprinklers popping up from the flower beds running along the castle's front face. They were nearly to the front door when his phone burbled at him. Hank paused, probably recognizing Rook's ringtone, but Dante waved him on. "Rosa's going to want to feed us or something. Let me see what Rook needs and I'll be right in. Try to convince her not to cook us a turkey dinner."

"Speak for yourself." His partner grinned back, patting his belly. "Wife's been into cleansing smoothies in the morning for breakfast. I'll take anything Rosa tosses in my general direction."

Shaking his head, Dante answered his phone. "Hey, babe. We just got to your grandfather's place. What's up?"

"Vicks is up." Rook sounded strained. "He followed me. To Bergan's, and after what happened, I think he wants to kick my ass. Well, not so much think as know. He's planning on chewing my head off like a female praying mantis, and I've come to knock on his back door holding a bunch of roses and a bottle of ketchup to make it all go down easier."

Dante's blood went cold in his veins, and he leaned against the car, holding tightly to the ends of his temper. Vicks worried him. The man reminded him too much of his old partner, Vince. Too eager to cut corners and too quick to hammer a nail into someone's coffin, whether they were dead or not.

"Okay," he finally said. "What happened?"

It wasn't hard to follow what Rook told him. If anything, his lover was skilled at leaving behind the charm he normally used to frost up a story. Sharp-minded and exacting, Rook'd have made a good detective, something he'd be horrified to hear, but he could strip down events to the bare facts, a skill most cops struggled to master. In the terse flow of Rook's recount, Dante heard Rook minimize Vicks's threatening demeanor, but the tautness in Rook's words couldn't be ignored. An angry spark erupted in Dante's chest, spreading outward until he was forced to tamp it back down, reminding himself he carried a badge and gun for justice, not revenge.

Their relationship was new, too new sometimes for Dante to deal with, because as right as they were together, some things were still being felt out.

Rook fit into him in strange ways, completing his life in a direction he'd never thought he'd take, and the fierce protectiveness he had for Manny oddly stretched over to Rook, but in a way that confused him. The odd-eyed man he'd fallen in love with would never stand coddling, but at that moment, listening to Rook relay how Vicks pushed at him, trying to dominate him, enraged a part of Dante's brain he didn't even know he had. Hot words from his childhood slid from his tongue before he could stop them, a filthy line of Cuban he'd probably learned from his father, but their malevolent promise to unman Vicks made him feel *good*.

"Okay, I don't know what that means," Rook murmured through the phone line, his smooth, silken voice lightened with amusement. "I'm going to need that in English, SoCal, Mexican, or Vietnamese if you want an answer, but I don't think that was a question."

"Sorry, *cuervo*. The less you understand, the less you have to admit to knowing. Vicks is an asshole, and if ever I have the chance, I'd like to twist the balls off of him." Dante turned to find Rosa staring at him from the open front door, a confused look on her face. Smiling, he waved at her, then mouthed Rook's name, getting a nod and a wave from the Hispanic housekeeper. She mimed drinking something, and he smiled back, holding up his hand to ask for a few minutes to finish the phone call, waiting for her to close the door behind her before continuing. "Tell me how you left it."

"The guy who owns Bergan's came up with a shotgun and pretty much kicked Vicks out. You know, the old guy?" Rook snorted through the line. "Apparently he's a hell of a lot younger than I thought he was—a clear-cut poster boy for the argument drugs do shitty things to your body—and he's also married to some guy named Thorkenberry over at Central. Vicks was out the door before Harsgard could call the cops in on him."

"Thorkenberry. I know him. He's in IA. Good guy. He handled the shit Vince and I got into with you." Bringing up the past was always touchy with Rook, but Thorkenberry did right by both of them, especially after Vince was shaken out of the force. His anger waged its silent war against the walls his rational, logical mind kept throwing up, screaming for Vicks's blood and possibly his head if Dante could get a good enough shot in. "You okay?"

A year or so ago—or even maybe last month—the Rook he'd first tried to pin down would have sidestepped and finagled his way out of answering. Now—this Rook—the one he'd woken up next to in the morning, who he'd wiped blood from his sharp, sweet face, who he'd buried himself into and pulled out screams loud enough to rattle the loft's expanse of windows, *this* Rook sighed and then broke Dante's heart.

"No," he whispered over the phone. "Fucker scared the shit out of me. Not right then. Not while I was facing him, but... afterwards. Yeah. I got fucking scared. He had me followed when I left our place this morning, Montoya, and I'm so fucking far out of the game I didn't even notice. Then my brain kept rolling over with the what-ifs. Suppose he'd been the one to screw with us at the shop? What's to stop him from dogging me while I go around LA and do business? And then, what's going to happen if one day I turn down the wrong fucking street and I find I can't get out without going through him? What then?"

Dante's fingers ached to break every bone in Vicks's body, until they were as shattered as Rook's voice. Gritting his teeth, he took a long breath, then another to squash his growing rage. Catching Rook's whispered *hello* in his ear, Dante pulled his focus in.

"He's not going to touch you. I won't let him, *cuervo*." Dante caught some movement at the front door, turning to find Hank standing on the top step, his expression filled with a questioning concern. Shaking his head at his partner, Dante waved him to go back inside. "Where are you now? Home?"

Home. Funny how *that* became the loft apartment over the store rather than the bungalow he shared with Manny.

"Yeah, I'm parked in the back. Just wanted to call you before I went inside." Something loud rattled through the phone, and Rook barked a short, hard laugh. "The store crew is going to love the fuck out of me. They're going to have to sort through about fifty pounds of tin toys."

"Tin… toys?"

"Yeah, and a few other things. Figured I owed the guy for pulling Vicks off my butt, so I kind of cleared out his third floor. They're dumping the larger stuff off later today. Seriously, I'd have bought out the whole damned store to thank the guy for saving me. There was a moment there, I wasn't sure, you know? I didn't *trust* him not to kick my ass. Like I said, getting sloppy."

"It's not sloppy to expect a cop to act like a cop," Dante replied softly. "And that doesn't include beating the shit out of someone just because you don't like them."

"Yeah, that's not the cops I've ever known," he murmured. "You're the first one I've trusted. Maybe the only one."

"What about Hank?" he teased, hoping to lighten the heaviness in Rook's voice.

"Fucker ate my carne asada tacos out of your fridge, babe," Rook reminded him. "Friends don't bogart another man's tacos. You know that."

"Fair enough," he conceded. "Tell you what. Let me and Hank talk to Sadonna about what Harold was up to, and maybe we can find something to lead us away from her and to the real killer."

"Yeah, about that," Rook hedged. "I've got some news from Vicks I'm not sure I should believe. He seems to think Harold got hooked up with some guy—the whole closet gay thing—and Sadonna was tired of faking a marriage and was on her way out the door."

"Wait, what?" Dante's brain shed its worry, latching on to Vicks's theory. "Harold wasn't gay. Okay, I'm lost. Explain to me what he said."

"Vicks dropped that Sadonna was trying to get a divorce out of Harold, but he wouldn't give her one. But some guy came along and hooked Harold. Sadonna got ahold of some pictures, then turned the thumbscrews to get out of the marriage without having to support Harold for the rest of her life. Hold on a sec, Montoya." Rook paused for a moment, and Dante heard a siren scream past, drowning out the call. "Sorry, some idiot hit a fire hydrant down the road. I think Vicks's looking at her like she's been Harold's beard so Archie wouldn't kick Harold out of the family or cut him from the will."

"That doesn't make sense." Dante thought back to the few times he'd been around Rook's cousin, but he'd spent more time biting the inside of his cheek and ignoring the digs tossed Rook's way by a few of his aunts than paying attention to anyone else. "What would Harold need a fake wife for? You're gay. Alex is gay. For all the crap he gives you, Archie really couldn't give a shit."

"Nah, he used to be a hell of a lot worse. Beanie—my mom—used to say Archie was the most narrow-minded, controlling racist asshole she'd ever known. It's why she left. But that was a used-to-be. He's worked his ass off to get his head on straight since I've been here." Rook tsked. "Okay, and so my mom's a druggie who wanted to sleep her way through the carnival, but she wasn't wrong about him. When I first came around, he was a raging dick. I almost walked a few times. Then he realized I didn't give a shit if he left me out of his will. He'd gotten too used to people rolling over and showing him their belly. Well, Alex didn't roll over, but he also didn't spend any time with Archie. He just never was around enough for the old man to get under his skin."

"Yeah, your cousin's more of a dodge and feint than an attack head-on kind of man." Dante chewed on his lower lip, thinking. "He'd avoid Archie rather than telling him to fuck off."

"Something I have a hard time *not* doing, so yeah, when Archie got around to meeting me, I'd already had *fuck off* on the tip of my tongue because of how Beanie used to talk about him when she was drunk. Shit got a lot better between us right about the time you decided I'd offed Danielle."

"Thought we worked that out. How long are you going to hold that over my head?"

"We did." Rook chuckled. "But it's always good to remind you about when you're wrong."

"Okay, focus now. Did Vicks give you a name of Harold's lover? Anything other than throwing it out there?

"Nope, Harsgard had him out the door before he said anything else. Maybe he thought I knew about Harold's boyfriend and that's why Sadonna hooked into me for help. I think he knows who it is but wouldn't tell me. Stupid though, wouldn't he know I'd go straight to Sadonna?" Rook hummed a bit, then said, "No, that's what he'd want me to do. He'd want me to drop something in her ear so she'd react. Do something stupid."

Dante bit back a laugh, amused at hearing Rook work Vicks's case out. "Academy's accepting applications, you know."

"Fuck you, Montoya. One cop in the family is enough." The *family* part warmed Dante's heart, breaking off the vestiges of anger knocking around inside of him. Rook cleared his throat, then rumbled through the phone, "Hey, are you heading back to the loft after you're done with Sadonna? I kind of need to talk to you about something. Face-to-face."

"Anything I should worry about, babe?" Concern crept back into the conversation, a discomfort in Rook's tone. "Something up?"

"No, not you. *You're* fine." Another chuckle, but this one was flat and bitter, a bit of tinfoil along Dante's teeth. "Today was... *fucked*, and I... miss you, man. Just come home when you can, okay? I just... need to see you, and then everything'll be fine."

"Love you, *cuervo*," Dante reassured his lover. "Don't forget that."

"I know, Montoya," Rook whispered back. "Just... hurry home and remind me again."

HE FOUND Hank sitting in the library with his hands wrapped around a pastrami sandwich the size of a small dog and chatting with the woman they'd come to interview. Sadonna looked up when Dante entered, her dazzling smile a practiced welcome laced with enough melancholy and sensuality to tug at a man's heart and tickle his crotch. For a grieving widow, she was an elegant shimmer of blonde hair, sun-kissed skin, and a brazen beauty groomed to make a man's pulse skip. Even with his own preference for long-legged, smart-mouthed men, Dante had to admit Sadonna Swann was a powerhouse of a woman, a classic, old-school sex kitten with a cunning intelligence gleaming in her wide, heavily lashed eyes and a hitch of promise in her sultry, smoky voice.

Hank hadn't stood a chance.

"'Nother sandwich over there for you, Montoya," Hank mumbled through a mouthful of deli meat, nodding toward a napkin-covered plate on a side table. "Rosa brought more coffee."

"We just ate lunch, Hank," Dante reminded him, then nodded at Sadonna. Sitting in a wing chair opposite her, he leaned back, taking in the room for a moment. She'd positioned herself beneath an enormous portrait of Archie in his later golden years, an unapologetic rendering of a man with a hawk-sharp nose, mismatched eyes, and steel running through his veins.

The two-story room was a temple to masculine traditions, steeped with Archie's presence and smug in its passing decorating nod to a Victorian gentleman's club with its dark wood bookshelves, overstuffed chairs, and Persian rugs. It was one of the few rooms not bristling with embellishments and oddities, its air fragrant with the smoky vanilla scent of old books and a hint of cherry tobacco left over from the days when Archie occasionally fired up one of the seasoned meerschaums displayed in a long glass case on the broad fireplace mantle.

"I don't know if you remember meeting me. I'm Sadonna. Sadonna Swann," she said, leaning over with her hand stretched out toward him. "Like Madonna but with an *S*."

"I remember, Ms. Swann. I'm glad you could meet with us." Her palm was soft and dry, no quiver in her fingers as far as Dante could tell. Then Hank's phone beeped with an incoming message and she flinched, drawing her hand back. Her smile tightened, and she tugged at the front hem of her shirt. "Check your phone, Camden. Might be the captain trying to get ahold of us."

He didn't know exactly how long Hank's phone had been left beeping, but it was only a few seconds after Dante'd hung up with Rook that he'd sent his partner the rumors from Vicks and a brief note about the detective's attempted intimidation. After a quick read of the screen, Camden's demeanor shifted and he put the half-eaten sandwich down on a plate, his face schooled into a neutral expression. Wiping his mouth clean, Hank finally glanced up at Dante, giving him a curt nod.

"Just my wife," Hank murmured, tucking his phone back into his pocket. "Wants me to remember where I live. Montoya, how about if you lead and I'll take notes, and let's see if we can't put this whole thing to bed."

"I appreciate you both helping with this." Sadonna reached for her coffee, her eyes mournful and worried. "I don't think the detective on the case is going to look for the real killer. And isn't he supposed to turn this over to the lawyers by now? He's already arrested me for murder."

"The DA hasn't charged you yet because what they have is too weak, but Vicks is probably going to work on building a case against you. That's why we need to produce someone for the DA to look at," Dante said, softening his tone. "Someone like the man Vicks believes Harold was sleeping with."

"Now's probably the time you'd want to come clean about possessing any tapes or photos you have of the affair," Hank interjected. "If you know who he is or how to contact him, it could go a long way in shifting the focus of the case from you to him."

"I don't…." Squaring her shoulders brought Sadonna's pert breasts up, but Hank didn't so much as flinch. She then cast a hooded, seductive glance at Dante, and he watched her expression change when she probably remembered she'd have no effect on him. Sighing, she continued, "I don't have any tapes or photos. I only told him that so he'd budge on the divorce."

"So he wasn't in a relationship with another man?" Dante pressed.

"Oh no, he was gayer than a flying unicorn with rainbow wings." She let a bitter laugh loose. "He just hid it because, well… Archie wasn't so tolerant before Rook sauntered in. Harold slept with any guy who'd have him."

"Then why'd you marry him?" Hank took up the questioning. "What was in it for you?"

"Connections. Harold's circle included a hell of a lot of movie people, and when you're a woman getting older in Hollywood, you need all the help you can get." Sadonna grimaced. "Things were going fine until Harold got it into his head that we needed to have kids, mostly to secure his place at Archie's Last Supper painting. The family's a wee bit threatened by Rook."

"So there's no guy?" Dante asked. There was something off in Sadonna's mannerisms, more than the habitual sex-kitten routine. Her attention slid away from their faces, focusing on other things in the room, and Hank pursed his lips together, sending Dante a dubious glance. "Well, no *one* guy Harold was seeing?"

"There is… was," she admitted. "I just didn't have anything to back it up. His housekeeper, Jennifer, delivered that delightful news one morning.

She never liked me, you know. Very loyal to Harold. Then one morning after I asked her to get me some tea, she told me to enjoy drinking it because it wouldn't be long before Harold's boyfriend moved in."

"And you believed her?" Hank inquired carefully.

"Yeah, I believed her. She'd do anything to get me out of that house. Between her and Harold's mother, it was like living on cracking ice sometimes. I'd have fired her, but—" Sadonna made a face. "—she actually works for Archie's company, so Harold was her boss, not me. Harold was a god to her. I wouldn't be surprised if that cracked bird statue that guy used to kill Harold ended up in her grubby little hands. It'd be the perfect thing for the Harold shrine she's probably got going on in her dining room."

"Huh," Hank murmured, sitting back slowly. "So, tell me this, Ms. Swann… what exactly *do* you know about the statue? And what makes you say that's what killed him?"

Nine

"WELL THAT was quick." Camden snorted as they walked down the front stairs and toward the SUV parked at the end of the drive. "I'd have laid money on her doing a smoke-and-mirrors act, not clamming up tight and booting us to the curb."

"Almost as if she's got something to hide." Dante opened the car door, then stopped to stare at the imported castle. The library's heavy drapes were drawn tight on the room's first-floor windows, blocking Dante's view of its interior. "I think there is a lover, but I don't think that's all of it."

"Still want to chase this down?" Hank glanced back at the house, the waning afternoon sun gilding his red hair. "We can leave this for the lawyers if you think she's playing us."

"Can't. I've got Rook in this," he pointed out, climbing into the SUV, then waited for his partner to get settled on the passenger side. "I'm beginning to wonder if she's the one playing him. Sadonna approached him to break into the house, allegedly to give Rook access to the movie prop Harold stole out from under him."

"Why?" Hank turned in his seat to face Dante. "Were they close or casual acquaintances? Why would she reach out to him? And why would Rook say yes?"

"Because he's a magpie, and deep down inside, gathering stuff up makes him feel safe." It was a truth Dante had been slow to realize, but the longer he knew Rook, the more he understood his boyfriend's avarice. The fascination of owning things drove the former thief, but it was the chase his lover got his thrills from. "He just wants them. It could be anything. Jewels, a plastic watch from the '50s, *anything* that catches his eye. I don't know if it's because he didn't have a home growing up and couldn't drag a lot of things with him or if he's just... a magpie. He hoards some things, but let's be practical, there's not enough space, so most of it gets discarded. It's the gathering he likes. Getting access to something—without breaking the law—would be attractive to him. So yeah, she played him a little bit."

"Surprisingly, he let her," Camden said softly. "He's leery of women. Especially after Charlene and her shit hit his fan."

"He said the same thing," Dante admitted. "That he had to stretch himself out to trust her. He's taking a risk with Sadonna because his gut tells him she's innocent, but that was before Vicks dropped the whole lover thing in his lap."

"No matter what, he's still in Vicks's crosshairs. That asshole's not going to peel off Rook just because Sadonna walked into the fire. So yeah, I agree with you. We're going to have to keep chasing this down. But where to next?"

"Let's see if the housekeeper will talk to us." He ran down what he knew of Harold's life. "There's also the cousin's mother. She doesn't like Sadonna, so that might be an avenue we can follow."

"How much do you believe in the whole Harold's-got-a-boyfriend story but he still wants to have kids with a wife he doesn't sleep with?" Hank tucked the paper bag of sandwiches Rosa packed up for them into the space next to his feet. "It's a little hard to swallow, but… this is Hollywood. Weirder things have happened."

"Yeah, I'm not willing to rule things out yet. Every time I think something sounds like it was cut right out of a telenovela, it turns out to be true." Dante started the car, glancing at Hank's snort. "What?"

"Kind of like an ex cat burglar gone straight and the cop who wanted him behind bars?" His partner laughed when Dante muttered a profanity back at him. "I'm just saying, sometimes life is weirder than we can even imagine."

"Right now, I could use a little less weird," Dante admitted. "It'll be good to settle back into a nice, normal routine."

"Don't get me wrong, Montoya." Hank chuckled, making himself comfortable in the SUV's seat. "But once you hooked up with Stevens, you pretty much kissed *any* kind of normal goodbye."

THE STOREFRONT'S sheet-covered wooden sign appeared to still have a few fans as Dante pulled into the drive. He braked to avoid hitting a bored-looking teen straggling behind what looked like his family on vacation, his face lighting up momentarily when they shuffled past Hizoku Ink's windows. The tattoo parlor had its front door open, a bit of wind tickling the tiny bell hanging from its frame, and the teen slowed his steps, peering into the shop before one of the older women in the group urged him to catch up.

Manny was waiting for him when Dante let himself into the building's side door.

It was still odd seeing his uncle on what was essentially Rook's front porch. The hallway was bright, and with its black marble floors, gleaming ivory walls, and elegant sconces, looked more like a hotel lobby than an access to an elevator leading up to a loft. The row of framed retro sci-fi and horror movie posters lining the walls was a dash of Rook's personality, as was the blue police box bas-relief fire door connecting the hall to the shop's front room. The other side of the door was a plain gray, and Dante overheard one of Rook's employees remark the blue build-out was on the wrong side, something Rook laughingly agreed to.

None of it made sense to him, even after Rook tried to explain it, but short of watching what looked like an eternity of television episodes to catch up on the inside joke, Dante'd just nodded his head and murmured something he hoped sounded polite.

A politeness mirrored on his uncle's face when Dante made sure the outside door was locked behind him.

"What's the matter, *tío*?" Kissing Manny's cheek, Dante spotted a tall cardboard box near the connecting door. "That something you need me to take up to Rook?"

It was better to come out and admit he knew Manny was worried. A few months ago, his uncle would hem and haw, then lead the conversation back around to what was bothering him. But that was before Manny began working for Rook. Now the soft-spoken and gentle man who he'd come to love and care for had a bit of steel in his spine, and from the firm quirk in his lips, Manny was ready to speak his mind about something, whether Dante was ready to hear it or not.

"There's something wrong with your man, *mijo*." Manny tsked. "He came in all worried and tight shoulders. Did you say something to him? Do something?"

"Not everything is because of something I said, Manny." Despite his words, Dante quickly rifled through what he'd said to Rook over the phone, then decided to place the blame directly at Vicks's feet. "Do me a favor. If a detective named Vicks comes around, call me. I'll see if I can find you a picture of him, but I'm not sure if it's something to involve the rest of the staff with. He came after Rook today. Had him followed, harassed him while he was at that store he goes to downtown. I don't like it."

"You don't like it?" His uncle frowned. "I know I don't like it. They let him go. No charges, right? Can he do that? This detective?"

"Something's personal for him in this. Rook's on the hook for a B and E, but they can get those dropped. Sadonna made a statement that she gave him permission to enter the house. He just broke in because, well, he's an asshole who wanted to get a cheap thrill," Dante grumbled. "Okay, maybe not cheap. He probably misses it. The breaking-in part. Probably seemed like a legal way he could do it and not be arrested."

"Instead he finds his cousin's dead body." Manny crossed his arms over his chest, a thoughtful expression flitting across his face. "What about the man who was at the house when Rook went in?"

"Vicks says Harold had a lover, and she says its true, but so far, I don't have proof. If he exists, then we might have another suspect, but right now, he's just a theory. Harold wasn't gay, or at least no one in the family thought he was." Dante mirrored Manny's grimace. "Yeah, it's too many whispers but no real evidence, but I left a message for the housekeeper. She worked for Harold for a long time, before he married Sadonna, so I'm hoping I can get something from her. After her, I've got Harold's mother on the line. Camden and I are clear for the next week, so we've got a few days to chase this down. If the lover theory is true, it could have been him in the room when Rook broke in. If not, then I have to find out who hated Harold Martin enough to kill him, because Vicks likes Rook as the killer with Sadonna pulling his strings."

"Sounds like a soap opera. The wife's probably guilty of something, but you don't know what." His uncle laughed softly. "And this Vicks doesn't know your Rook at all if he thinks anyone's going to pull *that* one's strings. Get me a picture of this detective so I know who to look for. In the meantime, carry that upstairs to him for me. One of the auction houses delivered it today for Rook, but I was busy when he stuck his head in."

Bending down, Dante picked up the long box, grunting slightly at its unexpected weight. "*Mierda*, this is heavier than it looks. What the hell is in it?"

"I don't know, but he gets things sent all the time, so wipe that suspicious look off your face. It arrived before Rook came in, but he had us running around with all the merchandise he brought in, so I didn't get it upstairs. We were busy. Funny how a broken window can drive up business. I'm letting my sign take the credit for that."

"Probably. Or at least according to Rook." Dante hefted the box up, tucking it against his side. "Don't wait—"

"Please, I gave up on you coming home two weeks ago." Manny patted Dante's face, his cheeks plumped with a broad smile. "It's nice living alone. I might get a boyfriend for some company. Or maybe a dog. Just be sure to stop by on Saturday to mow the lawn."

"Kicking me out of my own house?" Dante teased, hitting the elevator button.

"Yes, but let's face it, *mijo*," Manny replied warmly. "We might share a house, but here, you share a home."

THE LOFT'S heavy drapes were shut against the fading afternoon light. The Edison bulbs were lit, steeping the living space with a wash of sepia and gold. A soft vanilla scent teased Dante's nose, and he left the box on the kitchen island, then followed his nose to the bed tucked behind the wall of shelves separating the long space.

A few steps later, he found Rook in a pair of cotton drawstrings and a T-shirt, sitting up in their bed with his knees up, leaning against the headboard, his hands curled around a cup of sweet-smelling tea.

His lover was lost in thought, his animated face stilled and nearly blank of emotion. It was odd seeing Rook so silent, so quiet. He seemed to always be moving. Even when sitting down, his hands gestured or his eyes caught on every movement, tracking the world around him with a scarily attuned focus. Odder still was Rook *not* noticing Dante's entrance, because the man he'd fallen in love with vibrated in the presence of other people, hooked into even the slightest pulse when someone walked by.

Rook simply didn't see him, and that worried Dante more than Vicks's stalking, Sadonna's lies, and anything else nipping at Rook's heels.

"Hey, *cuervo*." Dante toed off his shoes, then padded toward the bed. "You look like you're chewing on something big in that head of yours."

Rook sat still and silent, watching with solemn mismatched eyes, only blinking when Dante's shadow from the lamplight fell over his torso. Dante took the cup from Rook's hands, not liking the chill in his boyfriend's fingers, and set the fragrant tea on the table next to the bed. The mattress dipped when Dante climbed onto it. He was about to say something to shake

Rook from his silence; then his lover reached for him, and Dante hooked his arms around Rook's slender waist, pulling him in close.

It felt *good* lying on top of Rook, letting his body settle into the curve of Rook's hip and the hardness of his belly. He shifted, sliding his legs over Rook's thighs to rest his weight on his knees, and Dante echoed Rook's sigh when he exhaled into the soft skin along Dante's throat.

"God, I'm glad you're home," Rook whispered, tightening his hold on Dante. His hands stroked along Dante's back, tracing the line of muscles still tender from his morning workout at JoJo's gym.

His lips found a tender spot on Dante's jaw, probably from the glancing blow he'd taken from Hank's ex-partner when they sparred. The slight ache tingled, strangely stoking Dante's arousal, and Dante embraced the spark of fire in his belly, letting it spread through him.

Rook Stevens was the one vice Dante could not live without. Even when he'd shoved Rook back into the shadows, condemning him as a con and liar, the sly-mouthed thief dug deep into Dante's soul, infecting his blood with an intense want for the one man he should have walked away from as soon as he'd laid eyes on him.

Now—Dante hissed at the sharp pain of Rook's teeth sinking into his skin—he couldn't imagine living without the worst-best mistake he'd ever made in his life.

"I'm glad I'm home too." He took another taste of Rook's lips, liking the smoky heat of his mouth and the sweet hint of vanilla and chai on his tongue. Rook's cock thickened, nudging Dante's hip, and he shifted, giving his lover's arousal room. He found Rook's nipple, rolling his thumb over its peak through the thin fabric of his shirt. "You've got on too many clothes, *querido*."

"Really? *Querido*?" Rook rolled his shoulders back, letting Dante slide from his body and onto the mattress. He made a move to sit up, then narrowed his eyes when Dante gently pushed him back. "What? Like I haven't been pushed around enough today?"

"You like it when I push you around." Dante tsked. "Let's see if I can remind you about that."

Undressing Rook was always a pleasure Dante drew out as long as he could. He loved watching his lover's body emerge from behind its cocoon of fabric and delighted in the glimpses of vulnerability in Rook's face as he was stripped. Laid bare and exposed on the bed, Rook's long body was a feast for Dante's lust, stoked to a high flame at the secrets Rook hid from the rest of the world.

Rook's past lovers were fleeting, shadows and echoes of sex, barely stopping long enough to make sure Rook got off, and if Dante were honest, Rook probably didn't care to remember a single one of them so long as he'd come. Relationships were chains, invisible threads binding Rook to someone he was sure would walk away as soon as the going got rough.

And for Rook, the going got rough pretty often.

His callused fingers caught on the smoothness of Rook's belly, snagging on the fine hair around his navel. Rook's breath hitched, his flat stomach twitching under Dante's touch, then settled when Dante pressed down on his skin, slowly exploring a terrain he'd never tire of.

There were imperfections, tiny scars and brown dapples where Rook'd been burned pulling cotton candy or popping corn kernels while working a carnival booth. Rook hissed when Dante slid the tip of his tongue into Rook's navel, and his hands clutched at Dante's thick hair when he moved farther down to suckle at the tip of Rook's cock.

"Fucking tease," Rook growled, straining to lie still when Dante laved at the ridge of his shaft. "Jesus, Montoya, you're killing me."

"Nuh-uh." Dante chuckled. "We've gone over this. When you're flat on your back and I'm with you like this, you call me Dante. Or did you forget that too?"

There were times when he'd ached to cuff Rook to their bed and take his time with his hands and mouth, but the man was impatient, always racing to get to the next place in his life. It'd been hard to pull back on the reins, showing Rook pleasure in taking his time. They struggled with Rook's fears and distancing, the micro-shoves away Rook did to give his heart some space so it could shatter in silence when it was broken... again.

Dante could spend an eternity holding Rook's heart in his hands, stroking at its wounds and kissing away its bruises, but only if Rook was willing to give it to him. Slowing Rook's pleasure forced him to trust, to lay himself open for Dante and let himself be stroked, coddled, and loved.

"Say my name, *cuervo*. Tell me you remember who can do this to you." Dante eased his thumb against the slit in Rook's cock, rubbing at the dampness along its velvet crest. "You can let go with me, Rook. If you forget everything else, please... for us... remember *that*."

The mistrust was there in Rook's gaze, a prickle of anxiety and flight ingrained from a lifetime of quick escapes and hard beatings. The scars on Rook's skin were nothing compared to the ones on his soul. Everyone failed Rook. There'd been no one to catch him when he fell, and he'd climbed out of the quagmire he'd been born into by sheer will and cunning, and Dante was determined to be the one Rook would turn to when his life grew too heavy to carry.

"I don't forget, Dante," Rook whispered, cupping Dante's cheek. "It's just... hard, but no, I don't forget."

He felt the moment Rook gave up his need for control when his lover sighed and the tension eased from his long, muscled body. From there, their hunger for each other took over, stoked by the strain of the day and Rook's need to be held, despite his unwillingness to admit it.

They eased into their lovemaking, Rook's soft murmurs on Dante's skin as gentle as his fingers around Dante's shaft. There was laughter, husky and rough, mellowed by the flush of need flickering between them, an ember banked under the ashes of a long, difficult day brought to life by the slide of their bodies.

Dante loved the feel of Rook in his hand, the soft crinkle of sparse chestnut strands at the base of his cock, and when the heat of his fingers warmed the powdery scent of Rook's inner thighs and sac, he adored breathing him in, amused at Rook's odd shyness at being explored. His own skin bore the marks of his lover's curiosity, his throat marbled with nips and his chest wet from tentative tastings.

"Lift your knees, baby," Dante urged, falling madly insane at the play of golden light on Rook's outstretched torso. He bent over, suckling at the tip of the black crow feather inked over Rook's hip bone, then clicked open the lube bottle Rook'd tossed at him. Dante used the tip of his fingers to pull Rook's chin over, guiding Rook's attention up toward him. "Look at me. I want to watch you when you feel this."

His fingers were hot with slick when he pressed two of them into Rook, easing them in halfway until Rook's eyes went dark, their contrasting hues bleeding to nearly black when he lowered his lashes and hissed. Dante kneaded at the spot, working himself into Rook's tightness, and when he thought Rook couldn't stand any more, he bent over to taste the moisture dewing Rook's cock.

Men with greater words described their lovers' spend with images of stars or ocean-kissed wine, but Dante *liked* the unbridled, unapologetic reality of Rook's salty-bitterness, a uniquely masculine burst of molten need cupped into the curve of his tongue. His lover didn't taste of the evening sky or a burst of the sea. Rook left the sting of a man's body in Dante's mouth, a mellowed sweat and musk he savored in the back of his throat and ached to delve into time and time again.

Something flashed in his mind, and Dante laughed, nearly breaking the mood between them. Rook's slight frown was something to be kissed away, and he'd nearly succeeded, but his lover pushed at him, aroused but curious.

"What is it?" his magpie poked.

"I was thinking you tasted a bit like the salt on a margarita glass, that little bit of bitter before the punch of tequila and sweet hit." Dante teased around Rook's rim, drawing his fingers out slightly as he slicked his shaft with lube. Rook's frown deepened, and his fingers found one of Dante's nipples, running a sharp thumbnail under its nub. "Hey, ouch. You wanted to know."

"Tequila. Bad things happen with tequila," Rook grumbled.

"I kind of like bad things," he said, nestling between his lover's raised knees. Bending forward, Dante guided the tip of his cock to rest against Rook's body, holding himself there as he kissed Rook long enough to leave him gasping. "Probably why I'm in love with you."

He captured Rook's mouth in a punishing kiss and slid achingly slow into his heat, gasping when Rook clenched instinctively down on his cockhead. Dante rocked his hips, stroking at Rook's belly. Their limbs were tangled, Rook's fingers digging into Dante's thighs, then his back and ass, pulling them in tight.

Dante let his weight settle over Rook's torso, bracing himself with his knees between Rook's legs and his hands flat on the bed. Hunched over Rook's chest, Dante grazed his mouth over his lover's parted lips, breathing in Rook's panting tea-scented huffs. A moment later, a single long push and Dante was seated into the damp heat he'd been needing since the moment he came home.

"Fuck, you're...," Rook rasped, hooking his arms around Dante's neck, letting himself be lifted up off the mattress and edged onto the pillows near the headboard. They were damp with the first sheen of sweat, a glisten nearly lost in the creeping darkness falling over the loft as the day rolled over the horizon. Another jut of Dante's hips and Rook grunted, furrowing his brow. "Dante...."

"Hold on to me, *cuervo*." He was firm, supporting Rook's back and shoulders with a shift of his hands. Dante curved his lover against him, and Rook's legs lifted, hooking over Dante's hips. "Just hold on."

It took them a few second to find their rhythm, a bit of slap of wet skin and a sharp pull of breath between Rook's clenched teeth. Then Dante found the angle he needed to make Rook moan. If poets dripped honey about the touch of a man's seed on their tongue, they'd have wept until they turned to stone if ever Dante could describe how he felt with Rook wrapped around him.

His world—their world—closed in, an aperture closing in tight to focus on only a sea of cotton and entwined bodies. Time slowed around them, every moment marked by a gasp or the slap of Dante's hips into Rook's waiting, needy heat.

Every thrust brought Dante closer to the brink, and he fought his urge to bury himself deeper into Rook. The delicious pull of Rook's edge along his cock feathered away his control, throwing his focus outward until Rook became the only point in his existence.

"Dante, so… damned close," Rook grunted, folding up to meet Dante's thrusts. "Fuck, hurry."

They flowed together, thighs and shoulders straining to deepen the beat they'd created, but the rush of pleasure building in Dante's balls threatened to break apart and drown them. Rook's nails dug into his shoulders, adding to the bites and bruises he'd gotten from his lover's ravenous flirting.

Rook's trembling, a slight shiver through his torso and down his belly, was all the warning Dante needed. He rocked in, rising to his knees, and hitched Rook's legs up, setting a pounding pace. Spreading Rook open under him, Dante found his own stars, his own universe unfurling around him when Rook reached down between them and stroked his own shaft.

The pleasure of Rook's warmth and the erotic hedonism of his lover's arched back, teeth dimpling his lower lip, and his unfocused, hot gaze broke Dante. He'd brought the flush of pink to Rook's high cheekbones, wrung out every gasping mewl with a graze of his fingers or a pierce of his cock into Rook's welcoming velvet clench. His lover's bite found his earlobe, a quick, decisive nip soothed over with a whisper Dante would never tire of hearing.

"*Mi cielo*, yes?" Rook's whiskey-rumble left a resonant thump in Dante's chest. "*Te amo*, Dante."

Dante slowed his thrusts just long enough to return Rook's nibble, then murmured in his lover's ear, "I know."

Rook's shock of laughter shattered the last of Dante's control. His unbridled, open joy brightened the shadows in the room, and the kiss he gave

Dante stole every ounce of thought from Dante's already overwhelmed mind. A shudder, then a splash of hot liquid on his stomach and Dante was lost. A few more thrusts, a threading spiral of sharp-bitter pain and he poured into Rook's body, his cock buried in as deep as he could get. They continued to rock, unwilling or unable to let each other go. The world snapped brittle, and Dante's mind went white, the tinfoil-on-teeth of his senses overloading fighting with the longing to spend his life wrapped up in Rook.

Lethargy took him down, and Dante reluctantly pulled free, collapsing beside Rook on the bed. They lay there, focused solely on breathing. Then Dante mustered up enough energy to roll over onto his side.

"You're going to break me one day, *cuervo*." It was nice to see the worry gone from Rook's face, but something lingered, an echo of a problem Dante hadn't quite eased away. "You were going to tell me something when I got home, but... I think you distracted me."

"Oh, is that what we're calling it?" Rook snorted. "Distracting you."

"You have all my attention," he admitted with a laugh. "I even forgot to tell you about the box Manny had me drag upstairs. He said it was something from one of the auction houses. Label said Natterly's. Now that I think about it, I shouldn't have brought it up without checking it out first."

"I wasn't expecting anything, but that doesn't mean anything." He shrugged as best he could in his nest of crumpled sheets. "Davis Natterly sends me stuff all the time to look at. If I want it, I send him a payment. If not, he gets a courier to pick it up. Totally normal. Last time it was a four-foot-tall Gojira rubber suit. Cut him a check before I even checked the damned thing's history. I'd say it can wait, but now you've got me curious."

"Wait here. I'll bring it over." Dante slapped Rook's thigh, grinning at the slight pink mark his fingers left on his lover's pale skin.

"Dick." Rubbing at the mark, he kicked at Dante's ass, scoring a hit on his thigh. "Let me open the box. Then we can talk."

The box was still heavy and sealed nearly airtight with thick bands of tape. Bringing one of the utility knives with him to the bedroom was a good enough idea to earn him a murmur of pleasure and a light kiss before Rook's avarice took center stage. Sitting cross-legged on the bed, a delectably naked Rook sawed away at the bindings, stopping to turn the box around when he found the package's opening. A piece of paper floated out of the exposed flap, and Dante caught it before it drifted to the floor.

"Probably an invoice," Rook explained, pulling the flap aside, tearing a bit of the cardboard away. "Shit, it's like they expected this thing to have a mummy curse or some—"

Dante didn't need to see the bloody rags and gore-splatted concrete bits sliding out of the box to know Rook needed to be as far from the package as he could get. Reaching for the box, Dante jostled Rook's elbow, and the flap flew open, sending what was inside tumbling to the floor.

He also didn't need to guess if the head striking the floor was a prop, not with the amount of splatter it left on the polished wood and the hard crack of its skull striking the floor. There was also no question about who it was. Dante'd stared at that face for more than an hour while Rook was being interrogated about Harold's death. After a few more bounces, Detective Mark Vicks's severed head came to a messy rest against the edge of the bookshelves, his open, lifeless eyes left staring up at the loft's open ceiling.

"Dante…." Rook's face was nearly as white as Vicks's bloodless expression, and he gulped, blindly reaching for Dante. With his hand gripped around Dante's upper arm, Rook stammered, "Help me get to the bathroom. I think I'm going to puke."

Ten

COPS CARRIED their own visual odor, a social pheromone Rook couldn't quite place his finger on, but he knew it was there. Some marinated in it, overblown and metallic, ruffling under Rook's senses until it seemed as if he were choking on his own blood, while others, like Dante and Hank, were subtler, giving off a firm stance of authority with a veiled suggestion things could go very wrong for someone who challenged them.

Detective Dell O'Byrne wore her copness like it was a second skin with no room for anything else in her life besides her badge and gun, and the flick of her inscrutable gaze over Rook's face when she walked into the room left him with no doubt she'd make short work of him if he fucked with her.

In the time before Dante, Rook would have given her a wide berth. Now he considered his options and decided he'd still probably cross the street if he saw her coming his way. And knowing O'Byrne, she'd probably follow him.

The weirdness at being interviewed in Manny's office did nothing to erase the image of Vicks's bloodless face or the wave of sick that followed. Stranger still to hear Dante's rumbling, softly accented voice outside of the door, but O'Byrne insisted on speaking to them separately in order to get an uninfluenced perspective of what'd happened.

O'Byrne set her phone down on the table, then hit Record on an open app, then rattled off the date, time, and the store's address. "I'm going to be recording this—"

"And if I said no?" He didn't have any objections, but something about the cop begged to be rattled, and the crawling panic in his gut needed something to do besides chew on him.

"Then we go down to the station, where you'll probably call in a bunch of guys in suits who'll make my life hell for a bit and nothing will get done," she said, a bit of steel creeping into her voice. "Let's not make this shitty for both of us, Stevens. Can you state your name, date of birth, and address?"

"Name's Rook Martin Stevens, birthday April first. Year unknown. License says twenty-six, but it's a crap shoot." He grinned at her frown. "Beanie—my mom—wasn't big on paperwork, so getting me a birth certificate wasn't at the top of her to-do list. And I live here. Above Potter's Field."

"Tell me about Detective Vicks. What happened?" Shifting in her chair, O'Byrne's jacket fell open, giving Rook a peek of her gun in its side holster. "Walk me through this."

"I don't know what else I can tell you other than I opened the box and Vicks's head rolled out. I don't know how he got there. In the box, I mean. Okay, I know how the box got here. It was delivered, but I wasn't here when it came in." Lazing back against the couch, Rook hooked one arm over its plump back and studied the detective sitting across of him. He couldn't read her face much, but her body language was pure cop with easy tells. Tense shoulders and a bit of a pull between her eyebrows was enough to let Rook know she believed he wasn't telling her the truth. "Look, Vicks came after me this afternoon. He cornered me at Bergan's. There were witnesses. Well, one witness but a pretty good one."

"Did you file a complaint about the attack?" She tilted her head, assessing him. "With someone other than Montoya."

"No, I didn't think anyone would give a shit, to be honest," he replied. "Montoya and I didn't get a chance to talk about it. Figured we'd get around to it later and he'd push me into it."

"Why don't you start with what happened there and then tell me everything right up until I showed up?" O'Byrne uncapped a pen she'd pulled from her jacket pocket. "And then I'm going to ask you about a few things we've found out since then."

It took him less than three minutes to tell her about Vicks's trying to choke him to death in an interrogation room many years ago, then the recent threats and theories about Harold's murder, and despite her deadpan expression, he caught a flush of pink across her face when he asked her if she really wanted to hear about how he and Dante passed the hour or so after the detective entered the loft. Moving him along with a muttered grumble, O'Byrne kept scribbling in her notepad as he described opening the package, then stopped when Rook got to the moment Vicks's decapitated head bounced along the loft's hard floor.

"And you know this auction house well? You said they send you things often?" She cut through his story, looking up from her notes. "How?"

"I'm friends with Davis Natterly, one of the owners. Well, friendly enough." Rook shrugged. "I've done business with him for years. Mostly high-end stuff. It's where the falcon was auctioned off. The one Harold stole from me."

"I've read the initial complaint. I don't know if Montoya told you there's a bit of a turf war going on over this case. West LA is gunning for someone's blood over Vicks, but so far it's in our house. He might have been an asshole, but he was *their* asshole. They're going to want to take a shot at who did this."

"So long as that shot isn't at me, I hope they find the guy." The comment got him a long cop look, and he snorted derisively. "This isn't the first time I've been in a cop's crosshairs. They're going to be leaning on me because his head rolled across my damned floor and he'd tapped me for a murder. You think his buddies down in West LA *aren't* going to be looking at me?"

"Not if I can prove you didn't have time to kill him, no. They won't." She went back to her notebook, flipping a few pages. "You said you came back to your business after you left Bergan's? Did you go anywhere or straight here?"

"Straight here," he offered up. "Bergan's guys loaded my car up with the toys I bought off of him, and when I got here, I helped Manny get the boxes unloaded. Spent a couple of minutes explaining how I wanted them divided up, then headed upstairs."

"Why didn't you stay in the shop?" she probed. "It was still open."

"First off, it was a shitty day and I just wanted to decompress, but mostly because I don't work the store." Rook shook his head. "It's a storefront for common stuff, throwaway merchandise for browsers. Trendy things or cereal-box toys. Some more expensive stuff, but not the really high-ticket items. Nearly all of the big money is with private collectors, but I wanted someplace solid, a brick-and-mortar store someone could come to if they needed to, and it gives me a spot I can unload medium to low-range items. Manny's in charge of Potter's Field. He and Ralph—that's one of the shift managers—usually price out new things using reference books, but I pitch in on the weird stuff. There were a couple of pieces I saved back, but most of the toys were run-of-the-mill. Nothing special."

"But you bought up all of Bergan's tin stock, you said. Why?" She dug in, trying to poke at sore spots in Rook's story. "Doesn't sound like it would be worth your while."

"Because the owner came upstairs with a shotgun and stopped Vicks from ripping my head off." Rook tamped down his irritation. "Hey, I didn't shake my ass at him and beg him to bite it. Asshole followed me to Bergan's, and Thorkenberry told him to take his shit elsewhere. So yeah, I took twenty pounds of toys off of his hands as a thank-you, because it would have been kind of weird if I'd dropped to my knees and gave him a blow job. What with him married to an IA cop and me being hooked up with Montoya."

He came off sounding aggressive, but Rook was quickly growing tired of a day full of cop games. He wanted Montoya next to him, but the detective firmly told his lover to stay outside while they talked, and now Rook could see why. The questioning sounded less and less like information gathering and more along the lines of setting him up. Rubbing at his face, Rook felt the fatigue in his chest settle down along his spine.

"I didn't kill Vicks, lady," he said, dropping his hands down into his lap. "I'm going to keep saying that until I'm blue in the face if I have to, but I simply didn't have time. I left Bergan's, came here to take care of the merchandise after calling Dante, then went upstairs. Montoya came home, and I didn't even *think* about Vicks until I saw his face staring up at me. And after that, I puked my guts out into the toilet while Dante called the cops. What the fuck else do you want from me?"

"I'm trying to help answer questions a hell of a lot of people are going to be asking, people who are going to want someone's blood." Her chin lifted, mouth tightening. Then O'Byrne said, "You seem a bit tense, Stevens. I'm not the bad guy here."

"Probably because it seems like you're trying to shove me into some corner," he replied. "I don't do well with cops. So maybe I'm taking you wrong."

"You do well enough with Montoya," she pointed out.

"Kind of different, I think we both can agree to that one."

"Agreed. Let's continue, okay? I'll try to make it fast." She consulted something she'd written on a previous page, glancing up when the voices outside of the office door grew louder, but the conversation was still too muffled for Rook to make out anything other than a murmur. "You told the responding officer you recognized the package as coming from the auction house. Didn't you question him sending you something without telling you first? Or does the owner—what's his name?—here it is, Davis, does Davis send you items all the time? So you wouldn't have thought it odd?"

"He's sent over a couple of things," Rook admitted with a shrug. "I didn't think it was that weird, but yeah, normally I get a heads-up on stuff. Jesus. That *wasn't* a pun. I swear to God, that wasn't a pun."

"It's fine. But Natterly didn't send you the piece you claim Harold stole? He let that go to auction, right?"

"Difference between a niche piece worth a couple of thousand and a documented movie prop, even one from a parody. Any Maltese Falcon coming to the market is going to get a stir. There's a lot of social weight behind it."

"But the one Harold got was a fake," O'Byrne interjected. "Not from the original movie, I mean."

"If you're counting the Bogart version as the original. There were others, but yeah, the statue Harold got isn't from *that* film, but still, the later film cast their statues from one of those used in the Bogie piece, right down to the chips in its beak. I wanted it because there's some... I was kind of raised by the guy who ran with the bird's original owner." Rook waited a beat, expecting O'Byrne to feint the conversation again, a common con verbal trick, and she didn't disappoint. "And here's where you change the subject and come back a bit later to feel me out."

"Bergan's—" She caught his smirk and returned one of her own. The expression changed her face, softening it, humanizing it, and Rook fought off the wave of empathy he felt toward her in that shared moment when she realized he knew she was trying to throw him off his game. "Okay, not Bergan's. We'll stick with the bird. If Davis didn't send you things out of the blue, why didn't you question this box?"

"Probably because I was tired, and well...." He shrugged. "I'd just spent some time with Dante, unwinding my brain. The last thing I wanted to do was think. Should I have checked it out? Probably, but I think a part of my head figured Davis was sending a sorry-I-fucked-up present. I get that sometimes if someone auctions off something I've already bought or screws something up. His people down there should have known better than to give it to Harold. Technically, he's already been angling to make sure I don't sue him for not delivering the goods."

"What happened with the statue? Why did he give it to your cousin?"

"He didn't. I'd made arrangements to pick it up after he came back, but Harold convinced the office staff he was buying it for me as a present." The anger he'd felt arriving at the auction house to find the statue gone resurfaced, and Rook swallowed it back down. "Davis assured me it wouldn't happen again, but by that time, Harold already had it squirreled away, and he wasn't going to hand it over."

"So you came up with a way to get it back?"

"Sadonna offered to let me take it back," Rook replied. "It was… just a fucking prank. Sure, I wanted to kick Harold's ass, but mostly because it's my damned bird. He just did it to piss me off."

"It's the you being pissed off part I'm concerned about, because Vicks alluded in his investigation notes that you had a hot temper, one fueled by ego. His theory was you and Harold's wife cooked up a plan to kill him but she double-crossed you." O'Byrne's expression shifted, going a neutral so flat Rook's hackles rose. "See for me, the box didn't make sense. Why send it? And did it come from Natterly's? So I contacted the auction house and spoke to a Jeremy there. He said you weren't scheduled for a delivery, so why did you open it? Do you know Jeremy? Would he have a reason to lie?"

"Jer? No, he's the other Natterly in the business. Davis's the guy in charge. He's the one I usually deal with. I do business with him about as often as I brush my teeth. The box had Natterly's labels on it, so that's why I didn't think anything about opening it up." His brain kicked in, trying to come up with a name, anyone who'd be ballsy enough to kill a cop and cold-blooded enough to send his head to the last man Vicks threatened to kill. "Manny said it was dropped off by the delivery guy, a courier, but that's normal too. No sense using a shipping service when Natterly's about two miles down the road. They have their own guys to cart stuff around the city. Lots of business in Tinsel Town. People like the past here. He does good business."

After unfolding a piece of paper she'd tucked into the back of her notebook, the detective slid it over for Rook to read. It was definitely a copy, one made off of the shop's own machine, judging from the familiar black splotch on the upper right corner, an imperfection the technician valiantly struggled to correct, but the machine'd faithfully captured a scalloped blemish on the original, darkening one side of the paper. Handwritten, the blocky words were sharp black slashes and bristling with menace, assuring Rook Vicks would never bother him again.

"What's this?" The words were chilling, intimate, and cloying. Rook didn't want to touch the note, much less have its contents burned into his brain, but his eyes kept moving over the message, unwilling to let go. "What the fucking hell is this?"

The note was short, but not very sweet, although the person digging the pen into the paper probably didn't think so. *Rook*, it said in long, hard lines, *Vicks said he was sorry about trying to set fire to your shop. It won't happen again.*

His breath couldn't seem to leave his chest, and he choked on the lump of air in his throat. Coughing, Rook's eyes watered, and his fingers slipped the paper back across the table at the detective.

"Jesus, I…," he stammered. "Where was this?"

"This was in the package along with Vicks's head. As you can see, it's addressed to you." O'Byrne's eyes burned with a dark fervor, a predator sighting on its prey. "So you tell me, Stevens, who do you know can kill a man in cold blood, saw off his head, and then mail it to you with a love note attached? Because I think if you can answer *that*, we would have found who killed your cousin, Harold."

ARCHIBALD MARTIN was used to getting his own way.

It was clear he'd grown up with an entire set of silver crammed into his thin-lipped mouth and expected to be obeyed after issuing an order. Shadowed by a phalanx of serious-faced people in suits Dante assumed were lawyers, Archie marched into Potter's Field with a gleam in his eye and all intentions of doing battle.

He met his match in Manny.

It was an interesting standoff. One despotic, overindulged head of industry crossing swords with a Latino former drag queen bearing breast cancer scars and a fierce protective streak where his loved ones were concerned. Archie might have gone toe to toe with the thickest-skinned hard-nosed men ever to walk the earth, but Manny'd taken Death down and had no intention of letting Archie railroad him.

Or that's how it played out in Dante's head. The reality of it was they'd taken one look at each other and bonded over the one thing they had in common—Rook Stevens.

"He needs to be moved into the house. At least until this thing blows over. All of the… you too. I'd feel better if I knew you were safe. I'm old. People need to understand my heart can't take much more of this shit," Archie groused, pacing in front of a long counter filled with fuzzy round balls, ray guns, and decoder rings. Gesturing toward the office door, he turned on one of his lawyers, a florid-faced man whose wide-eyed expression made him look like one of the alien-fish masks hanging on the shop's walls. "Go in there. See what that detective's up to, and—"

"She's questioning Rook, Archie," Dante interjected. "Standard procedure. And you're going to have to leave the shop before they kick you out. It's a crime scene."

"The lady cop…. O'Byrne said we could wait here." Manny tsked. "Only the receiving room is a crime scene. Well, and upstairs."

"Great, *tío*." He threw his hands up, more to tease his uncle than anything else. "*Now* you remember things people tell you."

"Don't get smart with me. And Archie, you're not going to get him to go with you," Manny said with a shake of his head. "The boy is stubborn. He won't like being chased out of his house. We might be able to get him to come to our place, but probably only for a night."

"Doesn't like to give up control," the old man grumbled, leaning heavily on his cane. "Okay, Sanders, why don't you take the other two and see if we can't get some idea on what they're doing with the murder case. The sooner we get that woman out of my house, the better. I don't know what I was thinking letting her stay with me. She runs the staff ragged."

Dante bit his cheek to keep from commenting, but he caught Sanders rolling his eyes as he left the store with the other suits Archie dragged in. Hank caught the door for them as they stepped out, waiting for the way to clear before coming in. Nodding to his partner, Dante murmured a soft "Excuse me" to Manny and Archie. The old man waved him off with a shake of his cane, not stopping to take a breath as they continued to talk.

"Not sure those two should be in the same room as each other." Camden eyed the older men chatting quietly near the counter. "Hell, I'm not so sure they should be in the same *state*."

"They're trying to come up with a way to manage Rook. That's going to be a test of the irresistible force paradox I don't want to be around to see." Dante jerked his head toward the front door.

"You're sexy when you talk science stuff." Hank leered playfully.

"Shut up, *pendejo*. Let's get someplace we can talk."

The cool night air was a relief after the stuffiness of the overheated store, and Dante sucked in as much of the cold as he could. His throat throbbed slightly where Rook'd bitten it during their lovemaking, and the ache was a good one, reminding him of the man he'd brought into his life. Or, to be fair, the one who'd slithered in through an open window and took up residence while Dante'd been busy trying to arrest him for a murder he hadn't committed.

"Thanks for coming down," Dante said as he fell into step next to his partner. A taco truck worked a corner a few storefronts away from Potter's Field, and Camden headed straight for it. "I guess we're going for something to eat?"

"Drink," he corrected. "I know those guys. They make a damned mean *horchata*."

"You know it's probably all just the same stuff they sell in those bags you can get downtown, right?" Dante snorted at Hank's disgusted scoff. "You *know* it is."

"They add something to it. Maybe more cinnamon. Just shut up and let me have my fantasies," Hank grumbled. "I don't say shit about you thinking Rook's going to settle into the white picket fence, two-car garage life you've got going."

"I think I gave that up a couple of days ago," he admitted softly. "I told Manny I'd be home in half an hour, and he called me afterwards to ask where the hell I was. Thought I was in traffic or caught up in a case."

"And you were at Rook's loft, huh?"

"Yeah. I was." The truck's line was long and slow, winding around an electrical box painted like a *calavera*. The artist's attempt at *Catrina* was a decent one, her hat crowned with red roses and oddly enough, a taco stuck into the band like a feather embellishment. Shaking his head at the art, Dante scanned the crowd, listening to the conversations around them.

The nearly East-Hollywood neighborhood seemed on the brink of gentrification, but it was also a part of the city destined to attract a blend of oddballs and wedges of ethnicities. The taco truck with its aroma of caramelized onions and browning carne asada was set up in front of a boba shop who'd sent out a young Korean girl with a shy smile and warm face to hand out half-off coupons to the people standing in line. Around its edges, the neighborhood still clung to some of its dirtier habits, a couple of porn shops and the occasional street-corner preacher, but for the most part, it fit around Dante much like Rook did, comfortable but always slightly unpredictable.

But right now, a bit too unpredictable for Dante's liking.

"I think I agree with Manny and Archie. I don't think Rook should be up in that apartment. Vicks's head... all of that... something's off." Dante tried to put his worry aside, but it was too strong, digging its claws into his head. "He's not going to want to leave. Rook's stubborn. "There's a note. To Rook. A scary one. One that my gut says is going to escalate into something more fucked than what we're in right now."

"Did he see it? The note, I mean. Not the head." Hank made a face. "Couldn't miss the head from what you said."

"No, he didn't, but I'm sure she's going to put it in front of him to get a reaction. O'Byrne showed it to me before she went into the office. Vicks either got in the way of someone *or* something. The writer claims Vicks did the firebombing, which knowing him, maybe isn't too much of a stretch. He was pissed off Rook slithered out from between his fingers, but... I don't know." Recalling the sticky affection inferred in the note and the bloodstains around the paper's edges, Dante's guts twisted with worry. "It was all very watching-you-through-your-window, and those kind of things never end well. I didn't recognize the writing, but that doesn't mean jack shit. I don't know anyone he deals with on a daily basis, and that's kind of scary if I think about it too long."

"You can say that about any relationship. You think my wife knows about the people I come into contact with every day?" Hank pointed out. "You, sure.... We're attached at the hip, but everyone else? She knows I work for a guy named Book, but beyond that, she probably couldn't name one person in the bull pen besides you. Big question right now is what are we going to do? Shook down Sadonna, got nothing from her. Now Vicks is dead, his body's missing, and your boy's going to have to be looking over his shoulder until we find out who did it."

"O'Byrne wants us off the case," Dante said, shoving his hands in his jeans pockets. "She thinks Book's crazy for letting us dig into this."

"What do you think?" Camden shuffled forward a step, smiling at a pack of kids in front of him. "Should we keep going at this? Because I'm up for whatever you want to do."

"What do you think?" He chuckled when his partner shook his head at him, then sobered as he sifted through his emotions. "My gut says trust O'Byrne if she gets the case, but my ego... man, my ego says I want to chase this guy down and drop him. He killed a cop, Camden. Sure, Vicks was a dick and that asshole spent his last couple of hours on this Earth fucking with Rook, but he didn't deserve what he got."

"So the game's afoot, then. Good. Because while your gut is trusting O'Byrne, mine's saying the thing with Rook is going to take a back seat to Vicks's murder." He pursed his lips in thought, rocking back on his heels. "Nighttime. Not many domestics work at night. Maybe after O'Byrne cuts your boy loose, you and I should go pay a visit to Harold's housecleaner. See what she has to say about this whole mess."

"That'll probably piss O'Byrne off," Dante warned him. "You know she's going to get tapped for this, and we're just going to be getting in her way. You sure you want to be with me on her shit list?"

"Yeah I'm with you," he shot back. "She might not know it, but I like her. I think Book's going to be stepping down in a couple of years, and he's going to want someone to step into his shoes. I'm backing O'Byrne, but she's got to know we've got her six just like we've got to know she has ours. So before we go any further, you and I fill her in on what we've got, then take off. What do you think?"

"Agreed." Dante nodded. "She should be about done with him. There wasn't enough time for Rook to kill Vicks and package him up, so he'll be cleared, but there's someone out there with a cop's blood on his hands. I just want to catch him before it's Rook he's gunning for."

Eleven

"I STILL think this is a very bad idea. You can't even use the bedroom until the hazmat people go over it. Why would you go to a hotel when Grandpa's got a huge empty house?" Alex shouted from his perch on the edge of the loft's long couch. "And Dante's okay with this? He's going to let you do that? Because the house has things like a security gate and sometimes even guys with guns around it."

There were a lot of things Rook liked—maybe even loved—about the cousin he'd shaken out of his family tree in the last few years. Alex Martin was smart, geeky, adorable but awkward enough he came off as endearing rather than an asshole like the rest of Archie's spawn. But sometimes that stumble of foot-into-mouth tendency in Alex's brain brought Rook up short.

Rook stared at the empty duffel bag he'd pulled out and put on the bench in his walk-in closet. He hadn't put anything in it or even opened a drawer to see what he had that was clean, but as soon as his boyfriend bit his lower lip after Rook told him he wasn't staying at Dante's *or* Archie's house, Rook knew he'd made a mistake.

Dante and Alex were right. He couldn't stay in the loft or sleep in the bedroom, and despite his outward calm, he was more than a little freaked out.

He just hated admitting it.

It was well into tomorrow. If the people poking at things in his bedroom ever cleared the scene and if he could stand the smell of puke in the air and a faint hint of bleach, Rook *could* stay in the living room and not be anywhere near the bed where he'd unwrapped the remains of a man's life. The dead didn't bother him, not normally, but this one did. He'd seen death before, too many times to count if he stopped and thought about it. Carnies were too poor for doctors, and a trip to the hospital was a declaration to have affairs in order, because the sick were never coming back. There'd been summers on the circuit where he'd knocked on a performer's trailer door only to find them bloated and ripe, their corpses cooked in broiling heat.

It was a hardscrabble of a life, one usually leading to a death from disease or booze and drug addiction. He'd wanted more than that for himself, but today broke him.

But he wasn't going to show it. Especially not to Alex. Tucked out of Alex's sight behind the bookcases cordoning off the living space, he shouted, "Did you just say... *let?*"

When Rook peeked out of the closet, the look on Alex's face was priceless. His owlish blink behind the faint sheen of his spectacles and the hesitant curve of his lip while he sucked in his breath to contemplate his options would have been comical if it hadn't been countered by the scowl on Archie's wrinkled face as he let himself into the loft.

In his relatively short time as a sentient living creature, Rook'd never met anyone who thought and felt like him. Alex came close, or so Rook let himself believe, but as he'd allowed himself to feel something for the Martins he'd met, it was Archie who simply *got* him.

Sure, the old man was cantankerous and a bully. He'd grown up on the opposite of the soup kitchen table, and his idea of struggling was running out of cream cheese for his morning bagel, when Rook'd fought for every scrap he could shove into his mouth from the moment Beanie popped him off her breast. Rook longed to be a better person, someone *like* Alex who saw the world bathed in bits of sunshine, and where there were shadows, it just meant he had to work that much harder to make it better. The reality? Archie was who Rook feared he'd become if he didn't let people into his heart.

The fright in Archie's eyes—so much like his own—smarted and left a sour taste in Rook's mouth. He'd put that terror there, and an icy sliver gouged out a piece of Rook's heart when Archie blinked, struggling to get his emotions under control before anyone saw him crack.

"Hey, Grandpa." Alex gracefully slid from the couch and strode over to Archie's side. "I was trying to get Rook—"

"Alex, can you give me a moment with your cousin alone?" Archie patted Alex's arm with shaking fingers. The gilding light from the Edison bulbs tinted Archie's skin to parchment, picking out the watercolor wash of his veins along the back of his hand. Alex hesitated, sliding a worried glance at Rook, his expression nearly a mirror of Archie's. Then their grandfather sighed softly and asked, "Please?"

"Of course, Grandpa." Alex's next look was harder, bristling with a firm warning, not something Rook would have thought his cousin had in him, but there it was, edged sharp and steely, promising consequences if Rook crossed any lines. "Is James still talking to Dante and O'Byrne?"

"If O'Byrne is that hatchet-faced woman with a stick up her ass, then yes," Archie muttered. "Go on. And can you see what kind of tea Manny made for me? I'm going to ask Rosa to get me some. Settled my head some."

"Sure." Pressing a light kiss on his stooped grandfather's temple, Alex said, "Don't chew off too much of his ass. Martin meat screws with your digestion."

Rook waited until Alex slid the heavy loft door open and left before he padded past the couches and stood toe to toe with his cantankerous grandfather. Archie grunted, clasping his hands over his cane's handle, leaning on it for support. Rook wasn't fooled. For all the years Archie wore on his skin, he was a hell of a lot stronger than he looked.

Usually.

Despite his claim of Manny's tea soothing him, Archie looked like shit.

"Archie, at least sit down before you fall over. I've seen more life in a Toronto trash panda pancake than I do in you right now." Rook slid his hand under his grandfather's forearm, gently tugging him toward the sofa Alex vacated. "I don't want to fight with you about this. You'd feel the same way I do if someone'd tried to shove you out of your house. You'd tell them to fuck off."

"I sit down, then you loom. Standing over someone like that gives you the advantage, and this is too fucking important to blow off," Archie grumbled, shaking him off. His temper was high, flushing his cheeks red. "You've got to learn to listen. Sometimes you have to do what you're told."

"I'm not anyone's puppet, Archie. *Sit.*" He gave another tug, and this time, Archie shuffled forward. "It's like pulling teeth with you sometimes."

"It's that way you with all the time, and now *this*. It's too much, Rook. This is all too damned much for me to take," Archie snapped back, his eyes lit with a fire Rook hadn't seen before. Something was wrong, something deep and broken, and it rose up, spearing Rook through his gut. "Sometimes I don't even know why I bother. Just like your mother. You're not worth fighting for, boy. I swear to God, fucking damned useless—why don't you do what Beatrice did and just walk away? Make it easier on everyone."

In that second, Rook bled, knowing something broke between him and Archie, ending them. The thin sliver of longing he'd nursed—the need to be folded into a family, even one as fucked-up as the Martins—finally died. He'd blinked, and without any fanfare, the breath he'd been holding in since the moment he'd first met Archie escaped; that foul, rancid stale hiccup of air he'd trapped in his lungs, waiting for when Archie shoved him away, finally left.

He just hadn't thought it would hurt so damned much.

Rook let go of Archie's arm, reeling back a step, then held himself back when the old man reached for him. It'd been a long time since he'd felt pain, *that* kind of pain. It sliced through Rook's throat, dragging down the front of his chest, then digging into his heart. A curdled bitterness flooded his mouth, and Rook wasn't sure if he was tasting actual bile or just the ichor leaking from his torn soul.

He should have known better. There'd been a small part of him waiting for that slap, the sane, rational, wary bits he'd stored in himself for that one day when he'd have to protect himself from the anguish of letting someone in. Someone like Archie. Even someone like Dante. It always fell apart, leading to nothing but a bone-aching pain dark enough to shatter his life into dust.

It was a fight to keep himself from showing his emotions, to mask the scraping rawness Archie left with his burred words, but he did his best, pulling himself up and squaring his shoulders. He wasn't going to give the man any satisfaction, not like he'd given others. Not like he'd handed his mother when she'd walked away from him for the very last time, rubbing his broken trust into the muck he'd landed in when he'd believed she'd changed.

"Don't," he croaked around the thickness in his throat. "Don't fucking *touch* me."

"I'm sorry. Boy... Rook... I am...." Archie strained to grab ahold of Rook's wrists, but he twisted away, snarling at the older man. "I.... God, you *know* I don't think before I open my mouth. I didn't mean that. I didn't—"

"Get the fuck out." He couldn't see anymore. The world was drowning, a painful sour plunge into salty tears and choked-off air. "Door's behind you, old man. Use it."

"Rook—" Archie's plea was cut short by Dante clearing his throat. "Good, Montoya. Tell him. Tell him—"

Hard as it was to believe, he'd missed Dante coming in, he had. His cop'd slipped through the partially open loft door and stalked in. He couldn't read Dante. Not now. Not through the tears he couldn't seem to get out of his eyes or even was brave enough to let fall. Rook wouldn't give Archie that. He could let himself—Dante was there before he finished his thought. His nerves screamed to shove Dante back when he got near, years—too many long fucking years—of keeping people away yanked at every rage-filled, agonizing need to pick up the pieces of his life and take it someplace else.

But not without Dante.

He couldn't live without the damned cop. *His* damned cop. The same cop who was now putting his hands on Rook, hands that stroked him to pleasure, the same ones who'd shoved him outside of the bedroom when Vicks's head fell out and then pulled back his hair when Rook puked his guts out for five minutes afterward.

"Stop turning that brain of yours in circles, *cuervo*," Dante whispered, wrapping his arms around Rook's stiff shoulders. "Don't run from this. I know you want to. I can see it, just… *don't*. Let me hold you for a second."

"Not going to. Not from you. Just from… shit, *don't* hold me. Makes me look… weak. I'm *not* weak," he stammered, and his spine rattled, a cold creeping out from his belly and icing over his nerves. Rook tried to keep the tremors from spreading through him, but he couldn't. Nothing he did, nothing he thought of could stop the minute shivers racking through him. "*Fuck*. Get him the fuck away from me. *I'm* fucking useless? After everything… screw this. I can't… *fuck*. I am *not* fucking useless, and I'm *done* being thrown away."

He needed to cry. *Needed* to fall to his knees and scream, because something *died* inside of him, a horribly cold excision of a dream, and it was changing him, closing Rook off and shutting him down. Dante's voice was a blur of white noise, and through it, Rook heard Archie pleading, begging for something Rook didn't want to hear.

Or rather, he didn't know if he was strong enough to hear.

Dante felt good, smelled wonderful, and most of all, was warm. Hugging Dante's waist, Rook pulled himself in as tightly as he could, wishing he wasn't smearing snot over Dante's shirt, but it couldn't be helped. He didn't cry well. Even when he ground his pain down, it surfaced, and Dante's embrace felt safe enough for him to let go.

Rook couldn't even absorb that. Tired, confused, and heartsick, he let himself be held—*let*—his brain snagged on the irony of a single word. He needed space to think, to breathe, and he took a step back from Dante, enough to let him pull in a bit of air *not* Montoya flavored.

Archie's words snuck in past the crumbling walls. "I can't let him…. Please, Montoya. Make him understand. I am *sorry*. I… reacted, and I—"

"I know, Archie. Give us a bit?" Dante's accent thickened, its fluid roll soothing a bit of the hurt away. He turned slightly, taking Rook with him, moving so Rook couldn't see Archie's brittle, agonized expression. "Words hurt, old man. And you two fight like cats and dogs, but sometimes, Archie, you bite for real."

"I'm not arguing with that. It was stupid, and… and *I am sorry*. My mouth ran, and before I knew it… I didn't mean any of that. I was just… *angry*." Archie moved, his cane thumping in an uneven rhythm across the floor, and the hand on Rook's back was cold, trembling, and tentative. "Rook, I am better than this. You deserve more than that from me, and I am *begging* you to please let me fix this. I love you, son. You mean the world to me, and… I'm scared. I hate to say it, but I'm fucking scared someone is going to take you from me… before I'm ready to let you go. Because I am *never* going to let you go."

"Archie…." Dante's chest rumbled, his deep voice lapping over the edges of Rook's panicked hurt. "He knows that. It's been a long day. For both of you. Let me talk to him. Manny's still downstairs—"

"I need him to know I mean it, Montoya," Archie snapped, hot and furious words at Rook's back. "I fucked up. I did what I did to his mother when she didn't do what I wanted her to do, and I'll be damned if I make the same mistake twice."

"*Cuervo*, what do you want?" Dante murmured gently, stroking the hair from Rook's face. His thumbs left a trail of rough warmth on Rook's cheekbones,

"I want to kick him in the balls and fucking laugh my ass off." Rook pulled back, then dug the heels of his hands across his eyes to wipe away the ache building there. "Then kick him again."

"*Rook*—" Archie stopped when Rook shook his head, his shoulders slumping. "I am *sorry*. I wasn't throwing you out. I promise—"

"I need to sit down." He pressed his fingers against Dante's hard upper arm, not wanting to lose contact but needing to separate himself. "I'm… off-balance."

"If you stop and think about what you've gone through today, babe." Dante brushed his lips across Rook's forehead. They touched noses, a brief moment of touch, and then Dante gave him room to move. "Both of you are… well, you don't have the best of tempers. Breathe and step back. Might do you both good."

Leaning on the back of the couch, Rook stared at his grandfather. Archie was a shadow to him, coming out of Beanie's stories in a rush of evil and malcontent. They'd fought before, slung words at one another in fits of rage, but always came back around to try again. They were too much alike, and if he was aching inside from Archie's heated exchange, then he owed it to the old man to hear him out.

He owed it to himself not to walk away from the only man who'd ever called him son… and meant it.

Dante was right. In the muddle of his overwrought emotions, his cop served him up a helping of common sense with a bit of tenderness. It'd only been a few hours since he'd opened the delivery box, and before that, he'd been cornered by the now dead detective, feared for his life, and then Dante peeled him open to expose him to an intimacy he wasn't sure he was strong enough to survive. Add Manny and Archie's attempts to bully him into relocating to the Martin estate and Rook stared at the smoking ruins of his day in a new light.

Because if Archie'd looked aged before he'd carpet-bombed Rook, he looked five steps away from death now.

"Okay, I'm going to check on Manny. Last I saw, he was trying to set O'Byrne up with someone. Hank and I were going to go talk to Harold's housekeeper, but it's too late now. We'll get back on the investigation tomorrow. I don't know who's picking up Harold's murder investigation, but I think we should still chase it down. All of this? It's connected. I just have to figure out how." He brushed his knuckles over Rook's chin, then stole another brief kiss, leaving Rook breathless. "What do you need me to do?"

"Let me talk to my grandfather. Then we can figure out what I'm going to need packed up." The relief in Dante's face stung a little, and he bit at his lower lip. "I don't know where we're going, but we'll figure that out too."

"The house is still open to you, son." Archie leaned forward, his hip resting on the edge of the couch. "I promise you I will never shut my door to you. No matter how much of an asshole I can be."

"Manny first, then I'll see if O'Byrne's wrapping things up downstairs. She's got a crew on tap to clean the loft tomorrow morning, so maybe just a hotel," Dante suggested. "Let's decide after you two are done. We've got lots of options."

He got one final kiss, a low, lingering simmer of a promise wrapped in the flick of Dante's tongue on his lips. Then his lover was gone, leaving him empty and with a relationship to patch up.

Then the couch's legs skidded on the floor, driven an inch forward by their weight, and Archie yelped, flinging his arm out to catch himself, but

Rook was already there, catching the older man before he fell. His cane shot forward, clattering loudly on the floor, but the edge of the rug stopped them from going any farther.

"Let me sit down before I kill us both," Archie rasped, his breath heavy. He limped around the sofa, letting Rook guide him. Then heaving a sigh of relief, he eased down into the cushions. Rook sat next to him, glad to be off his feet. "Damned knee is bothering me today, but that's no excuse for what I said. I'm just scared for you, boy. We're not… it's not easy between us. Too much alike. Too stubborn. And yes, you're like your mother, but that's because she's… she's the only one of my kids besides Alex's parents that I like. The others—well, that's something else. The bottom line is I fucked us up and I'm sorry."

The silence between them thinned, punctured by the pops of noise from the streets outside. There was a window open on the short wall of the living space, the slight crack of the sill barely wide enough to let the night in. Even in the early hours of the morning, Hollywood continued to dance under its own moon. A cat screeched nearby, its cry a long train whistle through the burble of cars rolling down the boulevard. There were still cops outside, the crackle of a radio echoing against the brick and stone exterior and the periodic punch of serious voices with the occasional rolling chuckle of macabre humor to lighten the weight they all carried with their badge.

It seemed like the perfect time to make amends, and Rook had every intention right up until the point his grandfather farted, a quick, explosive *brrpt* sound. Archie had the good grace to look sheepish after Rook broke out in a fit of laughter.

"Sue me. I'm old. You get gassy when you're old," the old man grumbled. "Wait until you get to be my age and they shove broccoli and salad down your throat. Damned nutritionist serves me up a kale and spinach smoothie every morning like I'm some damned cow. Quit your guffawing. It's not funny."

"It's a little funny. Serious moment and then armpit noises," Rook gasped out, wiping the corner of his eye. "How the hell can I stay mad at you when you're over there playing 'Oh Danny Boy' with your buttcheeks?"

"That's what I love about you, boy. You always tell me exactly what you're thinking." Archie's grin was a marvel. It cracked his face, wrinkling up his eyes, lifting the melancholy from his mouth. "I *do* love you. And I'm sorry. Again. Still. It's hard watching you make decisions I disagree with. I just want to shove you over until you're on the right path, even though I know it pisses you off."

"Yeah, no one pisses me off like you do. Not even Dante. And for what it's worth, I'm sorry too. I… flew off the handle." Rook got it out slowly, probing at the tenderness lingering inside him. "Today was *fucked*. Not as bad as it was for Vicks, but… it got to me, Archie. And *nothing* gets to me, but that… *his head*, man… *that* did. I lost it when you called me useless. *She* used to call me that, you know. Like I didn't matter. I couldn't hear it from you."

"You matter. God, you and Alex? You're my legacies. You'll see that some day. How much you mean to me." He paused, his eyes hooded and thoughtful. "I'm asking you to be patient with an old man. This old man. Because I'm stuck in my ways, and sometimes—a lot of the times—I punch when I should hug. Can I get a chance to show you that? Can you give me that?"

"Yeah, I can. Hell, I'll probably need that from you too because… if you haven't noticed, I'm kind of an asshole."

Dante's hugs were always warm, a blanket of protection, love, and a promise of pleasure and forever. The elbow-knock, loose-boned embrace he and Archie shared was not so much comforting as it was affirming. They were awkward, incapable of getting in a decent hug because they were sitting sideways, but to Rook, it felt good. It felt *real*. And after the day he'd had, he needed the *real* more than anything else.

"So we're good?" Rook asked when he let go of Archie's bony shoulders. The old man nodded, looking away to dab at his face. "Because we've got to take better care of us, you know? Neither one of us is good at this shit, and you've had a hell of a lot more practice than I have."

"I forget how young you are, you know? Maybe it's because you're with Montoya. Or that you've built all this. I forget you and Alex are the same age. Or is he older? I can't recall."

"Can't tell you, remember? Beanie doesn't know *when* I was born, and every time I asked, I got a different story and guy she'd hooked up with. Told me my dad was Sam Wong, one of the tent guys, because you know I look half Chinese."

"Um," Archie mumbled, sneaking a look at Rook's face. "Maybe?"

"Hey, if it were possible, I'd have been all in. Sam's cool. First gay guy I knew, but Beanie would have been the last woman he hooked up with if ever he even thought about it." The red tape of being Beanie's son was nearly more than Rook could handle. "She just makes life… *hard*. I get that. I don't blame you for butting heads with her. Hell, I just got a real driver's license a couple of years ago, and that's just because I got a lawyer to work through her being a citizen. Before that, everything I had was fake."

"She should have left you with me." His grandfather chuckled. "Although I don't think I could have survived both you and Alex. Bad enough he blew out one of the tower walls because some idiot gave him an old chemistry kit. Can't imagine the trouble you'd have gotten into, but… and know this, boy, I'd give my left nut to have had you. And that's the truth."

"I know, old man. I know." He blinked away the dampness in his eyes, and the pain in his chest receded, leaving behind an ache he knew would go away in time. "And now I'm going to say something I never thought I'd ever say… because God knows, they piss me off, but maybe you should give the others a chance. You've been kind of an asshole to most everyone else in the family for years, and it's like a damned gladiator's arena at that dinner table you've got going on Sundays. They're at each other's throats. Heck, they're at my throat, and I don't want anything from you or them. Maybe Harold would still be alive if he hadn't felt like he needed to pull one over on me."

"Harold dying had nothing to do with you, kiddo," Archie argued. "Someone killed him, and then someone else broke in for God-knows-what when you went in. I'm just thankful you didn't end up like that detective, and you could have. Bastard hit you on the way out, or did you forget that?"

"I didn't forget that. I was going to talk to Dante when he got home, but we got sidetracked. Then… well, shit hit the fan," Rook murmured, squeezing his grandfather's hand. "After Vicks left and I got to talking to Harsgard, I looked at one of the shop's old silver-backed mirrors, and the shadows kind of cut across my face. Then it hit me. Stupid how things come back to me later, but I'd seen just a little bit of the guy's face. It was quick, and I didn't get a good look because he had a ski mask he had pulled over his head, but swear to God, Archie, it looked like his eyes were two different colors. Like he was one of us. Like he was a *Martin*."

Twelve

"NOW HE remembers this?" O'Byrne paced off the length of her sedan, turning around to face Dante and Hank when she reached its trunk. As early as it was, the park had foot traffic. A pair of young Hispanic women dressed in hotel uniforms gave her a filthy look when she crossed the sidewalk in front of them, but the badge at her hip and the glare they got back probably kept them moving. "I've got Vicks's file burning a hole on my desk and West LA screaming for your boyfriend's head, and *now* he remembers something from the time he broke into the victim's house?"

It was early enough on a muggy Los Angeles morning for a trio of cops to get a cup of hot coffee and some freshly baked *conchas* from a food cart set up on the edge of MacArthur Park. The park was a vibrant, busy place before the sun hit, a far cry from the cesspool of violence it'd been a few decades ago, but there were still tense moments to be found. The park had a history with cops and not all of it good. Memories were long in Los Angeles, especially in the surrounding Latino and Korean neighborhoods. Sitting on the edge of a mixed plate of cultures and diverse incomes, the park anchored the district, providing a place for concerts and fairs as well as attracting more than its share of cops from the nearby beats.

Dante *liked* MacArthur Park, despite Manny's incessant need to break out into song every time they passed by the stretch of green with its massive fountain and lake. It was a good place to spend an evening listening to music, and he'd been meaning to drag Rook to one of the afternoon events but hadn't gotten around to it, if only for its food trucks rooted to prime sidewalk spots and battling for customers on a Saturday afternoon.

As for the concha seller's coffee, it was magnificent, and Dante gulped at his cup. It was black, sweet, and strong enough to burn Dante's nerves, but he welcomed its stinging hit, especially since he'd rather have been curled up around the warm, naked Rook he'd reluctantly left in a tousled bed to meet up with O'Byrne and Camden after only a few hours of sleep.

By the time they'd gotten to Archie's house, Rook was nearly insensible, and he'd been too dead on his feet to do more than strip off all of his clothes and fall into bed. He'd woken up to Manny and Archie in the kitchen attempting to master the espresso machine before Rosa showed up and a weary Rook lying on his back, staring up at their room's gaudy painted ceiling, then confessing he'd recalled something about the morning he'd found Harold lying dead on the floor.

"Montoya, I'm talking to you." O'Byrne now stood only a few inches away, passing over a handful of bills for a cup of coffee and a plastic sleeve of *arroz con coco*. "Did you tell Stevens to stay put where he is for a couple of days? I'd like to be able to get my hands on him after I see what the auction house has to say."

"It's cute you think Stevens is going to do anything someone tells him to do, O'Byrne." Camden sipped at his coffee, his eyes on the early-morning joggers and dog walkers streaming past them. He took a few steps to put their food on a bench, then took O'Byrne's cup to set down next to the paper bags so she could eat. "Dante might have a bit of sway, but Stevens is the kind of guy who'd pitch himself off a building just because someone tells him not to jump."

"He's not that bad." Dante's protests were met with snorts and eye rolls. "Look, Book said to keep you informed on what we find since we'll probably all be working parallel to you. West LA is good with Hank and I chasing down our own leads, but their captain wants to know what we find, and Book agrees to yank us if we get in the way."

"We're doing this on our own time," Camden grumbled at him. "And they get to tell us when to pull back?"

"If we want to keep our badges, then yes," he shot back at Hank, who grimaced ruefully. "Besides, Book said he's putting us back on the clock. If we're going to chase down a murderer with West LA, then he wants everything official."

"Makes sense. No minimal conflict of interest since, really, Stevens is pretty much cleared, even if the wife's still sketchy. I've got one of theirs coming over later to partner with me on Vicks. We're all crossing a lot of lines in this shit storm, but whatever's getting the job done," O'Byrne replied. "I think we'll all feel better if we can find out where Vicks's body is. Man's probably got family, and his house wants to do right by him."

"Good they're letting you keep the case." Extracting a concha from one of the bags, Hank asked, "Do you know what you're going to do first on Vicks?"

"I've got to do an in-person interview with the head of that auction house and his staff. Then I want to hear what Stevens thinks about what I find out. The big question is, was Vicks a message for Rook, and what were they saying? I'm not sure I buy this whole did-this-for-you thing, but as warnings go, it could have been stronger. Sure, your boyfriend's cute, but if someone's obsessing on him, I think he'd know. He's sharp." O'Byrne ripped the sealed plastic top of her container open, then dug into the cold sweet rice with a plastic spoon. "Did you talk to Book this morning or before you went to bed?"

"This morning. He was the second phone call I got. First was you." Dante held a napkin out to Hank as his partner bit into a concha, sending a spray of pink-tinted sugar crumble everywhere. "The West LA captain is a good friend of his. They're kind of in shock over there right now and said they're grateful for any bit of help they can get. Since Sadonna's still on the hook, I've been asked to keep tabs on her. She's not talking and apparently filed a relocation notice with the state and the LAPD for her mother-in-law's. I didn't think they'll let her go, but she's bailed for non-Martin pastures. Odd place to go since everyone, including Sadonna, says Margaret Martin isn't too fond of our widow."

"She doesn't want to stay at Archie's?" Hank's eyebrows lifted in surprise. "It's a damned *castle*. With hot and cold running coffee. With beer. And all-you-can-eat bacon."

"Archie's hard to live with, even when he's on his best behavior. He and Rook went at one another last night in the loft, and I thought it was going to go very bad very quickly, but they worked it out." Another sip of coffee and Dante felt the knot in his chest unravel a little bit. "Sadonna stepped wrong. She might not have meant to, but she did. Rook's one of his favorites, so him getting caught up in this goes ugly in the old man's book. I don't know if Archie actually likes her, and I think deep down inside, he believes she had something to do with Harold's death."

"What do you think?" O'Byrne prodded. "So far, Stevens is clean, and the only one West LA has to hang the murder on is the wife, but that's shaky. Somebody got to a cop. *That's* the person I want to get my hands on. I think he did Vicks to take the heat off of Sadonna and push it onto Stevens, but that's not how it reads to anyone in blue. If anything, the timeline clears Stevens, and I can't find anyone who'd do a cop for him. Not even Montoya."

"Thanks." Dante sent her a flat smile, and she grinned around a mouthful of rice. "Glad I'm not a suspect."

"Hey, consider *any* angle," she responded with a chuckle, then swallowed. "I eliminated you because of timing too, but there was a long second when you were right at the top of my list. I see how you look at Stevens. If you'd been there when Vicks bum-rushed him, we'd be having a conversation down at Central."

"She's not wrong, Montoya. You get kind of gooey and sick when Stevens is around. Now what I think we need to find out is who was in that room with Harold's body when Rook found him," Hank cut in. "And take a good hard look at which Martin has odd eyes. From what we know about Harold, he was pretty offensive. Someone else in the family could have wanted him dead."

"Not a lot of the Martins have complete heterochromia, but it definitely runs strong in the family. Rook and Archie both have distinctive shifts, but some of the others have partial or central. I haven't paid much attention to them because, well, they try to make Rook feel shitty," he confessed. "One of the boys has it, full shift, but he's about ten, so I think we can rule him out. But I wouldn't put it past the little brat. He's a piece of work."

"So asshole runs in the family too?" Hank teased.

"Learned trait, not inherited. A couple of them are okay, but I couldn't even tell you their names." Dante shook his head. "I don't even know how many kids Archie has. It was a hell of a time to figure out Alex's mom is Archie's kid and her husband's a second cousin so they're *both* Martins. Or at least that's what Rook told me."

"And you believed him because he's *so* trustworthy." O'Byrne snorted. "Could have been playing you to yank your chain."

"O'Byrne, let's get something straight... I trust Rook. Hell, with my life if I had to." He eyed Hank, daring his partner to make a joke, but Camden turned his head, suddenly discovering something interesting about the lake's spouting water feature. "He didn't like Vicks. No one did, but Rook didn't want him dead. Or Harold. He remembered something and told me, knowing we'd work with it. The heterochromia is a maybe. It could have been a trick of the light, but it's definitely something to watch for. Rook said he couldn't make out the exact colors, just that one was much brighter than the other. He'd thought blue or gray, but it was too fast. All he got was an impression."

"Might be something we'd chase after because we've got nothing," O'Byrne agreed. "I don't want to go looking for zebras just because we hear hoofbeats. I'd like you there when I question Rook. He'll be more likely to talk if you're around. How long is it going to take you to get to the housekeeper's place?"

"Not long. Her name's Jennifer Martinez, and she lives out in Pasadena, but she's house-sitting her sister's place over on South Westview and Seventh. I called her about five times last night and got nothing, so I thought she was blowing us off, but I got a text at about five while I was taking the dog out for its morning poop tour. She asked for a meet at the sister's place. Set the time and gave me the address. I texted back an affirmative, and that's the only reason I'm up this early." Hank balled up his napkin and tossed it toward the trash can. It hit the rim, sliding in easily. "Still got it. Anyway, she'd agreed to talk at nine, so we've got to get going soon. People get grumpy when the cops leave them waiting."

"We can probably be at Archie's place in a couple of hours. Maybe tag me before you head over and see if we're close?" Dante suggested, tucking his own trash into the bin. "Lot's changed since last night. Might shift again before noon. If you don't need us, let me know. Martinez might lead us to something else."

"Yeah, I'll tap you either way. I need to find out where he was killed. Maybe someone saw something. The killer knows Stevens does business with the auction house and about Vicks allegedly tossing those Molotovs into the shop, so it's got to be someone close to him. It's the *why* we don't have." O'Byrne squinted at the sun pushing its way through the trees. Pulling her sunglasses out of her jacket, she was careful not to flash her gun, angling herself in toward Hank. "West LA is working on reconstructing where Vicks went after he left Bergan's, but I don't want to wait on that. He called going in to interview someone but didn't mention it was Stevens he was shaking down. What he did after he left, I don't know, but I'm going to find out."

"You know, we could have done this all on the phone," Hank grumbled at them. "Yeah, I know… best *conchas* in Los Angeles and it's close to the housekeeper, but I could have gotten another half-hour of sleep in."

"It's good to have a huddle, Camden. Builds teamwork and all of that." O'Byrne slid her sunglasses on, Hank's reflection shimmying over her mirrored lenses. "Now let's go see if we can catch a bad guy today and not die trying."

"CAN'T BELIEVE you made me walk over here," Hank groused, lumbering beside him. "It's like… what? Two blocks? That's a marathon for a Californian. You wouldn't understand, coming from Texas."

"We don't walk there either. Not in Laredo," he replied, reading the street numbers on the buildings. "Well, not in the summertime *or* the spring sometimes. Good way to get heatstroke."

"You miss it?" Camden stopped walking, and Dante pulled up short, turning around to look questioningly at his partner. "I wonder sometimes if you miss it. I mean, I know you've got Manny, and well, Stevens, but you're the kind of guy who likes family. You let my kids climb all over you and call you uncle. You said you've got a lot of family back home, and I wonder if you miss them."

"Yeah, I do." He never gave a lot of time to thinking about his parents. He deeply missed his mother, and it was hard sometimes to see her in Manny's expressions and in his laughter. His father—*that* was complicated—and he knew he didn't have it in him to talk about it while standing in the middle of a Los Angeles sidewalk, but he gave Camden a smile, knowing his partner—his best friend—meant well. "I miss them, but there's no going back there. Not with how they feel. So yeah, I've got Manny and Rook, but I've also got you. And the wife and kids."

"And the damned dog. Don't forget the dog," Camden said, slapping him on the back. "If I could pull it off, I'd pawn that thing off on you so fast your head would spin."

"You love that dog. Besides, I don't know if Rook even likes dogs."

"He seems more like a cat person to me." Hank stopped in front of a red stucco two-story building, thick white security panels covering its windows. Two of the apartments had flower boxes, one with real blooms while the other sported a clutch of faded plastic pinwheels. An enormous calico stared back at them from its perch behind the whirling toys, its tail lazily twitching against a sheer curtain. "Looks like this is it. Apartment 104. Told me it's on the ground floor. No need to buzz her because the intercom's broken, but so's the front security door, so we should just go in."

"I don't know about you, but I like people knowing the cops are about to knock on their door, especially since most of these buildings have tight hallways." Dante looked around, trying to get a feel for the area. He'd been around these streets before, usually quick stops to verify accounts or to pull in an arrest. People in the area were more prone to look the other way than call a cop. "Want to ring her up again before we go in, or do you think we should surprise her?"

"Think there's going to be trouble? She's the one who wanted to do it here 'cause she'll feel more comfortable. She's expecting us." Camden's easygoing mask slid from his face, and he scanned the street, openly gauging the situation. "I say we just go in. What's your gut tell you?"

The street was relatively quiet, but there were signs of life. A bit of music flowed out from a nearby open window, brassy and sharp with spatters of LA Mexican crooning over it. Not more than a few feet away, a pair of men huddled over the open hood of a Honda, their faces screwed up in serious contemplation while a third banged at something with a wrench. It was a normal on-the-edge-of-poor neighborhood, a little too run down to spruce up and packed with people living too tightly against each other but nothing either one of them hadn't walked through before.

But there was something lingering on Dante's mind, an elusive, skittering thought he couldn't quite nail down.

"I'm probably overthinking it since I got no sleep last night," he confessed to his partner. "Book wanted me to talk to one of the outreach guys about Vicks, but I put it aside. I don't have time to deal with it. Maybe later, but—"

"You saw a cop's head roll out of a box, Montoya. In your bedroom. After you've just... well, you know what you did," Hank reminded him. "That's going to eat at a guy, especially since he was a cop and we wear a badge. Listen to Book. Find some time, because I don't care what O'Byrne says, that was a message to someone. Maybe it was Rook. Hell, maybe it was for you, or it could be for the aliens who abducted the sick fuck when he was fourteen and wanking off in a field of cows somewhere. For good or for bad, you don't do that to a man without something wrong going on inside of your head, and the asshole who did it is just trying to spread his sickness to you."

"Cows?" Dante snorted. "And the thing with Vicks, I can't let it crowd me in. I can't second-guess everything."

"Look, I saw the cow and went for it," Hank said, shrugging. "If your gut is telling you this is hinky, then we go in like it's hinky. Wouldn't be the first time your gut's saved our asses. Question is, do you still want lead?"

"Doesn't matter. Let's see who she responds better to. We need to get the names of who was at that party Harold threw—if she knows—and who he hung out with. He and Sadonna didn't mingle a lot outside of casual social stuff, typical Hollywood crowd, and Archie said he kept apart from anyone at the office. If she coughs up the name of this boyfriend, even better."

"A party says social, but no one in the family knows who his friends are? That's a sad kind of life. Morgue came back with him killed that night or early the next morning, right?"

"Yeah. So either he knew the killer—still holding out for that boyfriend—or the guy slipped in and hung around until everyone left, then came out when he was sure it was clear." Dante nodded at Hank's thoughtful murmur. "Harold was knifed. *A lot*. That says angry to me. Then someone came in to hit him on the head with that statue. The timelines are just weird. Maybe Martinez might not know who was at the party, but she might know who he felt comfortable enough with to let stay."

"It's a stretch, but we don't have a lot of choices." Camden sighed. "Let's go in and see what she's got to tell us."

Los Angeles's mugginess followed them into the building, and the tight shotgun foyer beyond the unlatched metal security door was dark and heavy with stale air. The end of the long corridor ended in a rectangle of bright light, a second security door probably leading to parking in the alley.

A few yards in, the hall split off into a cross leading to apartments on either side of the building, and a narrow, steep stairwell took up a good section of the hall's width, leading to the second story and down to a basement landing doubling as a laundry room. Dante peered over the railing, spotting mounds of wet clothing piled high in a couple of laundry baskets set near a churning dryer. One of the washing machines chunked through a cycle, slightly off-balance to Dante's ears. He couldn't help but grin, a familiar perfume carried through the corridor in a wave of heat from the tumbling machines. The sweet, soapy odor grew overpowering, and Dante took a step back, scraping at his tongue with his teeth to get the sting of cleanser out of his mouth.

"Fabuloso," he murmured to Hank. "But man, they used a lot of it. I can taste it in my throat."

"What?" Hank twisted his shoulders around, glancing back at Dante. "Are you looking at my ass?"

"No, stupid, that smell. It's a cleaner. My mom used to wash my baseball uniforms with a little bit of it in the water. God, that takes me back." He fell into step behind his partner, heading toward the back of the building. "Funny how your brain catches on certain things. My mom only likes the orange or pink one, but my aunt always bought the light green, like five or six at a time because they were on sale, then dropped them off at our house, so she was stuck with using it."

"Why didn't she just give them away or even—" Hank paused dramatically. "—toss them out?"

"Oh, you obviously didn't grow up with a mother from my neighborhood. I'd pay good money to see my mom's face if I came up with that as a solution." His thoughts turned somber, caught in a bit of melancholy from the heat and scents. "Hope she's doing okay."

"That way. Probably the end unit. Jesus, that stuff's powerful. Did they use the whole bottle?" Hank peered down the left corridor, then nodded toward the right. "Your mom. They'd call, right? If she wasn't?"

"Maybe my aunt, but I think someone would. At least they'd call Manny, since he's her brother. Or so I hope." Dante went down the short, lightless hall first, moving cautiously across its stained short-pile carpet. "You said one-oh-four?"

"Yeah. Shit, door's cracked open." Hank fit himself in behind Dante, his jacket pulled back so he could reach his weapon.

"Could be the heat. No circulation, and those AC units on the outside apartments looked ancient," Dante cautioned. "Just… let's keep our heads on this."

The corridor was hot and ripe, a floral overlay barely masking the rancid, greasy stink coming from the cracked-open door. Dante knew that stench and shuddered, breathing through his mouth as he pulled his weapon from his holster. Behind him, Hank'd gone silent, tucking himself against the wall. His partner's gun cast a shadow on the end of the hallway, a dark gray puppet poised for a curtain rise neither one of them wanted to happen.

A sweltering wave broke free when Dante pushed the door open, pouring into the hall and choking them with a foul tide of rot and death. Forcing himself to go inside, Dante kept his weapon up as he shouldered the door open, then gagged on the redolent air hitting his face.

"Go to your left." Hank choked, coughing when he came around Dante's open side. "I'll take the right."

The one-room apartment was barely large enough to turn around in, and someone had cranked the heater on despite the rising temperature outside. Desert-hot, the vents were angled open, cooking the walls and turning the studio into an oven. Three full strides would have taken Dante from the front door to the kitchenette on the far wall, and another five to the full-sized mattress and box spring lying under the studio's single window, its sheets rumpled and pillows tossed onto the carpeted floor. A beat-up sofa sat opposite the kitchen, a large badly done oil painting of flowers and butterflies hanging above its worn, lumpy back. A few books kept knickknacks company on a pair of leaning shelves on either side of the couch, and from the top of one, a one-eyed carnival-style purple dog forlornly stared out into the room, its white-striped face thick with spiderwebs and dust.

There'd been a glass coffee table in the middle of the room, but its frame lay in pieces around a facedown, headless man, his legs spread apart and partially sprinkled with the pebbled remains of the table's top. Three holes punctured his back, promising large exit wounds out through his chest cavity, judging by the damage to his clothes and the sinkholes in his flesh.

A few feet away, a young Hispanic woman in a yellow tank top and jeans lay slumped in between the bed and the sofa, her dark skin ashen and purple. Flies picked at her once-pretty face, black specks crawling over her swollen cheeks, and her bare shoulders were beginning to show sign of bloat, a rip forming along the ridge of her collarbone.

An LAPD detective's badge rested inches from the man's flung-out hand, his other hand tucked under his body. Dante couldn't see a gun, but he did spot the hacksaw balanced against the end of the mattress, its serrated edge thick with chunks of dried meat and skin.

"Shit, Montoya, that's Vicks," Hank gasped, swallowing against the gagging noise he made. "Okay, let's step out and call it in."

"Yeah, and I think that's Martinez. Or it should be." Dante swept the room one last time, covering for Hank as he fled the apartment. He was close on his partner's heels, stepping quickly to get out into the hall and catch his breath. Panting, he was grateful for the cloying flowery taint in the air, anything to mask the putrid reek of decaying human flesh from his lungs. "But *fuck*, if it is, then who the hell did you talk to this morning?"

Thirteen

THE WORN light-gray T-shirt Rook pulled over his head was too large, and if the size wasn't a clue the garment wasn't his, the roughed-up LAPD silkscreened across its chest was a dead giveaway. There were a few small holes on its front and an indeterminate stain along the bottom left hem, and it'd been cold, left folded in the bathroom connected to their room, probably set aside for Dante to wear to bed again later that night.

Rook's body heat quickly warmed it, and the fabric soon smelled deliciously of Dante, a whiff of his lemongrass cologne and the crisp brightness of his natural scent barely strong enough to tease Rook's nose. It felt stupid and juvenile to wear his boyfriend's T-shirt, a high school cliché for a man who'd not attended more than five days of school in a row during the sparse times he'd even been enrolled, but the urge to have something of Dante on him was too powerful to ignore when he'd seen the neatly folded shirt sitting on the bathroom counter.

He stood in front of the mirror with his mouth smarting of spearmint toothpaste, breathing in deeply and being caressed by the soft fabric, silently marveling at how the shirt clinging to his shoulders and ribs felt like one of Dante's gentle hugs.

A hug he was very grateful for when he came downstairs to find his aunt Margaret standing in the main study, examining an oil painting hanging over the room's massive fireplace, her elegantly boned face waxen and run tight with grief. Standing in a stream of milky morning sun, she looked more marble than flesh, a living, breathing Corradini reflecting on a pastoral, bucolic scene of long spotted hounds frolicking in the British countryside. Her pale blue eyes were unfocused when she turned at Rook's entrance, but they sharpened quickly, hot and furious behind a flutter of her mascara-darkened lashes.

Margaret never cared for him. She'd made that clear a heartbeat after meeting him at the first family dinner he'd stupidly agreed to attend. Archie'd introduced him, then abandoned the fray. It'd been a brittle, formal dance of icy barbs and cold bloodletting, an emotional fencing match where he'd taken a baseball bat where rapiers were the chosen weapons.

His relationship with the rest of the family had never recovered, and up until the moment he saw Harold's mother, Rook hadn't cared. Now there was no chance in hell she'd take any scrap of comfort from him, even when she needed it the most.

"Oh, I thought you were Archibald." She clipped her words, severing their ends with a snap, as sharp and clean a cut as faceting a diamond. "So you're living here now? Couldn't wait until Harold was cold in the ground before setting up house?"

There was not a scrap of warmth in her, and despite the mourning she wore on her face, her trim, slender body was dressed for battle in a cadet-blue sweater set and black pants, her long, skinny feet tucked into a pair of kitten heels. Any other time, he'd have chuckled at the double string of pearls draped around her long neck, but today she'd worn them as a suit of armor, the familiar and hard strapped to her body to protect her from further blows.

Death hung on her, its skeletal arms wrapped casually over her shoulders, and it was all she could do to bear its weight.

"Cops thought it was safer after… some stuff happened down there," he replied softly. "It's just temporary."

"Temporary. The last thing you are is *temporary*. You are like a tick no one can shake off." She sniffed at him, her tone brittle and glittering. "So what's on today's agenda for you? Headed to play down at the little store of yours? Not a care in the world when the rest of us are dancing around Archie's feet hoping for a scrap or two? Maybe you should take over for Harold down at the office. Since you're shoving your way into everything. He's just going to be swept under the rug, so you can walk all over his memory. Just like you walked all over his body that day."

"I'm not.… Look, I didn't kill Harold. I didn't want him dead. No one did," Rook said as gently as he could. "I just wanted—I wasn't there to hurt him."

"It doesn't matter what you wanted because it's not going to bring him back. He's dead. My son is… *dead.*" Her teeth were bared and her coral-lipsticked mouth curled up and stiff with disgust. "He spent years hiding behind that woman's skirts, pretending to be normal so his grandfather wouldn't toss him out. Then you stroll in and spit in his face. What makes you so special that Archie forgives you for being a fa—"

"Watch yourself, Margaret," Archie rumbled, his cane thumping on the floor as he walked into the room. The Pomeranian was on his heels, an orange poof of fur who'd inexplicably thought Archie hung the moon and the stars. "Losing Harold was a tragedy, but there's no reason to take it out on Rook. Boy didn't do anything wrong."

"He did *everything* wrong," she spat back, hands clenched into fists at her sides. "Harold tried to be who you wanted him to be, but it was never good enough. He was never *special* enough for you, but *this* one is? You're a hypocrite, Archie, and once you get Beatrice's son dancing to your tune, you're going to cut him loose just like you did Harold. My boy worked himself down to the bone for the company, for you, and the least you can do… never mind. I just came by to tell you they released Harold's body, so we'll be able to plan his funeral. I'm hoping you find some time in your busy schedule to attend. At least pretend he mattered to you. For the family's sake."

She was heading to the door before Rook could reply. He had the words. Soft, mournful, and consoling, but Margaret wasn't going to listen. He stepped in, hoping to… he had no idea what he was hoping for. Maybe to offer her something—anything—to make her feel better, but she shoved at his shoulder, stiff-arming him to get past.

"They're going to find who did this to him, to your boy. I promise you, Margaret, we'll find out who killed him," Archie called out to her, and she stopped at the door, her shoulders shaking beneath her sweater.

"*You* killed him, Archie. You killed him a long time ago. The first time you told him no grandson of yours was going to be gay, you stabbed him right in the heart." Margaret turned, her icy glare glittering with unshed tears. "And you continued to stab him every day after that. I don't care who killed his body, not when I know who killed his spirit. And Rook, enjoy this while you can, because he's going to turn on you. Just like he turns on everyone else. The only reason he's even halfway decent to you is because he feels guilty about your mother. I'll let you know when the funeral is, Archie. All I ask is that you show up. And *without* your pet poof."

Her quick footsteps echoed with a fading machine gun report when Margaret left the room. The dog tap-danced around Archie's feet, then dashed back out down the hall, chasing after Margaret. Rosa asked after her, an indistinct query returned with a sharp slap of a reply, but Rook couldn't hear what either woman said. Archie reached for him, clamping his cold fingers over Rook's upper arm and squeezing hard enough to make Rook wince.

"She's just angry, old man. And hurt." Patting his grandfather's hand, Rook nodded toward one of the room's broad chairs. "How about if you sit down, and I'll get Rosa to bring you some coffee?"

"No, Margaret's right. *You're* right. I treated Harold like shit. All of them like shit. I still do. Even Alex...." Archie snorted, shaking his head. "And that's right up there with kicking a kitten. I've got to do better by them. I just don't... know how." His grandfather eyed him, assessing Rook thoughtfully. "I need you to keep pushing these people... the cops... everyone in this. Your cousin should have been happy, and he felt like... I had a hand in keeping him from that. Leave the murderer to the cops, but... maybe you find out what you can about the boyfriend. Maybe I can at least do right by him."

"And if he's the murderer?"

"Then don't get killed." Archie sniffed. "Honestly, boy. It's like I've got to tell you everything."

"You're asking me to stick my nose in where Dante told me to stay the fuck out. As much as I love you, old man, I piss him off and my already messed-up life's going to go to shit." Rook held his hand up to stop Archie from chiming in. "I'm not going to promise it'll come to anything, but I'll ask around. I'll see if Davis Natterly knows anything about what was going on over there. He was friends with Harold. If I don't get somewhere, maybe Dante will have more luck when he talks to Sadonna again."

"Don't count on it," his grandfather rumbled. "That girl's sneaky. For all we know she's lying about Harold having a boyfriend to throw us off because she's the one who killed him. Just be careful. I've already lost one grandson. I don't want to lose another."

ROOK FELL in love the very first time he saw Los Angeles. It'd been after a long, hot few days, and through the dirty window of a Greyhound bus, his snotty nose pressed flat onto the glass so he could make mist ghosts with his exhaled breaths. He'd been young, maybe more than six but less than nine, a stretch of years where life was a blur of bruising knuckles, teary apologies, candy bribes followed by neglect. His mother'd gotten it into her head to break away from the carnival circuit and begin to systematically destroy any relationship she had in the city by begging to stay, then stealing either food, money, or husbands before dragging Rook off to her next victim.

Something happened, a huge yelling and screaming something, then a big boom, followed by an eerie silence Rook now knew all too well. Then Beanie rolled as much of their lives that would fit into a large duffel bag, and they'd stolen away into the night, somehow ending up on a bus from Nowhere Fucksville to Los Angeles. He didn't remember where they'd been running from—or even who—but he'd *known* he'd come home the moment he'd seen the city's skyscrapers cradled against the far-off blue mountains with the morning sun painting the sky a pale pink cotton floss.

He was tired of running, and as the city slipped around him, Rook realized for the first time in his life, he'd found *home*.

There was something inelegantly beautiful about Los Angeles. Its ugly-pretty streets and jumble of mean and sweet spoke to a thread in Rook's soul he couldn't capture no matter how hard he tried to grab it. He'd fallen in love. *Hard*, and the City of Angels became a sparkling dream, as elusive as a dust mote and as breathtaking as any starry sky he'd ever seen. Pulling into the Greyhound station, Rook drank the city in and swore to himself, one day he'd live there. They'd left LA much like they left everywhere else, too quickly for Rook to feel comfortable and leaving behind tears, screaming, and heartache.

They'd returned to the carnivals and came back to LA while on the circuit, but he'd not stayed. It was too soon, he'd been too broke, all of the same lies he'd heard from Beanie until one day he'd said enough to his old life and left it behind to chase a dream he'd had behind a wall of misted ghosts and through one fist-blackened eye.

"Different now," he reminded himself. There were other memories, warm enough to tighten his belly as he got caught at the light a few yards away from Potter's Field. His day was full of echoing images, welcome thoughts of a wicked smile, silken words slick and hot with a whisper of an accent, and strong, capable hands on his body. Shifting in his seat, Rook gave himself a moment, then frowned when a text from Dante lit up his phone. *"Going to be home late. Don't wait up. Eat something.* Nice, Montoya. You're worse than Manny sometimes. I'll grab something to eat after Davis drops by."

The building looked exactly as he'd left it, its front window still busted out but covered with a snarky wooden sign he loved. Cutting through the side alley, Rook pulled into his covered spot behind Potter's Field when a too familiar lanky Latina detective stepped out of an ugly green sedan parked near the shop's back door.

O'Byrne looked worn out, as if she'd shoved as much of the day as she could get in before her two-in-the-afternoon drop-in on Rook. Her jeans were creased, and a bit of her long black hair had escaped the ponytail she'd secured at the base of her neck. The woman's eyes were hard, nearly as flat as her mouth by the time Rook put the SUV into park and got out. Flashing her a smile did little to lighten her mood, nor did his casual offer to get her a cup of coffee as he strolled toward the store's side entrance.

"Didn't I tell you to stay put at your grandfather's?" she ground out, falling into step behind him. "Good thing I called before I headed up to the hills, or I wouldn't have found out from the housekeeper you'd come here."

"Forget the coffee. You need a drink," Rook muttered, juggling his keys until he found the one he needed. "Did you come bug me for something in particular, or you just couldn't find a dog to kick? And what the hell's wrong with calling me? Not like I don't answer the phone."

"Because sometimes, Stevens, I get better answers out of you when I take you by surprise." She snagged his arm, tugging him away from the door. Her hold was casual but firm, as unexpected as her presence. She caught his glance down and let him go, shoving her hands into her pockets. "Have you heard from Montoya?"

"Just a text telling me he's going to be late and to eat something. Why?" A frisson of worry cut through him, bringing Rook to full alert. He fisted his fingers in the overly large gray shirt he'd stolen from Dante, wondering impossible things in between staggered breaths. "What's—"

"Nothing's wrong. Montoya's fine. *Dante's* fine." Her reassurance was soft under the steel of her voice. "They… found Vicks. Montoya and Camden. I just came from there."

She sketched in as little as possible, but Rook didn't need much. He had enough of an imagination to fill in the blanks, possibly painting the details a bit more lurid than necessary, but there they were, trickling through the lines O'Byrne laid down for him.

"So the housekeeper… they killed her too? Why?" Rook choked on the lump in his throat. "What the fucking hell is going on?"

"I don't know, but I'm going to find out," O'Byrne promised. "So I'm going to ask you, Stevens, can you think of anything about that day that you haven't shared? Anything at all?"

"Seriously, I don't know jack shit. I got into the house, went upstairs, and there was Harold. I didn't even get far into the room when that guy came at me." It'd been a difficult thing to punch through, especially since he'd been flying high on adrenaline not more than a minute before. "He wasn't a good fighter, but it was tight, hard to turn around, and he flailed at me. The ground was wet, I remember that, but that turned out to be dog piss. Sadonna's dog peed on the marble floor, and it was slippery. I thought maybe it was… blood, but Harold was dead way before I came into that room."

"Did you pick up the dog?"

"No, I didn't see him until later. Shit, if only the dog could talk." He made a face. "It's Archie's now. I thought he belonged to Sadonna, but he was Harold's. My aunt doesn't want him. She doesn't like dogs, so Archie took him."

"You say you thought Harold was dead already," O'Byrne pressed on. "Why?"

"He wasn't breathing. I remember seeing the bird. The falcon. It was on Harold's stomach. Then it fell over, slid off really. I was looking right at him, and he was just *still*." He'd gone over everything he could, trying to dissect the flashes of memory floating through the shock of seeing his cousin spread out over the floor. "I got the impression the guy knew where he was. I mean, I knew the layout pretty much, but after he hit me and I went down, there wasn't any hesitation. He was gone before the dog… wait, the dog didn't bark. It knew me. I'd played with it at Archie's more than a few times, but it didn't bark when I came up the stairs."

"So it definitely knew the person in the ski mask," O'Byrne mused. "I'm not sure if your attacker killed Harold, but I'm going to guess he knows more than we do. He was there for something. Do you think he was after the falcon too?"

"Can't see anyone but a hard-core movie buff wanting it. It's not like… I mean it's cool, but the average guy off the street would probably want cash or jewelry out of the safe. If it was from the Bogey film, you'd be looking at a couple of million, but it's a replica from a parody. It's worth a bit, but not millions, and besides, the guy left it behind."

"True. And Ms. Swann said nothing was missing from the safe." She eyed him. "Did you get as far as the safe?"

"I wasn't going for the safe," he replied. There'd been a tickle of wonder at breaking through the mini-vault Harold had on the property, but he'd been good, or as good as he was going to get, leaving it untouched. "I was there for the bird, O'Byrne. Nothing else."

"Were you tempted?" The detective pushed, a gleam in her hooded eyes. "One last hurrah?"

"I had my last hurrah years ago. And no, no temptation. Dante's too important to me. I'm not going to fuck that up just because my ego's in a twist," Rook explained. "I like him coming home to me. There's something about—"

The sound of the bullet hitting O'Byrne's shoulder was a thick, sickening thud, and the wound's burst of blood surprised him, a violent rosette of sound and metallic red suddenly appearing above her breast. Another followed, plowing through her arm as the first spun her around, splattering Rook's face with her hot blood. The parking lot asphalt popped and sizzled, shots hitting the tarry surface, and Rook nearly turned around, foolishly wondering where the assault was coming from in the split-second before his brain registered O'Byrne was falling.

She was fumbling for her gun, fingers arched and twitching when Rook grabbed at her waist, her weight nearly taking him down to his knees when she tipped over. The shots kept coming, puncturing the sedan's back end, and a tire took a hit, blowing out in a rushing boom loud enough to rattle Rook's eardrums. His chest was wet, his shirt wicking away O'Byrne's blood, and he dragged at her, cursing when she pushed at him.

Everything smelled and tasted of blood and fear. Her blood. His terror. They were exposed, out in the open, and he couldn't tell where the shots were coming from. O'Byrne fought him every step of the way, her boots digging into the parking lot's squiggly black patchwork.

"Fucking stop." He didn't know who he was pleading with, the wild-eyed detective or the shooter, but neither one appeared to be listening.

"I'm fine." She was slurring, her eyes unfocused and drifting. "Get inside. Call 911."

A brick chip flew past his nose, scoring his cheek, and Rook tugged O'Byrne along, keeping his head down until he could get closer to the receiving door. A stab at the lock's three-digit combination and the door rolled up slowly, but he was under the metal slats as soon as he could. On her back, propped up against the building, O'Byrne had her weapon out, one hand limp at her side, but she held the gun steady, aiming it out of the cavernous opening.

"Keep going, Stevens. I'll cover you," she croaked, struggling to get to her feet, but Rook grabbed at her again, holding her in close. Her eyes rolled back, and she spat while he half dragged her behind a column. Another shot pinged at the entrance, but either the angle was wrong or the shooter was losing his nerve because it went wide, missing O'Byrne's foot by a good seven feet. "*Get down!*"

Pressing down on O'Byrne's shoulder, Rook cradled the woman as best he could, trying to keep their arms from tangling as she lifted her weapon up again. Flat on his ass and trapped by the detective's weight, he screamed in frustration when he couldn't reach the phone he'd slid into his back pocket. Twisting to get it, he winced when she groaned. Then the detective went limp, her arm dropping to the ground.

An engine roar broke through the Hollywood afternoon, and something heavy hit the sedan, sending it flying across the receiving bay opening. Metal and glass crunched into the building's fittings, jammed in tight, and Rook caught a glimpse of a gray quarter panel before the vehicle reversed out of sight and was gone.

Heart pounding, he finally got his phone loose, his fingers shaking when he tried to dial in to emergency services. O'Byrne's labored breathed stuttered, then steadied out when Rook pressed into the heavier wound again. A distant-sounding voice echoed in his ear, asking him for his emergency, and he couldn't find the words in his brain, hung up on the blood and pain reverberating through him.

"Rook!" Manny's voice seemed even farther away and for some reason, gray. Manny was never gray, but there he was, crouched over Rook and going grayer with every passing second. "Oh God, Rook. Let me—"

The pain hit him all at once, stealing his breath and filling his lungs with glass, and he tried to shift O'Byrne off of him, but his arms weren't responding, flopping about and too weak to get her clear. His shirt—Dante's shirt—was soaked through, sticking to his chest and ribs, and his side ached where the fabric clung, twisting around his hip and lower back. His stomach was wet, too wet to be just O'Byrne's blood, and when he tried to move, a shock wave of agony echoed along his spine and down his legs.

"Don't move, baby," Manny pleaded, the edges of his round, handsome face blurring where the light leaked in around him. "Just… stay with me, okay? *Please*. You've been shot, baby. Oh God, you've been shot."

Fourteen

"YOU'RE GOING to be the death of me, *cuervo*," Dante whispered, kissing Rook on the forehead. "I always figured it'd be Manny, but you... you're a solid contender."

"Hey, I didn't ask to be shot." It was a weak protest. He'd pretty much been asking for a bullet since the moment he'd laid hands on O'Byrne to pull her to safety, but Rook wasn't going to bring that point up. Not when he was propped up in Archie's study, surrounded by cops, and floating on a painkiller strong enough to make his face numb. "It's just a graze. Sure, kind of hurts, but not like it took a lot of meat with it. Docs were fine with letting me go. You guys should be thankful I was getting out of the way. If I hadn't moved, I'd have a bed down the hall from O'Byrne."

"Or Vicks," Dante's lanky partner rumbled at him, moving through the space, surprisingly nimble despite his size. "Sit down, Montoya. You're hovering."

"Rook was *shot*," Dante reminded Camden, but he settled onto the ottoman next to the club chair Rook collapsed into. "He should be in bed. Doc said rest and more rest. Not sitting around waiting for an interrogation."

It was late, nearly a quarter past ten, and as tired as Rook was, it felt damned good to sit in something more comfortable than a plastic hospital chair. It felt even better to have Dante's fingers wrapped around his. He'd caught the stumble of words from his lover. Their relationship was complicated, made more so by the apparent death wish Rook somehow picked up over the past week and a half.

"Here is some coffee and something to eat. If you all are going to be here, at least get something into you." Rosa pushed a tea cart into the room, cups and plates rattling when she hit the edge of one of the carpets. The fall of bells tugged at her attention, and the Latina frowned, shooting Dante a fierce look. "Were you expecting anyone else?"

"Detective taking over for Vicks is coming. Book called from the hospital. Said he'd send her around." Hank's enormous hand swallowed up the mug Rosa handed him, his fingers sliding under the handle. Camden's phone buzzed, and he reached into his jacket. "Hey, don't glare at me. Rook said he was up to it. I can grab the door—"

"We have people for that," Archie declared, hobbling into the room, circling Hank reading his phone screen. "And security. Someone will bring your cop in. Don't you worry about it. Rosa, make mine sweet and tan. I'm going to need the calories if I'm going to survive another night with this boy."

There was a bit of a fuss as his grandfather took up the chair next to him, Dante shuffling to the side to make room for Archie, but Rook caught the look they exchanged, one weighted with worry and a little bit of affection. Manny was somewhere in the house, hopefully asleep if Rook had his wish. The older Latino hung by Rook's side through the ambulance ride and then when the doctors began to stitch him up, only moving when Dante came through the emergency room's doors, Camden shouting for information above the chatter of the personnel telling them they couldn't be there.

"O'Byrne's out of surgery and in Recovery." Camden put his phone away. "Looks like she's good. Captain says her brother's there, scaring the shit out of the nurses. So I guess grumpy runs in the O'Byrne DNA."

"His sister's just been shot. He has a good reason to be grumpy." Dante stood, trailing his fingers along Rook's shoulder. "Rosa, you don't have to wait on us. We can pour our own coffee."

"Speak for your damned self, boy. I pay Rosa a lot of money to know how I like my coffee." Archie's hands shook when he reached for the half-full cup held out to him, and he grumbled when Rosa set it on the table next to him. The dog poked his head out from under Archie's chair, then scrambled out to beg at Rosa. "Damn it, woman. I can drink a full cup—"

"You're tired and should be in bed, old man. Be glad she even gave you some coffee and didn't just knock you on the head so Dante could toss you into your room." Rook sliced into the conversation. "And say thank you once in a while. Won't kill you."

His grandfather's eyes were pulling down at the edges, but it would be a long battle if anyone'd tried to get him to bed. Refusing to budge as long as the cops were in his house, the Martin patriarch was in for the long haul, firmly entrenched in his chair despite Rosa cajoling him to rest.

"I say thank you all the time," Archie grumbled back, but he muttered a bit of Spanish under his breath when Rosa placed a small plate of cookies by his elbow. "She knows I'd be lost without her."

"See? You didn't die," Rook shot back. "I'm only going to stay up long enough to talk to this new guy, and then I'm off to bed."

"No coffee for you," Dante grumbled at him, handing him a cup of something brown and fragrant. "Herbal tea. With sugar. You're on enough stimulants."

"I can't feel my toes," he muttered back, sniffing the brew. It was sweet and fruity, possibly mango or orange, neither of which displeased him. Still, the lure of the bean was strong, and he jabbed Dante's side with his finger. "I *need* the coffee."

"What you need is for that detective to get in here and we can all go to bed," Archie groused. "Rosa! Go see what's taking them so long to get that man in the house."

The sound of heels on marble brought them all up short, and Camden whistled low under his breath when one of the security guards led a sharp-featured blonde woman to the study's doorway. She was all angles and hipbones, wearing red heels, a pair of jeans, and a button-up white shirt topped with a navy blazer nearly the same color as her eyes. A gold badge hung from her belt loop, its metal winking under the light coming from the study's crystal chandeliers, and the glint of a holster flashed them before she tugged her blazer back down, covering her weapon. She crossed the room with a distinct purpose, holding her hand out to Dante.

"Detective Montoya? Detective Anna Cranston, West LA. It's good to meet you." Her fingers were swallowed momentarily in Dante's. She continued about the room, shaking Camden's hand as she took introductions. Cranston's eyes caught everything, skimming over Archie, then settling on Rook's face, flitting back to the old man for a brief second, as if verifying the genetic similarities she found between them. "I've heard good things about you guys. Looking forward to your help on this."

"That coming from you or something West LA told you to say?" Camden took over for Rosa and poured out another cup of coffee. "Milk? Sugar? Since I'm here."

"Black. I grew up on cop house coffee. If it isn't bitter, I wouldn't know how to swallow," she said with a laugh. "Heard about O'Byrne. I was hoping I could work with her too, but it's good to know she's going to be okay. I figured I'd make this as short as possible, and we can hook back up tomorrow once you've all caught some sleep. I appreciate you making the time to meet up. I'm playing catch up here. After what happened this afternoon, I didn't want to wait until morning if I could get the jump on things."

"How long have you been a cop?" Archie tilted his head back, his beak of a nose casting a shadow over his jutting chin. "You don't even look old enough to drink a beer. Don't hush me, Rosa. I'd like to know who's on this case and what they're doing to protect my grandson."

"You're being a pain in the ass, that's what you are," Rosa sniped back, but affection softened her words. "I'm taking Queequeg outside. And I'm telling you, he better learn *where* he can go to the bathroom soon or I'm going to put him in diapers."

"No one's wearing a diaper in this house. He just needs some discipline." Archie scruffed under the dog's chin before Rosa got out of reach. "Now, detective, answer the question."

Rook had to hand it to Cranston, because she was a master at handling crotchety old men like his grandfather. She countered his quizzing rejoinders with an ease he'd have loved to see on a carnie thoroughfare. When Dante pressed the tea into his hands, he'd clung instead to his lover's hand, stroking the back of Dante's fingers while Cranston laid out firm but polite answers to Archie's intrusive questions.

"Archie, I love you, man, but I'm dead on my feet here. Can you leave the cop alone so she can do her thing and I can go to bed? You didn't treat Montoya and Camden this way when they came over." Rook caught Hank's eye roll and Dante's snort. "Jesus, old man. Seriously?"

"I pay taxes, don't you forget." His grandfather took up his coffee mug, steadily bringing it to his lips. Slurping a bit down, he nodded at Cranston. "*You* I like. Those two… well, let's just say it took a while. Then that one brought one of them home, and now I'm stuck with the pair of them. Just catch this bastard so I can get my house back in order."

"I'll do my best," Cranston promised, a slight smile touching her lips. She flipped to a screen on her phone and asked Rook, "Do you have any objections to my recording this interview? I find it helps with my notes later."

"Nah, it's all good. I don't know what else I can tell you I haven't told O'Byrne. Shit, forgot she didn't exactly have time to tell anyone what we talked about." He shrugged and instantly regretted it. His side ached, and from the creeping tendrils of pain stretching over his skin, it felt like the painkillers were wearing off. "I went down to the store to meet up with Davis Natterly, but O'Byrne was there. Next thing I knew, someone was shooting at us."

They went over the incident with Cranston coming at it from several angles, probing gently at everything Rook said until he wasn't sure anymore if he'd been facing left or right when O'Byrne's shoulder was hit. She walked him back, asking his impressions of the day, and then circled back to something he hadn't thought about.

"Did Natterly ever show up?" The question was a soft one, lobbed innocently in the middle of a bunch of queries, but it brought Rook up short. "Did anyone tell you he came by? Did he leave a message telling you he wouldn't make it?"

"Um… I didn't see him, but we were supposed to meet later, so he could have." Rook shook his head. "I was focused on O'Byrne, and then well, the doctors had me on my back at the hospital. I never saw him. The only messages I had were from Dante, and then well, afterwards, they brought me here. A couple of mundane things about an estate sale I wanted to go to but nothing else. Not from Davis. But like I said, he could have shown up and one of the cops told him what happened."

"I have his contact number. I'll follow up with him tomorrow and find out if he came by at all. Does he normally not show up?" Something in her manner tickled Rook's attention, and he sat up straighter, handing his tea over to Dante. "Or is he pretty reliable?"

"Mostly reliable, but sometimes his brother, Jeremy, fucks something up and he's got to take care of things. Usually sends me an I'm sorry text afterwards."

"You think there's an issue there?" Montoya held the cup only long enough to put it aside. "We can have someone do a welfare check on his home."

"Might not be a bad idea," Camden interjected. "Peripherals seem to be this guy's MO. Hell, for all we know Harold was on the fringe of something and was killed just because he was in the way. There's a lot of loose threads and nothing stitching them together."

"So far, Rook seems to be at the epicenter of it all," the female detective conjectured. "Is there anyone you fought with before any of this happened? This seems to have started when you purchased an item from Natterly's and your cousin intercepted it. Was there someone else who wanted the movie prop? Someone who might have been angry about not getting it?"

"That I don't know. But the bird was there when I got into Harold's house. If the person who killed him wanted the thing, he'd have taken it," Rook pointed out. The sight of the Maltese Falcon sitting on his cousin's belly, then hitting the floor haunted him at the oddest moments. "The originals were about fifty pounds, but the replicas from the parody weigh a lot less because they're resin. I mean, the damned thing's still heavy, but it's easily carried. The guy who attacked me… who killed Harold… could have taken it with him."

"That's the curious thing about this, Mr. Stevens," Cranston replied, tapping at her phone to pull up a gallery of pictures. "Forensics found a couple of interesting things while going over the evidence for me today. First, there was a green contact lens in the bloodied debris near your cousin's right hand, so that seems like a very solid explanation for your attacker's oddly colored eyes. But what was more interesting than the contact was the falcon itself."

The picture she pulled up was of the bird, its backside coated in dog fur, blood, and flecks of things Rook didn't want to identify, but what caught his attention was the bright white gash cut into the statue's left wing. Flakes and dust coated the glove of whoever was holding the statue up for its close-up, vividly bright on the black latex.

"That's not resin," Rook mumbled, leaning in to take a closer look. The detailing along the wing was perfect, and the mimicked dents in the bird's body and beak were exactly as if it'd been cast from the battered original, but the damned statue was definitely flaking. "That's plaster of Paris. That bird's a fucking fake. That's not the bird I saw at Natterly's. I know it's not. They'd be different weights. I *held* my bird. It was real."

"Exactly what the forensics crew decided. So now, Mr. Stevens, I'm asking you again for your thoughts on this." Her smile this time was professional, a bit hard but inquisitive, drawing Rook out of his racing thoughts. "Who else wanted this statue? And more importantly, who'd want it bad enough to kill for it?"

"SO THE fake's a fake?" Hank poured himself what seemed like to Dante his fifteenth cup of coffee. "And we don't know where the original fake is or where the guy who sold it to Stevens is. This night just keeps getting better and better."

Getting Rook to bed had been simple enough. His lover was worn down to the bone, and he'd nearly fallen asleep during the quick hot shower he'd managed to talk Dante into letting him take. Keeping his stitches dry was an exercise in flexibility, and despite another round of reluctantly swallowed pills, he'd caught Rook wincing in pain when Dante helped him sponge off, sluicing bits of dried blood and dirt from his back.

The former thief was a fragile mess, and Dante hated leaving him alone, but tucked under the blankets, he'd grumbled about needing some sleep and was snoring before Dante could turn off the bedroom's lights. Walking away was difficult, and he'd stood in the doorway, debating telling the world to go to hell so he could crawl into bed with the man who made his heart stop.

Dante could still taste the fear in his throat, a lingering metallic stain when Manny'd called him to say Rook'd been shot. No amount of swallowing would ever clear it away. He was certain of that, even as he returned to the study to hear Cranston and Camden hammer at the edges of the case in the hopes of breaking something—anything—loose from the murderous knot someone'd tied around Rook.

"I'm interested in hearing what you think, Montoya." The West LA detective had her notes spread over the table, a makeshift murder board of Venn diagrams and lists. "You guys started this to debunk Vicks's investigation. I know about Vicks putting his hands on Stevens, but nothing was filed. There was an old arrest attempt on Stevens for a burglary, but that was years ago. Vicks wasn't primary on it, but there was a mark on the report that he'd handled the suspect—Stevens—a bit too hard. Do you know if he remembers seeing Vicks back then? I didn't find any indication that Vicks recalled that incident."

"Knowing Stevens, he took off after it happened," Hank remarked. "He was slippery back then. Kind of sad if Vicks assaulted his arrests so often he didn't even remember them."

"He wasn't the greatest guy to work with." Cranston ruefully looked down into her cup. "You didn't hear it from me, but he was always the short straw cases. No one wanted to work with him, led with his dick instead of his brain. I always thought he was hanging on by the skin of his teeth, but then the Martin case landed in his lap, and he seemed like he had a clear shot at the wife and, well, your boyfriend."

"Rook didn't kill Harold. Timing was off from the beginning, but I can't say the same for Sadonna. I've been trying to corner her to follow up after Martinez was found," Dante admitted, stretching his arms to work out a kink in his shoulder. "But I can't see Sadonna shooting at a cop, though. She confessed her marriage to Harold was a sham, then tossed in the maybe-boyfriend, but I'm still not sold on her murdering someone."

"But Martin *does* have a boyfriend," she pressed. "I spoke to his mother. She said he was in a relatively new relationship, one he kept quiet from the family. Which doesn't make sense. Why keep it quiet? The old man seems okay with Rook."

"Wasn't always the case. Harold's older and was around for the formative years of Archie's prejudices." Dante liked the old man, but from all accounts, he'd been an abusive asshole for a long time, riding roughshod over his family even after Rook showed up on his doorstep. "He's working to change his ways, but it's a hard go sometimes. I can see Harold... and the others... leading a double life to keep in his good graces."

"Keep the old man happy and you'll stay in the will," Camden commented softly, rocking back on his heels. "Then along comes Stevens and blows the whole thing up with his fuck-you attitude. That would stick in Harold's craw. All these years of hiding, fake marriage, and slaving away at the company farm, only then Stevens fucks with the balance of things."

"Rook's good at that," Dante agreed. "But Rook wasn't a threat. Not to the family. He's pretty adamant about not working for Archie."

"I like the wife for the stabbing," Hank countered. "She said she wanted a divorce... that she was the one pressing for it, but he wouldn't give her one because now he's thinking of setting up a nursery. I think she hacked at him, then ran."

"Then who was there at the house the next day?" Cranston asked. "Harold's dead. She'd have no reason to come back. I'd supposed it was the killer coming back to make sure he was really dead."

"Did Harold know he had a fake?" Camden frowned, studying the photos again. "He's not like Stevens. He didn't collect movie stuff, so would he even know?"

The detective sighed, sitting back in her chair. "Why even swap them out? Natterly's had to know they couldn't cheat Stevens, so whoever gave Harold the fake either knew they could get away with it or—"

"It was a mistake," Hank finished. "Forensics do anything to that statue other than pick at it? Maybe it's holding something. Drugs? The Holy Grail?"

"What, like x-ray it?" She shook her head. "No, they hadn't gotten very far on what we'd sent them. There's a backlog. O'Byrne was lucky enough to get the bird on a table as quick as she did."

"So you think something's inside that plaster bird?" Dante eyed his partner. "And Natterly's sent it to Harold by mistake. Then why go after Rook?"

"Because only the cops, Rook, and Alex knew the statue was recovered on the scene. Then Sadonna dropped the bit about the bird being broken, but she could have heard about that from your boyfriend. If you were an intruder… and say you worked at the auction house… wouldn't you assume Rook pocketed the thing?" Hank asked. "Thieves always assume the worst of people, your boyfriend notwithstanding."

"Oh no, Rook always assumes the worst of people. It's when he doesn't, that's when he gets into trouble," Dante replied. "Look at the crime scene photos. No one stepped in the blood. Our intruder didn't check to see if Harold was still alive…. He was there for something else. Rook surprised him before he could get out, or maybe he found out it was a fake, seeing the plaster, so he knew then it wasn't what he'd come for." Dante tasted the theory, liking its flavor. "The Natterly brother—Jeremy—told O'Byrne Harold had the statue picked up and delivered. Then today, Davis, the other brother, didn't show up for his meeting with Rook. Something's off there. Sadonna killing Harold doesn't make sense, but I'm liking one of the Natterlys for it. They knew him. Rook even said they'd done business with Harold before and Davis was a good friend. Suppose it was more than just friendship?"

"So what? Someone got pissy and Harold gets stabbed?" Hank rubbed at the short ginger scruff covering his jaw. "Why kill Vicks and Martinez?"

"Because they were loose ends. People digging into the mess someone'd rather be swept under the rug. Just like Rook. The shooter wasn't after O'Byrne. He was after Stevens but is a really lousy shot. That statue really is a MacGuffin, just like in the movie. The real problem was Harold's murder." Dante reached for one of the detective's diagrams, then grabbed a pencil from the pile near her hand, studying the sheet. "I don't think the intruder was there for the statue. He was there to clean up. That's why he wasn't surprised to find Harold. He already knew Harold was dead going into the situation. Maybe the boyfriend pushed Harold to crawl out from under Archie's thumb and they fought. Knives happen when tempers flare. There was a lot of anger in those stabs. They knew one another. Intimately."

"There wasn't any evidence of a relationship in Harold's bedroom. Nothing. No photos, sex toys, nothing to lead us to believe he was having an affair." Cranston huffed in a breath. "Hell, that's what the intruder was doing. Erasing the boyfriend. My life's full of my boyfriend's crap. Even if you were keeping it under a rock, things leak. Pictures. Clothes. Small things."

"My wife's leaked all over my life. I've got about an inch of bathroom space. The rest of it belongs to her and the kids." Camden nodded. "So assuming Montoya's right, then that begs the question of which one of the Natterly brothers was Harold's lover, and how far is the other one willing to go to protect him?"

Fifteen

"WHERE'D YOU leave it with Stevens?" Camden guided the unmarked sedan they'd been given through the posh neighborhood's curved streets. "He still feeling like shit?"

"He woke up long enough for me to press a couple of pills into his mouth, slosh some water over his tongue, then hold his jaw shut until he swallowed." Dante held up his still-throbbing fingers. "Fucker bit me, but he took them. Thought I was going in for a kiss, but that wasn't happening until he got some meds into him. He had a rough night. Stitches along the rib cage hurt, and he moves a lot when he sleeps. So wasn't a good night."

"Brave man, pilling Stevens like a cat. If I were you, I'd sleep with one eye open." His partner chuckled, reaching for his coffee.

"What makes you think I don't already?" It was a soft grumble, and the bite had been accidental on Rook's part, more a reaction from shifting across the bed and a flare-up of agony so intense he'd gasped and clamped down on the edge of Dante's fingers instead of letting Dante tip them into his open mouth. "Just… worried about him. Not used to that yet, I guess. I mean, sure… I had Manny, but this… this is different."

"Yeah, it is. I might give you shit about Stevens, but he's good for you. Loosens you up." Hank shot him a glance, one Dante couldn't read. "You're having fun now. Before it was all work, and then you'd go home and work some more. Stevens makes you a little bit crazy, but it's a good crazy. I don't know what you see in him, but shit, it takes all kinds."

"He makes me… *feel*," he confessed softly, flicking his thumbnail along the ridge of his coffee cup lid. "You find a guy who can teach a Latino about passion, you hold on to him. No matter how wild the ride."

"Talk to me about passion when you've been married for ten years and date night means cleaning the lint out of the dryer vent," Hank teased. "And you're thankful the kids have the flu because it means they're huddled in bed and quiet."

"Think about what you just said and Rook Stevens," Dante replied. "You see us with kids?"

139

"Why not? Stranger shit has happened. I'd hate to be your kid's teacher or, worse yet, the principal." His partner began to chuckle in earnest. "You'd need a fucking vineyard to keep them tanked up on wine to put up with any kid raised by you and Stevens. Kid'll rip you off blind, apologize, hand it all back, and do it again for shits and giggles."

"We haven't even talked about moving in together, and you're already giving us kids? One step at a time, Camden." Dante tapped at the dashboard. "Hey, back up. You just passed it."

"How the hell can you tell what the address is if everything's got these huge damned hedges?" Reversing the sedan, Hank took the curve a hair too tightly, squealing the tires on the bank. "Sorry. You sure this is the place? I got nothing but a wooden gate Godzilla couldn't get over and another damned hedge. Maybe we should find a white rabbit to take us in."

"Not a rabbit. Caterpillar. Blue hair. Wears a scarf." Dante smirked at his partner's withering look. "Hazard of hooking up with a movie buff. You end up watching a lot of weird shit. And yeah, this is the right place. Numbers on the curb match."

"O'Byrne must be losing her shit being flat on her back in the hospital." Maneuvering the car into the driveway, Hank pulled it in as close as he could to an intercom speaker mounted on an arm near the gate. Hank came to a stop, then rolled down the window to buzz the house. "Okay, one ding-dong, then we wait. No one answers, we're storming the castle. You spoke to Cranston, right? She's okay with chasing down the Natterly brothers while we're here at Margaret's?"

"Cranston's fine. She's digging out possible locations for them, but she's got uniforms on the auction house. Staff got a voice message this morning from Davis, the older brother, telling them he'd be out for the rest of the week. Jeremy's just MIA, but he doesn't have regular hours according to the receptionist. Mostly you're lucky... or unlucky... if he shows up for work on any given day." Dante snorted. "That must be nice. Just show up whenever you want to. Buzz the house again. Maybe they didn't hear you the first time."

"You'd be a twitching pile of nerves if you didn't show up for work. And we're murder cops. We don't show up, people don't get caught. People don't get caught... and there's a shit ton more murders," his partner pointed out with a laugh. "Seriously, thirty more seconds and we start knocking down doors."

The neighborhood was claustrophobic, slender winding streets with spaced-out houses shrouded with enormous hedges and thick groves of trees. Cut into the hills, the tiers ran around the dips of canyons and along short mesas, shoving estates in where they could fit and, in the case of one mostly glass-walled house up the hill, perched on thick stilts anchored along a short cliff face. There was an eerie, nearly postapocalyptic feel to the area, devoid of life or any movement. With the rest of the city tucked down beneath the hills, the only sounds Dante could hear were the wind moving through the trees and the faint whirr of a lawn mower echoing through the clustered houses.

"Still nothing from the intercom. Let's get out and stretch. I'll try the speaker again." Hank unclipped his seat belt, then opened the car door. "Why don't you go take a peek through the gates? See if you can catch any movement up there. Swann knew we were coming. She's even the one who set the time."

"Yeah, confirmed it again with her this morning." Stepping out of the car, Dante was grateful for the slightly muggy Los Angeles morning air. It was cooler than down on the lower streets, but not by much, but he didn't care. The unmarked's cooling system had two settings, stale and arctic, so the warmth felt good. Closing the door behind him, he stretched, feeling every sleepless second he'd spent lying next to Rook hanging on his bones. "Maybe the intercom's broken. Try giving her a call."

The hedges were recently cut, heavily fragrant with dried sap beading on the trimmed branches, brutally snipped to follow the edge of the gate's stone pillars. Peering behind the hedge, Dante leaned on the heavy wooden gates blocking the drive to get a good look at the wall when the right side swung wide, gliding easily on its heavy hinges.

"Shit and hell," Hank swore from his spot near the intercom. "Damned thing's not even—"

Dante heard the engine before he saw the car, a squat, pug-nosed European job with rattling hubcaps and blacked-out windows. A curve in the driveway and a copse of bristly palms hid most of the house, and for a brief speck of time before the gray-green rattletrap emerged, the car's ill-timed motor fired roughly enough for him to wonder if the lawn was being mowed. The sleek black drive was wet, or maybe the car's tires were balding, because when the two-door coupe barreled around the bend, heading straight for the gate, it began to drift, and its back end skidded around.

Straight for Dante.

He dove, a graceless tumble behind the metal post set on the side of the drive. Meant to stop the gate from swinging back, it was his best hope— his only hope, really—to not get smeared over the driveway. Hitting the cement curb with his shoulder, Dante rolled, shouting at Hank to get out of the way. He got a flash of a ski mask, blurred by the darkened windows and the speeding car, before a bush caught his back, crushing branches into his ribs, and Dante's wind left his chest, leaving him gasping. The car continued on, smashing into the gently swinging gate in a horrific tear of wood and metal, ripping the anchoring planks from their hinges. The coupe's front end glanced off the unmarked's passenger side, spinning it toward Hank, but the lanky detective dodged the sedan, plastering himself up against the hedge.

"Dante! You good?" Hank's jacket flared, flung aside as he pulled his gun from its holster, but the car gunned its motor, slipping around the bend. "Answer me!"

"Fine!" Gasping, Dante struggled to stand up, extracting himself from the tangle of leaves and small branches he was trapped in. "Gate's got cameras. Maybe a plate? Checking the house—"

"Got it. Calling in backup! Montoya! Don't go in if it's off!" Hank was already on the move, sliding into the battered sedan. The unmarked's tires kicked up a flurry of leaves, pelting Dante across his face. Camden hit the siren before he turned the car completely around, then punched it, barreling down the street.

His lungs burned, but Dante broke into a run, following the driveway line. His knee ached from something he'd hit, but the urgency of getting to the house drove him on. Going in hot without a backup was foolish, but there'd been no choice, no time. Not after seeing the aftermath of the killer's diligence painted all over Martinez's apartment. Sadonna was his only focus, and the very real fear she now lay dying or dead somewhere in the house kept him going.

The rose-hued stucco house was enormous, a multilevel faux-Spanish mission with sweeping balconies and a tall iron-studded wooden front door. Framed in colorful tiles, the door stood open, the space behind it shrouded in shadow. The driveway circled around a tiered fountain, its lower bowl ringed with splashes of striated pansies and orange mums, and its curved spigots misted the air with a delicate spray faintly smelling of chlorine. Trimmed juniper pines obscured most of the house's front, providing a bit of a break from the wind coming up from the winding scrub-brushed cliff face. From what Dante could see, the house sat back from the property's ridge, a narrow strip of land buffering the structure from the drop to the canyon below.

He drew his weapon, slowing his pace, and mounted the short flight of steps leading to the front door. There was a twinge in his shoulder and a bit of stickiness along his right leg. The wind bit through the wet, and he felt its chill on his skin, assuring Dante he'd torn the knee out of his jeans. An ache continued to stretch over his side, and he bit back a sardonic laugh, amused at the irony of mirroring Rook's injury.

There was no guarantee the coupe's driver had been alone or if he'd been fleeing nothing more dangerous than a breaking-and-entering charge, but the stillness in the house, the silent nothingness leaking from the open front door made Dante brace for the worst.

"Police! I'm coming in. Ms. Swann, can you hear me?" Pressing his shoulder to the door, Dante leaned toward the opening, listening intently for any response. "Mrs. Martin! Are you home? Can anyone respond?"

He stepped in, cautiously pushing the door open with his foot. A wail of a far-off siren was partially comforting, but Dante wasn't going to wait. Sweeping the front hall with a pivot, he moved in, systematically working through a sitting room, then the library connected to it, all the while announcing his presence. There were signs of a struggle, an occasional table tossed to the marble floor or a vase once filled with sunflowers smashed into pieces against a wall, the blooms trampled to a flat mush in a pool of cloudy water. Books were scattered around an eating nook in the kitchen, the end of a glass table fractured from something heavy, but there was still no sign of anyone in the house.

Finally, Dante heard something. A low moan, gurgling and pained, came from somewhere farther in the house, and Dante stepped up his sweep, hurrying through the seemingly endless maze of rooms until he came to a screened-in patio. One of the french doors leading to the space was off its hinges, the frame ripped from its moorings, and two of its panes were punched out, a glistening spray of pebbled glass crunching under his feet. The patio ran the length of the kitchen and formal dining room, cluttered with rattan furniture and overturned palms.

He found Sadonna on her stomach, her sunshine-bright blonde hair tacky with blood, its matted strands trailing down her bare back. A plush white robe bunched up around her knees, its collar pulled down to expose most of her shoulders, and welts mottled the expanse of her back, their edges just beginning to yellow. More blood dribbled from several shallow gashes on her right arm, a serrated steak knife wedged halfway into a rattan club chair's side.

Sliding his fingers over her neck, Dante breathed a sigh of relief at finding a pulse, its strong beat coursing beneath his touch. He had a quick debate on whether or not to holster his gun, knowing he hadn't cleared the entire house, when Sadonna groaned again, feebly reaching out to grasp his ankle.

"Help…. Oh God," she gasped, fighting to breathe. Turning her head, Sadonna winced, and her hair fell from her face. Her right eye was nearly swollen shut, and her lower lip puffed out, a corner split open and raw. "Hit my… chest."

"Hold on. I need to make sure they're bringing an ambulance." The sirens were louder, and Dante reached for his phone, connecting through to Dispatch. He made the conversation quick, verifying an EMT team would be arriving on the scene, then ended the call just as he heard a deep voice shouting his name from the front of the house. Raising his voice, Dante yelled back. "Back here. Need medical assistance. First floor only half clear! There might be someone else in the house." Leaning over, Dante pressed his hand on Sadonna's shoulder, gently urging her to stay down. "Medics will be here soon. I need you to tell me if there's someone else in the house. Is Margaret here? Or any of the staff?"

"Margaret," Sadonna croaked out, trying to twist under Dante's palm. Then she collapsed back down, panting. "I heard… her screaming. Taking a shower, so I got… I came out and…. Oh God, poor Margaret. I think they killed her. I heard her yelling, and then… it all stopped. She just… *stopped* screaming."

"SO STILL no sign of the Martin woman, and it's what? Eight at night now? No one's heard from her since before we showed up, and there's no ransom call. I don't like this one bit, Montoya," Hank mumbled, rubbing at his face, then exhaled a heavy sigh. "Got word from the hospital Sadonna's injuries aren't life-threatening, but they're keeping her for a couple of days. She got punched in the chest pretty hard, possibly with something more solid than a fist. Last thing the doctors want is Archie on their asses if she develops heart problems because they've missed something."

"Archie's probably lost his mind. I touched base with Rook to make sure he's still at the house and not at the hospital. I'd rather he stay behind a wall of bodyguards and security alarms than go traipsing off to sit in a hospital room. He gave me a tentative… sure, okay. I threatened to sic Manny on him. Hopefully he listens." Dante stared at the forensic team working over the mansion's kitchen. "Between Vicks and the note to Rook and Margaret disappearing, none of this adds up. Why take her and not ask for ransom? Unless he needs her dead for some reason, but if he's going to attack Sadonna, why leave her alive when he's killed everyone else?"

"Probably because we showed up. There's surveillance cameras at the gate and screens feeding live into the kitchen. I think us arriving and ringing the intercom scared the guy off." Hank chewed on his lower lip. "Could have been he got Margaret into the car and was trying to subdue Sadonna but we interrupted him. She was fighting him off pretty fiercely from the looks of it. IT guys are going to pull the tapes so we can maybe catch a break. There's eyes on the driveway too. We could have a good shot of the car's license plate or even our perp. What do you think? You saw him. Could he have gotten Margaret into the coupe?"

"Guy I saw was pretty slender, a lot like Rook described as the intruder at Harold's house. Vicks was a big guy. He'd have to be taken by surprise or… been incapacitated. The rest of them would be easier to take down. Harold wasn't in good shape, Martinez was slight, and Margaret is bony, more angles than muscle. Vicks would have been a hell of a lot harder." Surveying the damage scattered about the front rooms, Dante frowned. "Sadonna surprised him. He didn't have time to take her out like he did Vicks, and he couldn't overpower her. Or at least not easily."

"Tox hasn't come back from Vicks yet. Could have been drugged. We're assuming the kill site was the sister's apartment from splatter and just how hard it would have been to drag Vicks in there." Hank moved out of the way when an attendant tried to slip past him. "Cranston asked if we needed her here, but I told her not to head up. She's got a lead on the Natterlys. Parents owned a house out in Santa Monica. When they died, about fifteen years ago, the brothers inherited, and it was rented out up until about two months ago when the tenants left."

"Two months is a long time to leave a house empty. Especially in Santa Monica. Rents out there are crazy. Even if they owned it free and clear, it'll bring in enough income to pay property taxes and maintenance." Dante whistled under his breath. "They're rich enough to let it sit?"

"That's the million-dollar question, Montoya. Might be too late for Cranston to get anything done tonight, but tomorrow's good for that." Camden cocked his head, turning when one of the techs called his name. "Yeah? What's up?"

"Got the video transferred over, Detectives. Looks like we've got about an hour of activity, but it'll take us a while to go through it, and I don't know what we've got. It's pretty fried." The tech's frown crinkled his bald head, forming ridges around his brows and ears. "Problem is, someone tried like hell to erase it. Took me a bit to recover it from the drives, but I got some files. Give me a couple of hours and I can probably get you a face. Maybe even a plate off the car."

"That's really what we need. A plate." Montoya patted Camden on the shoulder. "Especially since you lost the car."

"Dude, garbage truck cut right in front of me. You should see the car. If that damned beater that asshole drove didn't wipe out the front end, the sanitation scow took care of the rest of it." Hank shoved at him lightly. "If we're lucky we can make it home before—hold on, my phone. Why the hell do they call me and not you?"

"'Cause you're the ranking detective." Dante grinned.

"By like six months. Hold on, it's the hospital. I think it's O'Byrne calling to chew me out. Woman's got informants, I swear to God." Hank held the phone up to his ear. "Yeah? Camden here."

He left Hank to the call, especially when it sounded like he'd been right and it was O'Byrne calling to catch up with the case. They'd cleared the front rooms out, working methodically through the connected spaces and gathering what little evidence they could. Upstairs was still off-limits, although there hadn't been any blood splatter or even evidence of a gunshot, but considering the house had about a million bedrooms, the lab techs hadn't processed everything they'd cordoned off for testing. There wasn't much chance for fingerprints, but Dante held out hope, especially on the knife he'd spotted in the patio furniture.

There was still a feeling of discomfort along his spine, despite all of the time he'd spent in Archie's house, surrounded by furniture and objects well outside of his income. Margaret's house was a tasteful display of antiques and delicate chairs stacked with throw pillows, too fragile-looking for Dante to trust under him despite Hank testing one. Everything gleamed, polished to a sheen and dusted ruthlessly, daring a speck of dust to settle anywhere near a flat surface. Now a few of the sparkling surfaces were powder-speckled from the techs lifting latent prints as best they could, considering the heavily carved pieces' turns and curves.

A baby grand piano ate up a good corner of the study off the foyer, and Dante wandered over, half listening to Hank's side of the conversation with O'Byrne. The framed photos on the piano's top were typical shots, poised family pairings of children and people Dante only half recognized. There were very few candid photos in the identical heavy silver frames arranged in a curved wave to follow the piano's lines, but Dante could see a few. Picking up a shot of Margaret and Harold, he studied their fixed half smiles, clearly uncomfortably captured on camera during what looked like a child's birthday party. There were no pictures of Margaret's ex-husband, Archie's son, but that wasn't a surprise, judging from the bitter, sniping comments Margaret made about the man after one too many glasses of wine.

Unsurprisingly, there were no photos of Sadonna.

"But she let you stay here with her," he muttered to himself. "Margaret hated you but moved you in. Because of Harold or something else?"

He was about to turn away to pay more attention to Hank's grumbling when something bright green caught his eye. At first thinking it was something reflected on one of the frames, Dante peered into the thick cluster of smaller frames in the middle of the spread, finding the shot that drew him in.

It was of Harold, taken someplace tropical and, from all accounts, after he'd been out in the sun for more than a few hours, because his shoulders were as bright pink as the umbrella-and-pineapple garnished drink he held in his hand. The verdant gleam didn't come from the lush palms framing Harold. Instead, Dante was drawn to the man standing next to Harold, his arm slung around the man's tender-looking shoulders.

He was young, much younger than Harold, and his eyes were shiny, an intense green too vivid to be real. Classically handsome, he had gold-streaked blond hair long enough to brush his shoulders, his smile wide and sensual with promise. Dressed in a T-shirt with a logo Dante'd seen more times than he could count, the younger man looked happy and way too familiar.

"Shit, I know him. And not just because he's wearing a Potter's Field shirt. I've seen this guy." Fumbling with his phone, Dante dragged up the particulars of the case, rifling through the photos until he found the one he wanted. Turning around, he was surprised to find Hank about a foot away, tucking his phone into his jacket, a storm brewing on his freckled face. "Hey,

I found something solid connecting the auction house with this damned case. Look. See this guy? With Harold? That's Jeremy Natterly. With green contacts, just like the kind they discovered on Harold's body."

"Well, that's good damned news, because we also fucking lost something." Hank's cheeks flushed, a sure sign of his rising temper. "Sadonna's not at the hospital. ER docs patched her up and put her in a private room, but when O'Byrne got it into her head to hobble over to talk to her, she was gone."

"Gone… how?" Dante's thoughts grabbed at the possibilities. "Someone take her? She walked out? What? She didn't have any clothes on her. She left here in a robe covered in blood."

"That is another question to add to the pile we've got building up, because I don't know, partner," Hank replied. "But what I do know is she's to the wind, and with her goes any chance we might have of finding out who the hell tried to kill her and what the heck happened to Margaret Martin."

Sixteen

THE JAB along his side woke Rook up. That and the cold draft down his spine. As comfortable as the bed was, he missed his apartment... *their* apartment. He missed his own bed and the ambient light Hollywood slipped into the loft when he'd neglected to draw all of the blackout curtains closed. There was too much quiet in the hills, and he discovered he hated the silence of the rich, and more importantly, he couldn't find the damned clock in the room to tell the time. All he knew was it was late—or very early in the morning—and Dante was not in their warm bed.

"Time?" It was a croak. An actual croak and Rook swallowed, tasting grit and stale air. "Shit, I hurt."

"You were shot," Dante said from somewhere in the milky darkness. "Well, mostly. Creased pretty badly. Stitches are going to hurt. Did you take one of the pills the doctor gave you?"

"Fuck the doctors," he mumbled into a pillow. "And okay, I forgot, but I'd rather have you."

Blinking was a chore, but Rook did it anyway, trying to peer around him to find his lover.

Dante stood at the end of the bed, shirtless and unbuttoning a pair of jeans. His belt lay at the foot of the bed, and a quick nudge of Rook's foot—a very painful, agonizing nudge—and the belt slithered off the mattress, hitting the carpet with a soft thud.

A glance up and Dante's amber gaze ran hot over Rook's face, traveling down his shoulders and coming to rest at the gauze taped to his ribs. The fire in his lover's eyes dissipated, quenched by the bandages and probably the bruises Rook now felt near his lower back.

The agony along his ribs and back dampened Rook's lust, but it flared and spat, refusing to die. Despite the haze of pain flittering across his senses, Dante was still hot, thickly muscled and lean-hipped, his hard abdomen dusted with a bit of black down around his navel, and the jut of his hipbones over the elastic of his briefs were hard enough to make Rook's mouth water. He loved Dante's wide shoulders, rippling and powerful from years of doing all the domestic, masculine things he liked to do with the house he'd brought back from the dead. Until he met Dante Montoya, Rook hadn't realized how sexy a man looked mowing a yard, sweat dampening his shirt and sticking it to the narrow of his back. Or how erotic it was to watch Dante drink from a shadow-cooled garden hose, shoving his head under the stream to soak the heat from his scalp and neck.

"*You* should be asleep." The reproach was firm, flavored with the promise of a tequila shot, a smack of lime, and deep kisses. Dante owed him a night of tequila, Rook mused, the two of them on the back porch of Dante's bungalow, listening to the city and dancing in the faint light of Los Angeles's spotty streetlamps. "You listening to me, Stevens?"

"No, I'm thinking of how good you'd feel stretched out next to me and warming the back of my thighs," Rook confessed. "But sure, I'll entertain all suggestions for my recovery. However the fuck late it is. Where's my phone?"

"Confiscated. It's over on the dresser." Dante grinned at Rook's frown. "Don't scowl at me. It was on the floor when I came in. Archie catch you up before you crashed?"

"Yeah. Remember? You sent me a threatening message not to go down to the hospital."

"Good call on my part. Sadonna skipped out. O'Byrne decided she needed to do something, so she lurched down to the room they'd put Sadonna in, but she wasn't there. There was supposed to be a uniform covering her door, but they hadn't gotten there yet." Dante's fingers were chilly on Rook's cheek, but he leaned into his lover's touch, biting Dante's thumb. "Tell me you've had a tetanus shot, *cuervo*. I can't afford to get sick. Not when we're trying to find your aunt. Sadonna pulling a Houdini—"

"More like a Crazy Ivan." The confusion on Dante's face was worth it. It was *always* worth it. "There is so much to teach you and so little time to watch everything. Gorram smuggler reference. Sets fire to the atmosphere and disappears, incinerating their pursuers. Really, it's like aliens dropped you on this planet without a guidebook. Go on about Sadonna."

"Not much else. Bottom line, Sadonna was hurt in an alleged home invasion, your aunt Margaret taken, and I was almost run down by the kidnapper. Her running out on us brings up doubt." The jeans were left open, and Rook tugged at them with his toes, trying to inch them down. Dante chuckled, slapped at Rook's foot, then bent over to pick up his belt. After coiling the belt up into a tight circle and securing its tang, Dante tossed it over to the dresser. "Honestly, there's way too much going on, and every time Hank and I get something figured out, it twists all around again. This is a Möbius strip kind of case."

"So Sadonna's back on the chopping block because she ran?" Rook contemplated the possibility of the vampish movie star plugging anyone full of holes, unable to imagine her standing over her husband's dead body. "Dude, you cracked your head. Sure, she's sketchy, but can you see her killing Vicks? Or Margaret? Maybe she ran because she's scared someone's going to finish the job they started."

"Maybe, but this makes her look bad. Especially since there's no one else left on the board for us to go after," Dante replied. "All we've got is theories, but so far the guess is one of the Natterly brothers is involved in something off, and somehow Harold got caught up in it. I found a photo of him and Jeremy at Margaret's place, so it's anyone's guess if that's the Natterly who's Harold's boyfriend or if they just knew one another. There could have been a fight and one of the brothers killed him or... something, but like Sadonna, them missing brings up doubt and more questions. Most law-abiding people find out the cops want to ask them a few questions and they're right there, ready to get us off their backs."

"Yeah, not in my world," Rook scoffed.

"Did you miss the part where I said law-abiding?" Dante teased, easily moving out of the reach of Rook's halfhearted kick. "What can you tell me about Davis and his brother, Jeremy? Could Jeremy be the boyfriend, or did Davis take that picture and he was the one Harold was with?"

"Jeremy, maybe." He bit back a groan, muffling it to a whimper as he eased back onto the pillows. "Davis is more... nonsexual. I mean, he's button-up shirts and horn-rimmed glasses. Very fifties-looking. He's... business. Always. No sense of humor but a decent guy. Jeremy's more... the poet type. Flowing hair, sensitive and distracted. I always got the feeling he's working there because he's got to, not because he likes the place. Davis *loves* it. He likes ferreting things out. Most excited I've ever seen him was when he got a line on a pair of ruby slippers and snagged them. You'd have thought he found Jesus's clay cup and drank from it."

"Just because someone's a poet doesn't mean he's gay." Dante tugged at Rook's nose. "We're all kinds of men now, remember?"

"Hey, you asked. I just can't see Davis getting excited about anything to do with someone's body. He's the type of guy who'd wear latex gloves to pop the lid off of a cat food can." His libido was doing serious battle with his fatigue, and Rook sighed. The sheets were soft, luxurious to the touch, and warmed from his own body, but Rook wanted more, something to anchor him in the freewheeling terror lurking at the edges of his mind. Flitting his fingers over Dante's thigh helped, as did the long pause his lover took, turning to stare down into Rook's face. "Why are you still dressed? Why aren't you in bed making me regret all of my bruises, but not giving a shit about the pain?"

"How about if I get you some of your meds, a glass of water, and tuck you in?" his cop offered, brushing a kiss over Rook's cheek.

"Tuck into me," he corrected. "Not tuck me in. Shit, you're crappy at this seduction thing."

"You were shot."

"I was *creased.*"

"You have stitches," Dante reminded him, but he let himself be pulled forward when Rook hooked his fingers into Dante's belt loops. "And need sleep."

"I need you more." Rook sat up, resting on his haunches, and gently tugged Dante's jeans down. Leaning into his lover, he traced Dante's belly button with his tongue, worrying at the rim with a delicate bite. He hurt. Ached, really, but Rook needed Dante's touch, longed for it. He needed a bit of *home*, and his heart skipped a beat when he realized home now meant Dante Montoya. The throb along his ribs began again, and he couldn't keep the grimace off of his face. "Okay, meds wouldn't be bad. But then after that, I need you, babe. I just… fucking need you."

"Meds first. Then… we'll see," Dante cautioned, stepping out of his jeans and kicking them aside. A few seconds later, Dante was back. "Here. Take these."

"No, not those pink ones." He accepted the glass of water and palmed most of the pills Dante got for him from the battalion of bottles lined up on the bathroom counter, but the sedative wasn't something he wanted in his system. Popping them in his mouth, he mumbled, "They make my head fuzzy. I don't want to pass out on you. The other ones take care of the pain. I don't know why they gave me so many of the damned things to take."

"Passing out isn't a bad thing," his lover said, but Dante dropped them into a shallow dish on the nightstand, taking the mostly empty glass from Rook when he was done, placing it next to the discarded pills. "Move over a bit. That way if you fall asleep, you're not on your hurt side."

The medications worked quickly, and Rook exhaled, testing the tightness across his ribs while he rested his head on Dante's shoulder. The tickle of fingers moving up and down his spine bled away some of the tension in his belly, and Rook eased into the crook of Dante's arm, forcing his taut muscles to relax.

"Shit, I'm going to pass out. Goddamn it." Sleep pulled at his eyelids, weighting them down. "I wanted to take advantage of you. I wanted… everything. Want everything. You. Us. Maybe a goldfish."

"A goldfish?" Rook felt Dante's chuckle echo through his chest, and he flicked Dante's nipple with his fingers, grazing it with his nails. "Ouch. Hey. Watch it."

"I'm not responsible enough for anything smarter than a goldfish." The tired was getting to him. His body was sloughing off the desire he'd built up, despite the warm, gentle stroking of Dante's hand on his arm and back. "I'm going to fall asleep on you. Like… right now."

"I know, *cuervo*." Dante's voice was as warm as his fingers, brushing over Rook's temple. "I'll be here when you wake up. We can talk about goldfish then."

THE DAMNED bed was not only empty next to him, but it was kind of cold. Flipping over seemed less of a chore than yesterday, and Rook gingerly slid from the bed, carefully putting his bare feet on the floor, testing for any pangs along his ribs. A little bit of pulling but nothing he couldn't handle, and the non-ache held up when he pushed off of the bed, bending forward to minimize stretching the skin across his ribs.

"Oh God, I need to pee." Despite the rug, the floor was chilly, and Rook shuffled quickly to the bathroom. A few minutes later, he'd swallowed his morning dose, changed the plaster on his side, and began brushing his teeth when the door opened behind him and the mirror reflected a worried Dante back at him. Frothing, he mumbled, "What?"

"Nothing. Just hoped you'd still be in bed when I came back." Dante waited while Rook rinsed his mouth out, then gently turned him around, pressing Rook up against the counter. "How are you feeling?"

"Good. It doesn't hurt as much today. Stitches look good, no pinkness." Eyeing the cop, Rook asked suspiciously, "Why?"

"Because Book told me to come in later, and since you and I haven't had a chance to catch our breath since all of this shit's gone down, I wanted to spend a couple of hours with you. I see you put your shirt back on. That's… unfortunate." Dante sucked at Rook's lower lip, playing with its firm flesh, then letting go when Rook growled softly. Stroking at Rook's sides, Dante murmured, "I brought you coffee and some food. Thought I'd feed you and we can talk."

"You and I have very different ideas on how to spend a couple of hours in bed. I want sex, and you want to… peel me grapes?" He shook his head, bemused at Dante's husky laugh. "Not cool, Montoya. *You* are a damned—"

Dante's mouth swallowed his teasing, stealing the breath from Rook's chest and rushing the blood through his heart until his eardrums ached from the increasingly pounding beats under his rib cage. He sipped at air when he could, but Dante wasn't letting him go, refusing to break the connection between their mouths. He felt nothing beyond his lover. Dante's hands were gentle enough, but the rasp of his roughened palms stoked an ember in Rook's belly, especially when the man's clever fingers skimmed the waistband of his sweats, tracing around the ridge of bone and muscle on Rook's hip.

He was left gasping, aching for more when Dante pulled back, arms braced on the counter and the small of his back pressed into the hard, cold marble, a keen contrast of sensations after Dante's hard, long body held him captive without so much as a sliver of air between them.

"No grapes," Dante murmured, nipping at Rook's throat in hard, sharp bites, leaving a trail of stair-stepped burns on his skin. "Strawberries, though. And coffee. I'd have brought champagne, but… work." Another dig of teeth, this time into Rook's bared collarbone, and he gasped, jerking back, but Dante wouldn't let go. Not until he'd had his fill. It took an endless second of momentous torture before Dante moved on, the throb he left behind a clear promise of a mark Rook would wear for days on his pale skin. "*Dios*, you're like fire in my hands, *cuervo*. I stroke you just a little bit and you… you are hot enough to consume me."

They made it to the bed. Barely.

Rook's elbow caught the tray Dante put on the nightstand, and they had a brief flash of coffee and fruit flying over the room before Dante grabbed at its edge, snagging its lip, then righting it. Half on the bed, Rook stretched out onto his back, his arm flung out and grunting when Dante stretched out on top of him, their feet hanging off the mattress.

"Am I hurting you?" His lover shifted, easing the press of his weight on Rook's torso. "We don't have to do anything—"

"No, I'm good. Some meds, a little horniness, and I don't feel jack shit. If I don't get some release, I'm going to break." His dick was hard and tight, trapped between Dante's hips and his thigh, but the friction felt good, welcome even. "'Sides, I was freezing before, and you, Montoya, warm me up just fine."

"I was just saying that about you." Dante moved to the left, and Rook slid his hand down the back of his lover's sweats, cupping his ass. The response from Dante was immediate, a thick ridge of arousal pressing into Rook's thigh. He shivered at Rook's questing touch. "What did you do? Stick your hands in ice water?"

"Told you I was cold," he groused playfully, squeezing Dante's ass. "I like the no underwear. Makes this a hell of a lot easier."

"You've got some on?"

"What? Underwear?" Rook crinkled his nose. "Yeah. Want to help me take them off?"

"Best offer I had all morning." He cocked his head, grinning. "Okay, second best offer, because Rosa helped me make the coffee."

"Dude, if I'm coming in second after Rosa with an offer to get nude and bump uglies, then I am definitely doing something really fucking wrong here." Rook bit at Dante's chest, closing his teeth over his lover's nipples. "Want to get me naked? Or do you want to spend a couple of hours drinking Rosa's coffee?"

"Okay, I am very sorry about bringing up the coffee," Dante murmured, sliding his hand under Rook's shirt. "Move your arms up. Help me get this off of you."

The slither of cotton across his chest and back only made Rook harder, and when the cool air grabbed at his skin, it pulled out a shiver and a prickle of goose bumps. He was stripped quickly and carefully, with Dante pressing a kiss on Rook's left hipbone before peeling Rook's pants and underwear off. Dante's sweats were easy to shuck off, the waistband curving down over the Latino's firm ass and then down his powerful thighs. He kicked them off, sending them over the edge of the bed. Lifting himself up, Dante rested his weight on his knees, dimpling the bed next to Rook's prone, half-naked body.

Dante literally stole Rook's ability to think. The churning thoughts bouncing around his head, random bits of information and whispers running noise through his mind quieted when Dante's honey-brown gaze settled on him. Nude and in repose, his hands resting on his thighs, his cock jutting out from his body with its slight curve to the right, Dante's powerful shoulders, arms, and legs were long planes of muscle and sinew.

His flat, sculpted abdomen twitched when Rook ran his fingertips through the silken, soft hair trailing around his navel and down to cup the base of his rampant cock. His dark brown hair stood out around his strong face, pulled askew by Rook's hands threading through the strands, but the disheveled toss of mink and ebony around his face softened his hard cheekbones and scruffy jawline, gilding a vulnerability onto Dante's intense masculinity.

"Damn, you are gorgeous, *cuervo*." Dante's rasp underscored the heat in his accented words, his husky voice thickening with want. "I am a *very* lucky man."

Running his hand slowly over Rook's long thigh, he leaned over, kissing Rook deeply. Their tongues did a slow dance, a flick against teeth, then another slide into the depths of each others' mouths. Dante tasted of a nipped strawberry and a faint whisper of mint, but Rook wanted more, needed more of his lover in him.

There was a bottle of lube liberated from a nightstand drawer, but the quick search was punctuated by nibbles and kisses, with Dante guiding Rook across the bed to lay his shoulders on the nest of pillows Rook'd gathered up from the rooms around them. A buttery morning sun poured in between the slightly parted gold curtains draped across the bedroom's french doors, the patio beyond damp from the heavy dew left by LA's marine layer. The shimmering fabric frosted the room in a faint glow, bronzing Dante's tanned skin.

His lover wasn't perfect, not by a long shot. He carried scars from a childhood played out on asphalt-hosted football games, and there was a slight chip on his right cuspid, a remnant of a battle fought over a game controller with a cousin wielding a broomstick. Rook knew the catch of that tooth on his tongue, felt the sharp ridge on his lip when it left a deeper, harsher mark, but they were all imperfections Rook loved to explore.

He knew the whorl on the back of Dante's head, intimately scritching at his lover's temple with his fingernails while sitting behind him on the couch while Dante watched *fútbol* on the floor with Hank's kids. There were golden spots along Dante's shoulders and a tiny star-shaped dimple from a fishing cast gone wrong. Rook loved Dante's right ring finger with its hooked-in first joint, the curve formed by a word-mad young Latino boy who'd written poems and stories before someone told him to stop dreaming and do something with his life that mattered.

The stories were lost to time, but the desire was still there, burning in Dante's soul as hot and furious as the desire in his expression at Rook lying on the bed. Reaching up, he cupped Dante's face, his palm roughed by the shadow of Dante's beard.

"You are... *everything* to me, Montoya," Rook whispered, unable to gather more than a bit of air past the lump in his throat. He was speechless with want, aching for anything Dante would give him. "I've never ever wanted anyone like I want you. Not... I can't *not* have you with me, and it fucking scares me, babe. You fucking scare me in so many ways, but each time, my heart tells me... reminds me... that I'm yours and—"

He couldn't think anymore, and Rook surrendered to Dante's mouth, losing himself in Dante's exploration. There were aches still, a bit of a twinge along his ribs, and when he hissed, Dante stopped, hair loose around his face and a questioning expression filled with concern and something tender on his face. Rook worked his fingers into the soft strands and pulled Dante down, capturing his mouth in a demanding, punishing kiss.

"What do you feel up to, babe?" Dante licked at Rook's jaw, then gnawed playfully at his earlobe. "Tell me. Anything you want."

"I want to have you around me," Rook whispered, kneading his fingers into Dante's shoulders. "Do you mind?"

Sex in the past meant quick and hard, sometimes with barely a glimpse of a face before hands were peeling him apart, and a hasty grind to get himself pleasure. Dante made him want to take his time, taste and savor every inch of his lover and bring a gasp or a smile to Dante's lips. Still, asking... talking about what he wanted... was still too new, too raw, and Rook stumbled over his desires, trying to remind himself he was worth being loved... having Dante's love... while holding his breath for his lover's no.

"Go slow," Dante warned, touching at the edges of Rook's plaster. "Don't... overstretch. Or better yet, lay back and let me do all the work."

Their laughter was as hot as the lube was cold, especially at Dante's exaggerated hiss as Rook's teasing fingers circled his entrance. They went slow at first; then something shifted, an urgency overtaking their desire. Perhaps it was the looming unknown waiting for Dante once he strapped on his badge and gun to face the world, or even the shadows closing in on

Rook, trapping him inside of Archie's elaborately decorated castle, a rambling sanctuary made into a prison by the insanity someone threw at them.

The sun stole away, leaving behind only a brush of light, but Rook didn't need it. Dante's body was a treasure he'd drawn pleasure from time and time again. Working his fingers into Dante, Rook reveled in every soft cry and kiss Dante left on his shoulders and throat. Easing the way for his cock to fill the sweet velvet of Dante's body, Rook spread the slick oil around, then coated as much of himself as he could reach while Dante moved to straddle him.

Dante held himself up, angling his back and resting on his shins, moving carefully around Rook's hips until he could reach back and grasp Rook's shaft. He played with Rook, teasing at the ridge of his cockhead until Rook mewled and ground out a nonsensical threat. Placing his hands on either side of Rook's face, Dante tipped the end of his tongue against Rook's nose, making him squirm.

"I kind of like you like this," Dante teased. "Try not to wiggle too much. Don't want you to bust your stitches."

Gripping the base of Rook's cock, Dante eased over him, enveloping Rook in a soft, tight heat. It seemed to take forever, and Rook fought the urge to push his lover down, but he kept his hands tight on Dante's hips, letting the other man have control. It was an intimacy he wouldn't have allowed with any other man. No one ever came close to Rook's heart, and he'd more than a few times marveled at how Dante could flay him open with a simple touch or loving word, then shelter him from the storm of his own doubts.

Nestled down on Rook's hips, Dante began to move, slowly working his body forward and rocking along Rook's length. They began their dance, moving together in an off-beat rhythm slowed by frequent kisses and teasing words. Their words became panting breaths, gasps run taut as the pleasure built up between their bodies. Rook's stomach clenched, his balls curling up and rolling under Dante's ass, and he tamped down on his orgasm, stroking at Dante's cock as it wept with the beginning of his release.

The anticipation crested, tearing apart Rook's control. A drop of Dante's sweat hit his chest, the splash wetting his nipple, but it was gone in a second, absorbed by the damp sheen on his skin. Unable to stop himself, Rook thrust up, meeting Dante's hip rolls, pushing as much of himself into Dante as he could. He'd have loved to watch Dante's body unwrap with their movements, clasping him in the rough tumble of their lovemaking, but the ride was beginning to take its toll. His side burned, a small flicker of pain quickly swallowed by the delight of Dante's ass clenching around his dick.

A squeak of the bed frame tapped at Rook's common sense, and he slowed his rocking down, stopping the headboard from slamming into the wall. Dante bent forward, pushing down on his knees, and anchored his hand on the tufted leather behind the pillows at Rook's head.

"Hold on, *cuervo.*" Hoarse with lust, Dante groaned, his cock heaving in Rook's clasped hand. "*Dios.*"

Rook lost the rest of it, drowned in the spill of his body's pent-up need. His cock jerked and teased, his hands clamped down over Dante's hips, filling his lover with every drop of his release. It was nearly too much to bear, too tender of an explosion, and Rook shook with the force of Dante's come splashing over his belly and chest, a musky wave of sex and potent emotions.

The world grew gray, softening at the edges as Dante slipped off of him. As much as Rook mourned the lost of his boyfriend's body on his, the tightness on his torso eased from the lack of weight on his hips, and when he sucked in a breath, his ribs trembled from the effort. Patting at his side, it took a bit for him to find the bandage he'd put on that morning, a twisted nest of gauze and tape stuck to his thigh instead of covering the throbbing stitches in his skin.

"Ouch." Peeling the taped-up tangle hurt nearly as much as the gash, but it soon faded, leaving only the abused stitches with their dull ache in its wake. Rook was sticky and pretty sure his hips were coated with lube, a surefire way to end up stuck to the sheets if he didn't get cleaned up. "Hey, babe, help me—"

Dante stood at the side of the bed, his phone in his hand and an expression Rook recognized as Dante's cop face plastered firm and tight where his lover's laughter once held court. Crawling to the edge of the mattress, the fire started anew across his ribs, Rook reached for Dante, tugging at his wrist. He was immoveable, a hard granite-and-amber monolith standing off in the ruined shadows from the insistent morning light.

"What happened? What's wrong?" There were too many people... too many missing pieces of the fucked-up puzzle of the case for it not to be someone Rook knew, perhaps even loved. His brain scrambled, finding horrors he hadn't even begun to fold his thoughts around—scared shitless that maybe the killer found Manny or perhaps even Archie, peeling them from Rook's life with the same careless brutality he'd used on Vicks and the others. "Dante, talk to me. What the fuck's going on?"

"I've got to go in, *cuervo*." Dante exhaled, dropping the phone onto the bed. Running his thumb over Rook's mouth, he pressed into Rook's chin, then said, "They found Sadonna in the water off of the Santa Monica Pier. I don't know how she is or even if she is alive, but… they've found her." Dante's kiss was salty, stained with an edged anger mingled with a terror Rook knew all too well. "So if you love me, Rook, you will do this one thing—this one *small* thing that I'm asking of you—stay here. Because without you, I have nothing else to live for."

Seventeen

SALT STUNG Dante's nose, the sea's briny mists clutching at his lungs as he walked the length of the pier, tiny droplets dappling his black peacoat. Hank stood at the end of a row of squat buildings, and Dante hurried, listening to Camden's thinner trench beat at his partner's legs, the slap-slap of fabric on Hank's shins sounding off an odd applause for Dante's arrival on the scene.

The landmark's massive Ferris wheel creaked ominously, its metal baskets swaying in the brisk, cutting breeze, and while someone'd turned off its flashing lights, its music jauntily played softly on, a muted jolly mocking of the pier's recent tragedy. A flight of seagulls hovered a few feet off the walk's edge, their wings pumping lazily as they rode the hard, icy wind currents, maddeningly out of reach of the torn-eared ginger tom squatting near the ride's compressor. There were uniforms swarming the pier, a flock of blue wraiths moving through rides and shops in a focused search for evidence.

Sparrows pecked at bits of food stuck in between the double pier's planks, scattering, then regrouping when Dante crossed over the boardwalk. Dante's partner moved closer, waiting near a roundabout kiddie ride of wild-eyed painted resin horses, swatting at a gull diving down to snatch at the scrap of muffin Hank had in his hand. The bird won, sweeping off with the pastry, leaving Hank swearing in its wake.

"Should I have brought a loaf of bread with me?" Dante teased. "So you can feed the birds?"

"Screw you, Montoya. And it's 'bout time you got here. Morgue sent a newbie. Think his name is Taylor. Um…. Chase Taylor," Hank grunted, jerking his chin in the direction of a slender young man with hair nearly as vibrant as Camden's. The tech must have heard them, because he looked up from his tablet and waved at Hank, his mouth turning up into a wide, enthusiastic smile. "He's like an American cheese sandwich with mayo on white bread and a bowl of Jell-O. God, were we ever that young?"

"Never," Dante asserted. "I also don't think I've ever had a cheese sandwich in my entire life. Grilled, yes, but plain?"

"Think really crappy tasteless quesadilla that sticks to the roof of your mouth and you have to use your tongue to get it off." His partner chuckled. "I used to eat tons of them after school before dinner. Man, they're like the shittiest thing to eat, but it's childhood, right? Like mixing uncooked ramen noodles with coleslaw. Good stuff."

"There was something seriously wrong with your childhood, Camden." His throat was closing up at the thought of cabbage, ramen, and mayonnaise. "*Dios*, even Rook eats better than that, and he was raised in a circus."

"Scratch at that sometime and ask him," Hank retorted. "Bet you find something fucked-up, like he ate Cheetos and milk like cereal for breakfast. Let's find Cranston in this mess. She's probably got something for us to do."

"Any news from the hospital?" Dante stepped over a garden hose, its jet attachment spurting a thin spray from its threaded end. "Last I heard, they revived her in the ambulance, but it was touch and go all the way in. Surprised Cranston wanted to meet here instead of there."

"They were still working on her. That's all I know, but the sweep down here came up with something. That's why Cranston wanted us down here." Tugging at Dante's sleeve, Hank leaned in. "Text said to go straight down the right side of the pier, then hook in at the Ferris wheel to get to the back. Do not pass Go. Do not collect two-hundred dollars. And do *not* pet the cat."

"That cat looks like it can fuck me up, so no, I'm not going near it," he replied. They gave the feline a wide berth, and the tom flattened himself when a gull landed on one of the rain-damp baskets. "Cranston's over there. This place is insane. Between the Ferris wheel, the roller coaster, and those rinky-dink rides back there, how the hell does anyone walk around this place?"

"Doesn't help half of Santa Monica's beat cops are here." Hank glanced around. "Why the hell are they all here? And actually, why is the tech here? They pulled Sadonna out of the water."

The petite blond detective waved them over, motioning for the partners to circle around an ice cream kiosk. Like Camden, she wore a beige trench, but hers seemed to be lacking the inevitable jelly stain most of Camden's jackets bore on their hems. They ducked and cut under a small roller coaster's tracks, Camden grumbling about nearly striking his head on the bright yellow curve. She shook their hands firmly, but there was fatigue dragging at her face, tightening the corners of her mouth.

"When was the last time you got some sleep, Cranston?" Camden barked, frowning at her. "You look like you could use a three-year nap."

"Don't mind Hank. He doesn't like the ocean. Makes him skittish," Dante commented softly. "Something about crossing running water."

Hank snorted loudly. "There's things in the ocean that will literally eat all of you and leave like… your eyeballs behind. Bobbing around, washing up on the sand to scare the shit out of some kids playing Frisbee."

"Don't be silly, Camden," the detective retorted. "Eyeballs are soft meat. Gelatinous even. They'd be the first to go."

"Unless they're cooked," Dante pointed out. "Then they turn into white marbles, but those would sink."

"Oh, you two need some therapy," his partner shot back when Dante smirked at him. "So, what's with all the uniforms? Way too many for a drowning. And if it was an attempted suicide—"

"It's not a suicide. Someone stabbed her, in the shoulder. The blade caught on her ribs, and her attacker tried to pull it out. We got it on tape," Cranston corrected. "Come on over here. Behind the booth. I need to show you what the divers are looking for in the water."

"Why'd you need divers?" Hank peered over the blue railing. "Water that deep? Shit, it's like pea soup down there."

"Better question. How did she get in the water? That top rail is pretty high." Dante moved in behind his partner, comparing the bar's height with his memory of Sadonna's measurements. There were three divers he could see, layered with black wetsuits and listening to a fourth off to the side. His words were caught up by the wind, making it impossible to hear everything, but it sounded like they were heading back down to work another section under the pier. "How'd she go over? This is elbow height. How good is the tape? Do we have a clear face shot of her attacker?"

"We've got one good camera angle off of the coaster, and well, there was a struggle, not a long one, but it seemed heated. I've watched it, but I want your impressions." She pointed to a white ball hanging under a jut in the ride's structure. "It's cued up over in the office. That door right there."

The musty office was cramped, barely enough space for two institutional desks set back to back in the middle of the square room, and its plain wood paneling outer walls each sported a narrow sash window with metal screens fixed over the glass. Stacks of stapled papers covered half of one desk, while the desk closer to the door held an old, scuffed laptop and a small boxy television connected to a hard drive.

"Let me guess, you have to be two-dimensional to be hired here?" Hank glared down at the tight space between the desk and one of the rolling chairs, then shook his head. "Before we get started, who found her?

"A couple walking their dog on the beach. Spotted her arm caught up on one of the pier supports. Guy went into the cold water to pull her out and performed CPR until the EMTs got here. Reports said she was blue and unresponsive, but once she warmed up, they found a pulse." Cranston fiddled with the TV. "Let me get this started."

"Surprised they didn't call it." Camden sat on the edge of the desk.

"Could be they thought she was still alive if she'd kept bleeding out of the wound," Dante offered. "Fifty-fifty if it was pink because she was in the water, but once they got her stripped and it ran red and hot, they'd work harder. Even if the blood's sluggish."

"It was very sluggish, but yeah, she wasn't going to go on those guys' watch. Here we are." She angled the small screen so they all could see the grainy, gray-flecked recording. "Equipment's not great, and there's no sound. The security guys are pulling the other cameras, hoping we can get a better face, but so far, this is the only one with any action."

The recorded feed was choppy, a staccato replay of two shapes played out on a pixel canvas, reminding Dante of a yellowed zoetrope Rook showed him during a scrub of the shop's back room. A familiar-shaped woman with blonde hair trotted out onto the pier, her thick-heeled boots creating ripples in the wide puddles around the roller coaster's perimeter. Her hands were shoved into a heavy jacket, but she'd left her head bare and pushed her hair from her face when the wind whipped it about. She paced, looking over her shoulder and peering off into the diminishing shadows around the cluster of booths and sales fronts arranged around the larger rides.

When she turned her head to look back at the street, it was clear the woman was Sadonna Swann, but it was a shock to see the dark bruise across her cheek and swollen eye, its savagery vivid even in the muted palette of the coaster's security camera.

"She just walked out there. No one stopped her, but this place is twenty-four seven, right? All access, all the time? Where was the security guard?" Hank asked. "Is there one?"

"Guard makes a long round," she answered. "Sometimes it's up to an hour before he makes the next sweep. Or that's what he said. I'm guessing it's even more."

"This early, though, only die-hard surfers if the waves are good and a couple of crazy health nuts, but someone might have seen something. We just need to find them." Hank tapped at the time stamp on the screen. "Sun's not quite up but enough ambient light to see. Out in the open, so she doesn't trust this guy. Caught a full ID of her face there, but where's our attacker?"

"There. See." Dante saw a sliver of darkness move, detaching from a bank of shadows nearly outside of the camera's range to the right. It was hard to make out anything other than a dark hoodie, sweatpants, and running shoes, but then the figure gestured and he spotted the person's bare hand. "No gloves. So that means prints someplace."

"That's why we've got the crews in. Uniforms to keep everyone off and the tech crew working to get anything they can off really crappy surfaces." Cranston bumped the feed down, slowing the action. "Watch what's next."

The argument played out like a Punch and Judy puppet show. The attacker struck first, but Sadonna saw the hit coming, blocking the other's fist with her arm. The fury on the movie star's face was palpable, anger turning her face ugly, and she gestured furiously, her hands slicing through the air. The yelling was a pantomime of open mouths, flapping hands, and silent roars, but Sadonna's attacker kept to the shadows, giving tantalizing glimpses of a nose and chin every so often. Their body language was angry, stiff shoulders and then a shove at Sadonna's chest, pushing her back a step.

"Sadonna's pointing to something. Back towards the shore," Dante murmured. "She's pissed, but she's standing open, throwing her arms out. She's not defensive yet. She knows this person. Look how close they're standing. You don't stand that close or that loose unless you know someone."

"Then why meet out here? Because it's public?" Hank pressed. "There's some distrust but not so much that she wouldn't come out here at the crack of dawn."

"Here. Right here." Cranston slowed the video further, gesturing with the slender remote. "Something the other person says ticks Sadonna off, and she takes a swing at them."

This strike found its mark, and the other person's head rocked back. Hank whistled under his breath and muttered, "Damned good right hook."

"There's the knife. Yes?" Cranston nodded, and Dante tracked a glint of something light in the other person's hand. The angle made it impossible to see the attacker's face, and as close as they were standing to Sadonna, Dante guessed they were taller than the injured woman. The jab was quick, nearly too quick to see, and Cranston backed the tape up so they could watch it again. "*Jesus*. Straight through. No hesitation, and that knife, that's sharp. And you said he or… she… didn't get it out?"

"No, she went over the railing first." The detective advanced the speed, taking the play back to normal. "There. She turns around and catches her foot on the bottom bar. The railing's new, it should hold her weight, but either she's lost her mind or she's willing to risk the cold water because—"

"There she goes." Hank puffed out his cheeks, exhaling hard. "I'll be damned. She pitched herself over to get away. That thing was down to the hilt in her. Did you see the guy trying to jerk it loose? Well, maybe a guy. It's hard to tell. We'll need to do some measurements. Get a gauge of height and weight at least."

"How heavy is the current? Did they give you any clue if there's a chance it's down there?" Dante glanced over at Cranston. "We could really use a print."

"Divers went in for it, but so far, nothing. Not even her purse, and you saw how big that thing was." She thinned her lips, then said, "Frustrating, because I'd hoped we'd catch a break."

"Detective! We've found something!" The shout brought them to the door, and Cranston shoved herself off the desk just as the ginger-haired tech they'd seen earlier pushed into the office. His elbow caught Hank in the ribs, and he blurted out an apology, backpedaling into Dante. "Oh, crap. Sorry. Sorry."

"Back up. We'll follow you out," Hank ordered, shooing the young man back out the door. He caught Dante's reproachful look and shrugged. "Look, we're like sardines in here. Let's go see what they brought up."

"If it's the knife, I'll pull every favor I've got downtown to get the prints run," Cranston promised. "I want a win on this, boys. My house's hungry to pin Vicks's killer."

Emerging from the office was a step into a brine-scented sauna. The sun was out, breaking apart the marine layer into patchy clumps, its heat turning the smaller puddles along the wooden walk to a swampy steam. The tech Hank thought was named Chase hurried ahead of them, going past a circle of booths to the other side of the pier, leading the detectives. A cluster of cops stood around a drape of decorative netting and plastic starfish, its folds shoved aside into a mound, and one uniform held an umbrella up to keep the rain off of a small cardboard mailing box laying on its side, its flaps open, its walls bowed in from being soaked from the damp. Natterly's logo was bright across the fragmenting white cardboard, and a scattered nest of thin wood packing curls was darkened from the water the porous material wicked up from the wet pier.

It was too familiar of a sight, and Dante slowed his steps, bracing himself for another shock. The last box he'd come across had a dead cop's head in it. Taking a deep breath, he lengthened his stride, matching Hank's long ramble. The uniforms around the box didn't seem distressed, more curious than troubled.

"Crap, why isn't that bagged?" Cranston snapped, hurrying across the pier. "Why is it open?"

"It was like that when we found it." Chase hustled out of Hank's way. "One of the guys kicked the pile, and the box tumbled off those post things. It kind of broke open when it hit the ground. I went and got you before—"

"Get some cover for it. Water's going to eat through that box," Camden snarled as another tech, an older woman with a scowl on her face, came around the other side of the booths, her arms full of plastic bags.

"Wait, I know what that is." Dante grabbed at Hank's arm, holding him back.

If the box looked familiar, the broken pieces of what it once held were like a shattered memory of hours spent watching black-and-white movies on Rook's big-screen television, his lover rambling on about things Dante couldn't even imagine retaining. The squat black resin bird was intact, its judgmental, haughty gaze staring out over the ocean, but it was sheared off its base, its claws and tail forming a jagged crown around the detached square pedestal. The delivery label on the box lay under a crinkled plastic sleeve, but Dante could still make out Rook's name and the shop's address written in heavy blue lettering.

Even in the faint sunlight, the base's contents glittered and sparkled, grabbing at every bit of light and churning out prisms across their faceted sides. Most were small, about the size of a pinky nail, but there were a few larger pieces, including a faint pink-washed emerald cut about the length of Dante's thumb. A few were wedged in the cracks between the pier's planks, winking under the water gathered in the wood's grooves.

He didn't know a lot about diamonds, other than what commercials told him were good to buy or the lines rattled off during a film, most of which he took with a grain of salt. Rook would know their value, mulling over each rock and discarding the ones he didn't think were worth his time. They'd talked about those days, times when he slept with one eye open and a crick in his back from sliding through windows and launching himself over fences to escape dogs he didn't know were there. There'd been no mention of actual jobs, nothing to incriminate him, but the sharing of the thrill he got opening a door locked against him was all Dante'd needed to understand the man he'd fallen in love with.

"Jesus, do you see that?" Hank whistled low, his eyes widening in shock. "Those can't be… real. Shit, if they're real… crap, they were going to Rook, Montoya. Your boyfriend's—"

"Is not a thief." Dante rounded on his partner, his fury at Camden's words tempered by the years of friendship between them. There were a lot of explanations for what was going on with the statue. A few even made sense in the noise of Dante's racing thoughts, but there was one thing he was sure of. "Rook's clean, Camden, but somebody isn't. And that right there is why people are dying around him, and we don't have a damned clue who's killing them."

Eighteen

"WHAT DIAMONDS? What bird? Where…. I swear to God if this has a 'There Wolf, There Castle' punch line, I am going to find you and piss on your shoes." Rook rubbed at his eyes, stumbling out of their temporary bedroom. He grazed his elbow against the doorframe, hissing when his funny bone began a tingly, numb dance, and he shifted his phone to his other ear, tilting his head to wedge the device against his shoulder. "Dude, I haven't even had coffee yet. What the hell are you talking about?"

"We found the missing falcon statue. The real one." Dante sounded strained over the line. "Any reason it would have diamonds in its base?"

"Well, I'll be fucked," he muttered back. "That old son of a bitch."

"Which old son of a bitch? Archie?"

"No, Travis Bluthenthal. He was the falcon's owner. Well, right up until he died." Rook padded down the front staircase, mentally counting the steps as he always did, satisfied he had the same number as before when he got to the main floor. "Remember I told you guys he'd kind of raised up Hawkins? Where did you think I learned my shit? Hawkins's guy was a cat burglar. Legend really. Old-school kind of shit. Ropes, rappelling in, seducing the housekeeper to get inside the house he was going to hit. Very Cary Grant. Like I said, *legend*."

Dante's sigh could have been used as a sound capture for a flattening tire. "Only you would think someone like that is a legend."

"Hey, I'm not the only one. He's Old Hollywood. People used to invite him to all the big parties because he agented for a few stars for kicks. Got them some big bucks, from what I hear. Shit, he was still at it right up until he died a while back, but it took a bit for the estate to clear. When it did, stuff went up for auction." He sniffed at the air, noticing the lack of coffee aroma. "Crap, Archie's at an appointment, and I think Rosa's off grocery shopping. She asked if we wanted anything, so I asked for black pitted olives, ube ice cream, and tamarind candies. Not the plain kind. The spicy ones. I think she might have told me to go fuck myself, but it's hard to hear her when she mutters. Have you noticed that?"

He wasn't uncomfortable talking about his old life, but there was something protective bubbling up inside of him over Bluthenthal. Rook had an odd fondness for the thief, mostly fueled by the stories he'd heard from Hawkins and a few of the carnies who'd been done right by the aging burglar. From all accounts, he'd been a class act, willing to lend a few bucks to help someone out, even when things were tight.

Someone he'd wanted to be when he grew up.

Dante held a long, telling silence, then said, "You're fooling no one, *cuervo*. You knew about this man. Maybe even liked him?"

"Never met him." He chuckled at Dante's disbelieving snort. A barefooted saunter through the first floor came up empty of people, and after taking a last peek into the conservatory at the back of the castle, Rook began the long hike to the kitchen "Seriously. I thought he'd died yeas ago while I was in Seattle or I'd have tried to reach out to him. He taught Hawkins a lot of tricks… and those were kind of passed down to me when… you know… so it kind of felt like Bluthenthal was… my grandfather. Sort of. He died… shit… a year ago? I'd gotten wind of it and tracked the estate, mostly to see if there was something I could remember him by. The parody falcon seemed… ironic. Fitting, even."

"Let's get back to Travis. So you knew he was a thief, and that's why you bought the statue?" A horn honked near Dante, and he let a profanity slip, his low muttered Spanish outburst a sharp cut about a driver's intelligence. "Did you know or think at any time he might have stashed something inside of it?"

There was a little bit of a threat in Dante's words, or perhaps Rook was simply imagining the ominous tone. It didn't help that he was standing in front of the library with his grandfather's narcissistic lord-of-the-manor oil painting staring down at him through the open french doors or that, when he turned around to ignore Archie, the cabinet of tchotchkes across the hall was dominated by teary-eyed porcelain dolls dressed in elaborate Russian costumes, their sightless gazes plaintively judging Rook's existence.

"Babe, what kind of idiot would hide his stash in a movie prop? It's the first place the cops would look, don't you think?" He winced, crossing his fingers in front of him. "Wait, those things are resin. How the hell did you guys get it open? Or was it a plaster like the one they found at Harold's?"

"We're going on the assumption the one at Harold's was a decoy meant for you, something someone at the auction house cooked up so they could swap it with—what was his name?—Bluthenthal's original. I'd have put money on the goods being in the plaster statue, but it makes more sense it would be in the resin. That would be harder to break. This one was cut open. That's the only way we knew what it was holding." Dante's voice went soft. "You never answered me, *cuervo*. Did you know Bluthenthal had those diamonds stashed in there? Is that why you wanted that statue?"

Honesty was a funny thing. People around Rook demanded it of him constantly, and while he'd spent a good portion of his life dodging the law and stealing, he'd always been mostly honest. With Dante in the picture, the *mostly* was tested time and time again, especially when he'd tried to dodge telling a lie. This time there was no dodging, not with Dante pressing in on him.

"I knew he had stuff stashed somewhere. Or at least figured he did. We all do. At least if you're smart you do. For that day… when everything goes to shit and you need… *out*," he admitted softly, swallowing at the deep thumps of his heart when its beats thundered through his throat and chest. "But in the falcon? I really did get it because I wanted… I don't know… a piece of this guy I had a connection with. Even if he didn't know me."

More silence and the street noise stopped. It was unsettling, nipping at Rook's nerves, tearing snippets off to feed his fears. He heard the distinct click of a door closing and another sigh, followed by a stretch of silence so heavy Rook couldn't ignore its pressing down on him.

Then Dante spoke.

"The stolen gems returned to Central. That was you, wasn't it?" Rook didn't answer. He didn't need to. The truth hung between them, a guillotine sharpened by Rook's mistruths and whose blade was poised to fall, slicing them apart. "Where were they?"

"In the warehouse." The truth seemed to be difficult to put back in once it came out, bubbling out of Rook, a malevolent genie he'd shoved into a rusty lamp the moment he pocketed his first haul. "There's an Ark of the Covenant prop at the warehouse. It's got a false bottom, probably to stash explosives or something, but they never used it. The ark's where I stashed my stuff. *That* stuff."

God, he hated the silences. The dread of them. How they held his life in the nothingness, and Rook stumbled toward the wide staircase a few feet away, blindly finding one of the steps to sit on. There was nothing on the line, not even breathing, and he didn't know the damned rules… the magical words to fix what he might have fucked up in the past. There was no damned manual to work the lock of a relationship, no tricks of the trade to coax something along so he could breathe easier.

"I think you and I need to talk. Face-to-face," Dante finally said. "Are you at Archie's?"

"Yeah." Rook held his tongue, biting back the edged words his brain flung to protect him. His stomach roiled, acid burning his throat, and he swallowed, tasting ashes and bitterness. "You told me to stay put, remember?"

"Like you ever listen to me," he rumbled. "I'll be there as soon as I can, okay? Don't go anywhere."

"Nope," Rook choked out. "Staying right here."

"Good," his maybe-not lover replied. "And *cuervo*...."

It was harder to speak, especially when his mind was racing with all he'd have to do to abandon his life. "Yeah?"

"I love you," Dante murmured. "We just need to... let me clear something with Camden and I'll be right up. We're at one of Natterly's warehouses. It won't take me long. It's right off of Larabee. But remember, I love you."

"I love you too," Rook whispered back, rubbing his hand through his tangle of hair. "I just...."

"Fifteen minutes, babe. I'll see you then." This time the silence was finite, a click and the call was over, leaving Rook stewing in his own worry.

"*Fuck!*" The urge to throw his phone into a wall was strong, overpowering Rook's common sense. Gripping the device, his knuckles were white by the time reason returned. Taking a deep breath, he scrubbed at his eyes with the back of his hand, not surprised to find them wet. "Didn't used to cry before I met that damned cop. Jesus, this was so fucking easy before."

It was also incredibly lonely, his brain whispered, ignoring the pangs from Rook's torn emotions. *You want to die alone like Hawkins?*

Fifteen minutes seemed a long time to wait just so his heart could be broken, and Rook didn't know if he'd be relieved when he heard Dante's car pull up or if he'd empty his stomach out into the nearest trash bag and do the one thing he'd promised himself he'd never do... apologize for who he'd been and beg for forgiveness.

"Okay, grab your own balls and pull up, Stevens," he muttered at himself. "Get some coffee made and... you can do this. He fucking loves you. He keeps telling you that. You love him. Shit... he knows who you are. Who you were. Stop fucking sabotaging yourself. It's not like Montoya's coming to kill you."

"No, Montoya might not," agreed a cold voice coming from Rook's left.

He stood, alarmed at the pale, taut-faced woman standing by the front door. Margaret was dressed all in black: a pair of yoga pants, long-sleeved pullover, and ballet flats, but the wicked, heavy gun she pointed at him brought him to his feet. Her eyes were flinty, hard and boring into him, and she calmly strolled forward, the weapon steady in her hand as she moved noiselessly across the hall's marble floor. Smiling didn't soften her features, and they turned ugly, her expression soured by the caricature of a grin she'd plastered on her face and the purpling bruise swelling along her right jaw.

Cocking her head, Margaret remarked with a hint of mocking amusement, "But I certainly intend to. In fact, I've been wanting to kill you since the moment you first walked through that damned front door and into Archie's life."

ROOK STARED Margaret down, looking past the black steel piece she held in her hand and straight into her narrowed eyes. He took a step forward, bringing his feet off of the staircase when footsteps echoed from down the hall, short clipped ticks of hard heels on expensive marble. The man emerging from the shadows should have swaggered down the hall, especially since Margaret was the one holding the gun. Instead he partially slunk out, checking the various nooks along the way.

His dishwater blond-brown hair was neatly combed in a style Rook personally thought belonged in Mayberry, not Hollywood, and it did little to cover the growing bald spot at the back of Davis's head. His soft hands trembled when he reached behind a few of the larger vase clusters Archie insisted on cluttering the main hall with. If the study and inner halls were a treasure trove of odds and ends, the front foyer boasted the grander pieces of Archie's collecting obsession. Davis spared Rook a glance; then his pale blue eyes flicked over to Margaret, his enigmatic face shifting to something warmer for a brief moment, but Rook couldn't tell if it was anger or lust.

"I'll be damned. Davis," Rook spat at the man. "What the hell are you doing? Shit, what are both of you doing?"

"Where's the statue, Rook?" Margaret stepped in closer, her nostrils flaring, widening her pinched expression.

"There's statues all over this damned house," he snapped at her, inching a bit away from the gun.

The best mask for a lie was anger. Most people went with outrage or even incredulity, but Rook always preferred to use a bit of prissiness with a dash of snark. Subterfuge was a delicate thing and, much like a curry, required a gentle hand with an array of emotional spices. Too much rage and the lie was too hot to swallow. But from the look on Margaret's face, she wasn't buying anything Rook served up.

Or so he guessed, because she pulled the trigger and fired her gun, aiming straight at Rook.

Mostly.

The bullet went a little wide, shattering the lip of a stair behind him, sending bits of marble and rug flying. Ricocheted pieces hit Rook on the arm, and he was turning to protect his face when Margaret struck him in the ribs with the butt end of the gun. Either the sex he'd had with Dante tore Rook up, or his side hadn't healed up as much as he thought, because the pain across his side struck him like hot copper being poured into his eyes. His teeth ached from the blow, and Rook went down on one knee, the spot enflamed with a throbbing agony.

Saliva flecked over his lips, and Rook tried to swallow, but his tongue got in the way. His throat was parched, withering around the sick threatening to come up from his empty stomach. Everything now hurt, from his knee where he landed to the spot on his hip he'd smacked against the stairs' heavy end post when he fell.

"Jesus fucking Christ, woman! Are you out of your goddamned mind?" he gasped, bending over and panting to breathe through the pain. "What the hell is *wrong* with you?"

"What's wrong with me?" Margaret leaned over, and Rook pulled his head back, recoiling from the tequila-scented waves of her breath washing over his face. She smelled drunk, hammered beyond belief, but she held herself without wavering, the gun resting in her hand once again. Shoving the weapon into Rook's neck, she dug the hot sight as far as she could, searing his skin. "My son's dead. *My Harold.* And for what? No, the idiot had to go fuck some stranger he met at his party, and that stupid boyfriend of his caught them—"

"It wasn't Jeremy's fault." Davis spoke up, pulling his head out of a tall packed-tight china cabinet. "He said it was an accident."

"Wait, Jeremy killed Harold?" Rook rubbed at his side, not liking the damp beneath his fingertips. The area was tender, and the bandage he'd put on earlier wasn't as tight as he'd have liked. "And they were... really?

Jeremy and Harold? I mean sure, he was your kid, but you've got to admit, Harold was punching way above his weight with Jeremy."

"What does that even mean? Punching above his weight?" Margaret stepped out of Rook's reach, the sting of the recently fired gun fading on his skin.

"It means he thinks Jeremy could have done better than Harold." Davis sneered at Rook, but his heart didn't seem into it. "Jeremy could have done better, but Harold was... good for him. Motivated him. Cheating on him was... wrong. He shouldn't have done that to Jeremy."

Something in the way Davis muttered those last words tickled Rook's suspicions. There was something missing in the narrative, a disconnect of personalities and motivations. The Jeremy he knew would have drifted off, possibly screamed at Harold, but picking up something to stab a man didn't seem like the scatterbrained young man's style.

"You think Jeremy was too good for Harold? He was *lucky* Harold even looked at him. That boy's like talking to a rock. He's the reason we're in this mess, Davis." She turned, gesturing wildly with the gun. "If he'd only sent the right damned statue, we wouldn't be scrambling to fix his crappy mistakes and I wouldn't be trying to get this damned asshole to tell me where the resin bird is. Someone took the statue Jeremy brought over, and if it wasn't Rook, then Jeremy had to have taken it when he left."

"Let's get back to the statue thing later. First, there's no way in hell Jeremy killed Harold," Rook muttered, unfolding himself so he could lean against the post. It dug into his back, and he needed to shift to take the pressure off of his side, but Margaret seemed less interested in shooting him and more into complaining about Jeremy. "He was stabbed what? A gajillion times? That's someone with a fuck ton of rage and focus. Jeremy can barely decide on what kind of tea to have every day, and he's going to lose his shit and reverse-porcupine Harold?"

"Shut up, Rook," Davis growled. "You weren't there—"

"Oh, I can believe it was Jeremy I saw at the house that day. He'd want to make up for whatever crap happened by delivering the resin statue, but actually stabbing Harold?" Rook shook his head. "Doesn't have the balls. Or the strength. The only reason he took me down is because he got in a lucky punch."

He had Margaret's attention, and oddly enough, Davis seemed to stiffen to the point of breaking. Rook nodded toward the man and began to lay down the first foundation of doubts for Margaret to build on. She was on the edge, riding it hard until she bled on its sharpness. It wouldn't take much to tip her over, and Rook knew he'd only have one chance to persuade her.

Especially since she was the one holding the gun.

"Here's what I think happened," he started. When beginning a grift, it was important to be soft and gentle, a soothing, conciliatory voice in the chaos of the mark's life. She pivoted, her shoulders angled between him and Davis, a telling sign of her indecision. He only had to get her to turn the rest of the way. "Did Harold cheat? Yeah, probably, because he made bad life choices. He married Sadonna, hooked up with Jeremy, and stole my bird. He had a hard time holding on to the good things in his life. Jeremy showed up at the party with the statue—the one he thought was real because he didn't know any better—and he found Harold with… well, it doesn't matter who. They fought and Jeremy left.

"He didn't kill Harold. They probably fought, but Harold was alive when Jeremy left." Rook paused, gently laying the hook out for Margaret to snag herself on. "*If* he'd stabbed Harold to death in a fit of jealousy, he also would have killed whoever Harold was with and taken the bird back. But if that was Jeremy who hit me, he didn't have anything with him. Only reason he'd take it back would be because he knew what was inside. That's not something you'd have told Jeremy."

"He didn't know because I didn't want him to go to jail if we got caught. Jeremy's not *stupid*. It was just better if he was kept out of it," Davis snapped. "Why are we standing around listening to this? Have him tell us where the damned statue is! You're the one with the gun!"

"Margaret, sure you hate my guts, but let's face it, I've never lied to any of you. I've been flat-out since the beginning. If I knew where that statue was, I'd tell you. What do I care about it?" Rook leaned forward, hoping to create a sense of intimacy with his aunt but also to ease away the growing knotting pain across his ribs. "The bird had to be shown as delivered to the estate. Natterly's needed to show it getting to the auction winner, and Davis couldn't risk either the fake or the real bird getting to me, so you guys had it go to Harold instead."

"This isn't getting us anywhere," Davis spat.

"Oh, give me some time. Here's what happened, or at least what I think happened, so see if this makes sense," he reasoned. "Jeremy sent the wrong statue, the one you guys were going to give me—hopefully after you added some weight to it. The plaster bird went to Harold's house, and after either Davis or Jeremy realized they'd fucked up, Jeremy decided he'd drop the real bird at Harold's. Because that was what he was supposed to do. Small steps. Focused task. Jeremy needs that."

"He does," Margaret agreed, a bit of a slur on the end of her words. "Harold liked that about him. He liked explaining things to Jeremy, leading him."

"Unfortunately, Jeremy found... a situation there, tossed the box with the bird into the room, and left," Rook continued. "And then he went straight to the one person who fixes everything for him, his brother, Davis."

"Shut the fuck up, Stevens, or I'm going to bash your head in," Davis growled, then snatched up a hefty silver candlestick from the cabinet. He took a few steps toward Rook, but Margaret brought her gun up, finally turning her shoulders to face her partner in crime. "Come on, Margaret. You can't believe this crap."

"Gets kind of tetchy, doesn't he? Especially about Jeremy. Hell, look how he is right now." Rook edged back from Margaret, taking himself out of her line of sight. "Nah, it wasn't Jeremy who stabbed Harold. It was Davis, because Harold fucked up things with his baby brother. But he probably didn't know about Jeremy bringing the resin statue until it was too late and Jeremy told him he'd gone back to get it. And then of course, that he'd seen me there.

"What I don't get is what does Sadonna have to do with this?" He caught himself before a cough rattled through his chest, staving off a painful retch.

Pressing his hand down on his side, Rook panicked at the wetness under his fingers and how far it'd spread through his shirt. He didn't know how much Margaret heard of his conversation with Dante, but he was gambling she'd missed the part where they'd found the statue, especially since she insisted he knew where it was in Archie's house.

"She knew the bird had diamonds in it," Margaret said softly, but her attention never wavered from Davis. "Bluthenthal was her agent in the beginning, and the old man used to get drunk all the time, talking about what he'd done in the past and how he'd set himself up a few nest eggs here and there. One of them was the falcon. It's how we knew about the diamonds, because she'd convinced Harold to bid on the statue. They— Davis, Sadonna, and Harold—were going to split the money from the diamonds, but she double-crossed us by sending you to get it."

A part of him should have been hurt about Sadonna's backstab, but he didn't have proof of anything other than her keeping the diamonds a secret.

For all he knew, she'd have split it with him fifty-fifty once he brought it out. Margaret and Davis were the immediate problem, especially since talking about Sadonna was leading his aunt away from the problem at hand. He needed to push her back, a subtle, gentle shove toward the truth.

"It's too bad I have no fucking clue where it is. I wouldn't be here if I had that much of a stash. I wouldn't need to be hanging around Archie, licking up his scraps," he lied. "But if Sadonna brought it here, someone would have seen it. You can't miss that ugly thing. In fact, the only person who had their hands on the real one was Davis. He probably told Jeremy to get a delivery notice for Harold's place, and Harold was going to take the hit by saying he'd arranged the statue to go to him. It would take fucking forever for the courts to hear about it, and by then, you all would have been long gone.

"So where the hell is the statue? Davis has it. Davis, who went to Harold's house that night after Jeremy told him about what he'd seen there and stabbed Harold to death for cheating on his brother. Then he plays dumb, but he's stashed the bird someplace safe, and now he's just waiting for you to get caught so he can walk away with the diamonds and with Harold's blood on his hands," Rook finished, hoping his lies were strong enough to persuade Margaret to take a second look at her partner. "Vicks died because he walked in on Davis killing Jennifer Martinez, who had to die because she might have seen him at the house. Davis needs to get rid of everyone who knew he was connected to Harold. Including you, Margaret."

If anger rode Margaret hard before, it'd unleashed a Wild Hunt on her now. Furious, she brought her arms up, falling into a stance, and aimed her gun at Davis. Alarmed, he flung the candlestick he'd been holding at Margaret's head, but it went wide, going end over end until it smashed into a wall behind her. The crash was horrendous, the impact rattling a set of frames hanging above the wainscoting, and they tumbled from their perches, their glass shattering when they hit the marble. Rook lurched to the side, huddled around his leaking wound, but he reached out, hoping to grab at Margaret's arm, but she was too quick for him, stepping aside with a reptilian grin plastered on her face once again.

Then she pulled the trigger and fired.

THE SOUND of a gunshot coming from the house terrified Dante. Pulling his weapon, he went in hot, ready to kick open the front door, but the latch turned and he was in with a shove of his shoulder, slamming the heavy wood against the wall.

There was blood, a tiny trail of red smeared across the marble floor, and Rook lay on his side, tucked in against the heavily carved newel post. Dante's heart stopped beating, frozen in a clench of icy fear, but his emotions were wild, scorching hot and liquid. He had to shut them down, but they roiled, spilling over his reason. Dante couldn't look at Rook. Not if he wanted to keep his head and neutralize the situation, but his gaze couldn't seem to stop drifting from the other two people in the foyer.

The foyer looked like a small bomb had gone off in it. There was an ugly blocky candlestick lying on the floor near the library's open doors, and a small grouping of pictures were now on the floor, a sea of broken glass spread over the marble tiles. One of the stairs was missing a good portion of its lip, a thick crack running its breadth. Then Dante saw Rook's face break out into a smile, one warm enough to chase away the chill in Dante's tightened guts.

"*Cuervo?*" Rook was moving, shuffling along the wall in a muted, painful half crawl, but Dante needed to hear his lover's husky, golden voice. "You alright?"

"Yep. Probably popped some stitches," Rook grunted, and his laugh was rough. "Good to see you, babe."

"Good to see you too." He stepped farther into the foyer, trying to make sense of what he saw. "Margaret, it's good to see you too. We were worried about you."

Dante locked in on the gun the woman held, sparing a momentary glance at the man trembling against a shot-up cabinet. His arm was bleeding and seemed to be missing a fairly large chunk of meat near his shoulder joint, but the hutch and its knickknacks took the brunt of whatever Margaret was packing. The cabinet's side was blown through, and its broken contents were lightly splattered with blood. He knew Harold's brittle mother immediately, but it took a few seconds for him to recognize the injured man as Davis Natterly.

"Ma'am?" Dante kept his gun trained on Margaret. Where there was one Natterly brother, he had to assume the second was lurking about, but he had to make sure. "You doing okay, Mrs. Martin? Is there anyone else in the house besides you and Davis? Can—"

"He killed my son," Margaret accused, motioning with the gun at the cabinet and Davis. "Archie's blasted pet grandson figured it out. God, I am so damned blind. He killed Harold and tried to blame it on… his own brother. His stupid brick of a brother."

"Rook is lying, Margaret. You *know* you can't believe a word that comes out of his mouth. For fuck's sake, the only reason he's sleeping with the damned cop is so he wouldn't go to jail." Davis snarled at Dante, his chin tilted up, defiant despite the pain etched onto his face. His shoulder bled, darkening his clothes, and he turned to protect it, then lashed out again. "You don't actually think Archibald Martin's grandson would sleep with some border-trash cop? Don't you remember what you told me about Beatrice? How she'd whore her way through her teachers just to get a good grade? What makes you think Rook's any different? He's only saying these things—"

"You can shut the fuck up, Davis," Rook snarled from behind Margaret. He straightened, then took a hesitant step toward the other man. There was a fury in his mismatched eyes, and the curl of his lip was pure Archie, disdainful and withering. He was wobbling, and his T-shirt was scarily soaked through and dark where his hand clutched at it, but Rook was nearly to Margaret's shoulder before he stopped. "You can say anything you want about me, but Dante? I'll fucking punch your face in."

"Not helping, babe. Rook, step back. I need you to *not* be in front of me," Dante muttered, then shifted his focus to the angry woman. Rook moved, cradling his side, with an uneven limp. He was slow, achingly painful to watch, but once Rook got out of the way, Dante moved in closer, keeping his aim firm. "Margaret, let me take care of this. I'm going to need you to put the gun down, but I'll deal with Davis. But you have to drop your weapon or things will go very wrong very fast."

"Why should I?" Her breath was volcanic, steeped in alcohol fumes, and Dante had to blink to clear his eyes. "This was supposed to be simple. Harold was supposed to win the damned auction, but no, your boyfriend there just had to have that stupid bird. Like he has to have everything. He could have just let Harold have it. Just have one *damned* thing."

"Rook *had* to get a delivery. The bird was a gamble, *remember*? If it's empty, I lose my license for not delivering the damned thing and have nothing to show for it. Did you forget that, you stupid bitch?" Davis barked back. "You and your stupid son weren't worth me losing everything I built up. Not after the mess my parents left us in. We don't even know how much the diamonds are worth, if they're even there."

There were times when being a homicide cop was hard. He'd gone on one too many death notices, held too many hands shaking from shock, and offered up millions of tissues to dry tears he knew would never stop falling. The grief, horror, and anger in Margaret's face and stance were as familiar to Dante as Rook's kiss. Her world began crumbling the moment someone—possibly Davis Natterly—drove something sharp into her son's body, and it would continue to fall apart every moment she lived, a vast, echoing void she couldn't ever fill again.

Today was going to be a hard day. Maybe even catastrophic. Hard couldn't even begin to explain the torture Margaret would be going through for as long as her memory held. For all her faults and the constant sniping digs at Rook, she loved her son, and now all she had left of him were the shadows living in her mind.

Killing Davis wouldn't stop the ache. Dante knew that, but Margaret wouldn't have cared, even if she heard *anything* he had to tell her. So when she raised her gun again, bringing it up and poised to plant a hole in the middle of Davis's face, he knew he was going to have to shoot her, if only to stop her from ruining what little soul she had left in her.

Or at least he would have if Rook hadn't tackled Margaret from behind.

His boyfriend hit her hard, around the knees, and they both went flying, the momentum of Rook's tackle pushing them into a glide across the foyer's slick floor. The weapon discharged, clipping the chandelier, and a rain of crystals pelted the hall. Dante went in as Davis attacked, rushing Margaret and Rook with the twin to the candlestick lying on the foyer floor held up over his head. Rook continued to skid over the marble, frantically trying to grab at the loose gun, when Margaret punched his side, a weak blow softened by her out-of-control slide. She came to a jerking halt when her foot caught on a table, toppling it down on top of her, and she rolled over, resting at Davis's feet.

Staggering forward, Davis brought the weighty piece around, smashing Margaret in her temple as she was getting to her knees. She reeled, her eyes rolling, and she fell, landing on her hands. Blood dripped from a cut across her forehead, and she moaned, swaying back and forth.

"Davis! Drop it!" Dante swore when the man ignored him, bringing the blocky silver piece back around again. "Don't make me shoot."

He had no choice. Davis was in too close, and he'd chosen his weapon well. The single hit across Margaret's skull left her senseless, and Rook was on the floor, gasping for breath, his face screwed up in pain. A few feet away, Margaret's gun was within Davis's reach, and when the man's eyes lit up, Dante knew he'd spotted the weapon.

Davis was going to take the gamble. Dante saw it the moment before Davis tightened up his muscles and made a decision Dante knew he was going to regret. Tracking Davis's leap for the gun, Dante gritted his teeth and shot the man who'd come to take Rook away from him.

Epilogue

IT WAS a party of sorts. A tossed-together potluck, washtubs filled with ice and beer, and too many people in the house and backyard to move around without elbowing someone else kind of party Dante's house was used to having. Soft music was playing, something mournful and Mexican, but it was hard to hear through the chatter. It was a party mostly to celebrate still being alive, and at some point in the night, someone would break a glass or throw up in the bushes, but Dante expected all of that. In a crowd of drag queens, cops, and sundry other crazy people, including his partner, Hank, and his wife, Dante felt oddly normal.

"Where's Rook?" Manny shouted at him over the grill on the back courtyard. "I thought he'd be with you."

His uncle's stocky chest was covered with a ruffled white apron he'd given Dante a few years back as a joke but had taken to wearing when cooking outside. Bleach hadn't done the garment any favors, leaving behind sauce and marinade stains until the apron looked like it'd been used to clean up a crime scene. The carne asada Manny was flipping over smelled damned good, but despite the two days of no sleep, paperwork, and sour coffee, Dante wasn't hungry.

"I don't know," he answered loudly. "I was hoping he was out here. I needed to take a call from Book, but when I came back, he was gone."

He hadn't seen much of his lover, and there were words between them, emotions and arguments left on the broken floor in Archie's house Dante still needed to clean up. Tonight was the time to blow off steam and maybe mend a few things he'd shattered. He'd just had enough time to kiss Rook hello when the captain called and he ducked into the downstairs office to take it. When he'd emerged, the living room was full of everyone but the one man he'd wanted to see.

Wandering through the house, Dante shook hands and clapped shoulders, stopping only long enough to say hello. Hank grabbed his arm before he could get past the living room couch and pulled him toward the hall. It was quieter than the living room, but not by much, but he didn't need to hear clearly to see Hank was concerned.

"Book texted me about your desk duty. Said he'd talked to you." Hank pushed in close, ducking his head down to keep their conversation between them. "You're riding with me on Monday, then? 'Cause I love you, man, but tomorrow's our normal day off, and I've got dad things lined up, so as much as I'd like to share a car with you, I'm busy."

"I think Monday's fine." He pushed at Hank's shoulder. "And yeah, Book said IA cleared me. Went quicker than I thought it would."

"Dude, it was a righteous shoot," his partner pressed. "I saw that thing. I'm surprised he didn't kill her the first time. As it is, she's rattled in the brain. He broke her skull and was going to round two. She wouldn't have survived it."

"Yeah, they called it." Dante shook his head, Book's reassuring words leaving him more unsettled than he'd care to admit. "Doesn't feel like one. I took a man's life, Camden. I swore to protect and serve—"

"I'd have done the same thing, Montoya. You know it. You know in your gut that you did the right thing. Now Margaret's getting the help she needs, and Sadonna doesn't have to worry about Davis slitting her throat. He killed—*what?*—three people, man, and was aiming to kill a fourth, fifth, and maybe a sixth." Camden clasped Dante's shoulder, shaking him lightly. "Sadonna's alive. Charges… well, we'll see what the DA says, and Rook's all stitched up again. Life is good. We just need to get the brother boxed in."

"DA's letting Jeremy go. Book just told me," Dante said, and Hank scoffed loudly. "No evidence against him. He'd come by that night to drop off the *plaster* statue, because he thought *that* was the one Harold wanted. Sadonna intercepted the resin bird and put this whole damned thing into motion. She had the falcon with the diamonds in it all along and played Rook so she could screw over Harold and everyone else. If Rook'd taken the fake, the Natterlys would have been clear, but they'd all have been out the diamonds without anyone knowing Sadonna stashed them, but no one would have died."

"*Maybe.* I think this all wouldn't have happened if Archie didn't play his family against one another. Perhaps not all of it, but you've got to admit, as much as I like the old man, he's rough on that inbred clan of his," Camden remarked. "When we were up at the house yesterday getting statements, I heard the old man talking to Alex and James. Apparently he's seen the light and is going to loosen up some of the family purse strings. You want to know what I think?"

"I have a feeling you're going to tell me no matter what," he teased.

"Well, that too. But maybe they all need to learn to stand on their own two feet. Sure, Rook used to steal for a living, but he got his shit together, and Alex lives pretty well, not above his means except for that rocket he drives around in." Hank shook his head. "That family's not fucked-up because they're rich. They're screwed-up because they think they *deserve* to be rich. There's a difference."

"Can't say I disagree with you, but I've got the Martin who squirrels stuff away for a rainy day." Dante shook his head. "It's like living with those two gophers from the cartoon. There's shit stashed everywhere. Speaking of Rook, I've got to go find him. What with everything going on, we haven't really seen each other."

"Ah, saw him go out the front door." Hank peered over Dante's shoulder and nodded. "Okay, wife's calling me. Must be time to eat. I'm going to pile a plate up with food so she can pretend she's not hungry and pick at my dinner."

"Why doesn't she make her own plate?" He frowned at his partner. "Manny bought hundreds of the damned things. Forks too."

"Because it's a thing she does, and well, if there's one thing you should learn about being in love, Montoya—" Hank pulled him in for a fierce hug, squeezing the air out of Dante's chest, then patting his shoulders when he let go. "—you don't mind all of the stupid shit they do, because they're yours. The wife likes to eat her way through my dinner, and well, your boyfriend likes to stumble upon murder investigations and get shot. Between me and you, I'll take the plate thing any day of the week. Go find your guy. I'm going to go feed myself and the wife."

Dante found Rook straddling a broad bench on the side of the house, his long legs stretched out with his sneaker heels digging into the gravel. He was on the phone and, from his side of the conversation, talking to Archie. His back was to the front of the house, so Dante made sure he was making enough noise for Rook to hear him coming down the walk. Rook glanced back at the sound, spotting Dante, and the light played over his widened odd eyes, catching the silver and gold flecks in them. From the tumble of ruddy brown and caramel hair swept across his forehead, Dante guessed Rook'd been raking his hand through the strands, probably to ease the frustration of reasoning with Archie.

He came around the bench and swung his leg over it to sit down facing Rook, careful not to hit the other man's knees. Rook pulled his legs up to give Dante room, listening to the stream of brash noise coming from the phone's speaker, and smiled when Dante put his hands on Rook's thighs.

It was that smile—that sweet, secret, only-for-him smile—that brought Dante to his knees.

The first time he'd seen that particular smile was when the lights suddenly came on in the club he'd gone to find someone to hook up with, anything to get his mind off of the lean, sexy thief he'd been chasing for nearly a year. He'd found someone in the shadows, drawn to something about the way he moved, and when the dark peeled back and Dante found himself face-to-face with the man he'd gone there to forget, he'd laughed hard enough to bring tears to his eyes, and Rook simply smiled.

That smile.

He'd fallen halfway in love with the one man he never should have looked at right then and there. It'd taken a couple of murders, a lot of craziness, and some unorthodox seductions for him to tumble the rest of the way, but he'd gotten there.

It would be hours before the sun fully set, but the city was already pulling on its evening colors, coating the buildings with a muted blue wash, and the subdued light softened Rook's sharp features, blurring the innate wariness in his expression. Someone—probably Manny—turned on the outside lights, firing up the faerie lights they'd spent a long afternoon stringing through the tall hedges lining the side and back of the property. Their glowing sparkle played over Rook, warming his skin to a golden ivory, and Dante chuckled when Rook rolled his eyes at him.

"Archie, I'm fine," Rook said into the phone. "No, Montoya's here. Where the hell else would he be? This is his house. I'm going to hang up now. Nope, probably won't be coming back up there tonight." A pause and then Rook sighed. "No, I don't know where I'll be sleeping. We'll figure it out. Hey, listen, okay? I love you, old man. Don't forget that shit. I'll be up there tomorrow sometime. We can watch a movie and drive Rosa nuts. I'll bring Alex." He waited a second, then grinned. "Yeah, see if some of the others want in on that. Give me a time and I'll be there. With bells on."

Dante leaned in for a kiss, not surprised to find Rook meeting him halfway. It was gentle, a brush of lips and a slip of Rook's tongue. Then his lover pulled back, breaking them apart. Rook tasted of something sweet and fruity, probably a piece of sticky candy, since he seemed fueled by sugar, coffee, and popcorn. He smelled like *heaven*, a hint almost citrus, sundried cotton cologne, and the spicy richness of his own skin.

Inhaling deeply, Dante held his breath, then opened up the can of worms he'd been carrying since the moment he called Rook a few days ago. Clearing his throat, he said softly, "*Cuervo*, I think it's time you and I have that talk."

"OKAY." ROOK exhaled the breath he'd been holding in since Dante shot Natterly and Margaret fell apart. Its sour stench whispered out from his soul, a smoky dread he'd been carrying in him. Squaring his shoulders, then wincing when his side reminded him it was recently punched through with stitches again, he braced himself for what Dante had to say. "Let's talk."

He'd been avoiding Dante. Rook was man enough to admit that, but not quite adult enough to face things head-on. He knew that about himself. There was no denying he'd spent a lifetime hop-skip-and-jumping ahead of the law and relationships. Buckling himself down to one spot meant getting into the ugly of people's lives, and he'd thought he was ready for it.

Facing Dante across the bench—his heart aching and pounding with a low-grade fear—Rook finally understood he not only wasn't ready for it, he also had no idea what he was doing falling in love.

Taking a preemptive strike, he murmured, "I told you guys, I really didn't know about the falcon—"

"I know, *cuervo*. I believe you." Dante inched closer, taking Rook's hands in his. "At the time, I wasn't sure what to think, but now, after all of this... after I processed what you said to me, what you'd done before, and how hard that was for you, I wanted to tell you...." His lover inhaled sharply. "This is between you and me. No cops. No lawyers. Nothing but us talking, okay? And I want you to be honest with me. I will listen to you and not judge. I promise you that."

"Yeah, sure," Rook agreed, scrambling through his memories to see if he was still on the hook for anything he should avoid. He came up with nothing. He'd been so careful, watched his steps so he could one day live a life without looking over his shoulder. The diamonds had been the last of his old life. The one tie he'd been reluctant to break but one he'd severed for the man who now held his hands, called him crow, and kissed him under a bower of sparkling lights. "What are you not judging me on?"

"The diamonds you turned in…." Dante made a small hissing sound when Rook instinctively began to deny his involvement. "Babe, we're past that. Right?"

"Habit," he confessed. "Hey, I stopped. Okay. The diamonds. That was it. Those were my… safety net. In case this all fell apart. And by all, I mean the shop, Archie, and everything. I had them stashed before I met you, and then, well, afterwards…." This time the breath he held was sharp, a cold, cutting slice of air he'd regret taking in if he didn't release it a moment later. "I knew I had to let it go. In order to have you… to love you… I couldn't… hold on to that part of my life, even if it meant I'd lose what I saved to fall back on. Because if I held on to it, I wouldn't be able to go forward… with you."

"There were millions of dollars in gems in that bag."

"Oh, you don't need to tell me how much fucking money was in there," Rook snorted. "I know *exactly* how much that bag was worth." Stroking at Dante's hands, he said in a low voice, "I was taking a gamble that you'd… I was betting that you were worth it. That you'd be the one who was worth all of that and… I didn't want to fall in love with a cop. Fucking hell, that's the last thing in the world I'd ever imagined doing, but one morning I woke up next to you, and those diamonds—all of that—they became just *rocks*. They were an anchor I'd tied around my neck, Montoya, and if I didn't cut myself loose from them, they'd drag me down and kill me… kill us."

"*Nothing* is ever going to kill us, Rook." Dante's arms wrapped him up, dragging him into an awkward embrace. "I promise. *Nothing*."

Their legs were tangled, and the twist of his side against Dante's torso flared a warning twinge, but Rook adjusted, working himself free until he was straddling Dante's lap, facing the back of the house. Settling his hands on Rook's hips, Dante sought his mouth, drawing him into a long, simmering kiss. It was enough to sit under the fake stars caught in a stand of mock orange bushes and drink from Dante's mouth. His lips felt bruised, a bit swollen and tender when they finally came up for air, but Rook stole another quick kiss before settling back on Dante's crossed legs.

"I love you, *cuervo*," Dante whispered.

"I know," he teased, then yelped when Dante slid a hand down the back of his jeans and lightly pinched his ass. "Sheesh. Dude. Watch the meat. I love you too. I just… fuck up, babe. It's what I do."

"We've got to work some things out. I hate to ask you this, babe, but… I've got to know if there's anything else you're holding on to. Anything…."

Dante stopped himself, and his face shut down, going cop and hard. Rook's belly twisted, and as much as he hated reacting to the sternness in Dante's expression, he went a little cold along his spine. The authoritarian mask Dante pulled on lasted only long enough for Rook to gather up his thoughts. Then Dante's hands roamed up over Rook's back, soothing away the tenseness in his muscles. "Okay, see, here is where the problem is. It's not you. It is me—"

"Don't like where this conversation's starting off, dude," Rook interjected sourly. "Just saying."

"No, no. That's not what I mean." Dante shot Rook an off-kilter smile. "See, it's always me demanding things from you. I'm asking you if there's anything else you have stashed away. Anything illegal. Or I'm telling you to stay put or do this. I ask you to trust me, but I'm always poking at you, not trusting you when you tell me you've gone straight or at least pushing at you until I'm certain you're telling the truth."

"I broke into houses and cleaned people out, Montoya." He layered on as much sarcasm as he could, but still it didn't seem enough to get his point across. "And I was never caught. Not exactly the model citizen you'd hoped to bring home to Manny."

"That's where you're wrong. Or right. I don't know, *cuervo*." He leaned back a little, obviously studying Rook. "I knew who you were when we started this. I knew that bag was from you. I didn't need you to tell me that. The statutes ran out on all of it, and there I was, picking at you to make sure you had nothing else. I can't keep asking you to live by my rules and me not giving you some slack to live by yours."

"Once again, *cat burglar*." Rook tapped his own chest, then ran a hand over Dante's collarbone. "You're a cop. You've got a shit ton of rules, and I've got... well, none. Your life... your rules... make things a bit sticky, but hey, like you said, I knew what I was getting into. Here and now, I am totally clean. Now, since the falcon was mine fair and square, if you guys want to hand over the shit that was inside of it, I wouldn't say no. Because, babe, as much as I love you, handing all of that over the first time hurt as much as it felt good doing it."

"You're always going to be a thief." Dante chuckled.

"Yeah, it's kind of like an addiction." He shrugged, tangling his fingers into the hair along Dante's nape. "Or maybe it's just who I am. I don't know. But I've got other things to keep me occupied now. The store. Archie. *You*."

"I'm looking forward to keeping you occupied." Dante's voice went low, husky with a hint of lust. "As soon as that side of yours heals. You shouldn't have tackled Margaret—"

"Dante?" A woman's voice sounded out from behind Rook, and whoever it was made Dante stiffen. "Is that you?"

The sun was nearly gone, leaving shadows behind to swallow up the side of the house, and the faerie lights cast only a soft glow, a brush of gold on their bodies and face. Dante didn't say a word as he carefully eased Rook off of him, gently untangling their limbs. Then he slid off of the bench to stand at Rook's side, a silent monolith rising to face who was there.

Rook turned, and the woman stepped into the circle of light coming from the front porch. She was short, thick-waisted, and wore a knee-length floral dress covered in orange poppies with nearly matching tangerine-and-black flats. With her long silver-streaked black hair pulled back into a ponytail, her round face was hauntingly Manny's, round and creased with deep laugh lines bracketing her wide full mouth, her bright red lipstick a vivid slash of color against her shocked-to-pale skin.

Her eyes, however, were Dante's, rich with amber and honey, thickly lashed and tilted up at the corners, and when she stepped forward, she nearly stumbled, catching herself against the house with the flat of her hand. A carry-on purple suitcase sat on the cement walk behind her, matching the bag she clutched tightly in her free hand, and it trembled in her grasp, rattling until she carefully slid it between two of the porch's slats.

Turning back to face them, she squared her shoulders—another too familiar gesture—and asked, "*Mijo*, Who... who is this?"

Dante glanced down at Rook, as if seeing him for the first time, and Rook swallowed, trapped between a rock and a hard place he'd never guessed he'd have to squirm out of. Standing up, he was ready to make an excuse—any excuse—when Dante took his hand and held it, gently pulling Rook closer to his side.

"*Hola*, Mama." His smile was sad, resigned even, but the fire in his eyes was fierce, even in the dim light. Then Dante swallowed and said, "This is Rook, the man I hope one day I will be lucky enough to call my husband."

RHYS FORD is an award-winning author with several long-running LGBT+ mystery, thriller, paranormal, and urban fantasy series and was a 2016 LAMBDA finalist with her novel, *Murder and Mayhem*. She is published by Dreamspinner Press and DSP Publications.

She's also quite skeptical about bios without a dash of something personal, and really, who doesn't mention their cats, dog, and cars in a bio? She shares the house with Yoshi, a grumpy tuxedo cat, and Tam, a diabetic black pygmy panther, as well as a ginger cairn terrorist named Gus. Rhys is also enslaved to the upkeep a 1979 Pontiac Firebird and enjoys murdering make-believe people.

Rhys can be found at the following locations:

Blog: www.rhysford.com
Facebook: www.facebook.com/rhys.ford.author
Twitter: @Rhys_Ford

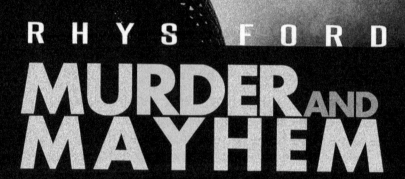

RHYS FORD

MURDER AND MAYHEM

Murder and Mayhem: Book One

Dead women tell no tales.

Former cat burglar Rook Stevens stole many a priceless thing in the past, but he's never been accused of taking a life—until now. It was one thing to find a former associate inside Potter's Field, his pop culture memorabilia shop, but quite another to stumble across her dead body.

Detective Dante Montoya thought he'd never see Rook Stevens again—not after his former partner falsified evidence to entrap the jewelry thief and Stevens walked off scot-free. So when he tackled a fleeing murder suspect, Dante was shocked to discover the blood-covered man was none other than the thief he'd fought to put in prison and who still makes his blood sing.

Rook is determined to shake loose the murder charge against him, even if it means putting distance between him and the rugged Cuban-Mexican detective who brought him down. If one dead con artist wasn't bad enough, others soon follow, and as the bodies pile up around Rook's feet, he's forced to reach out to the last man he'd expect to believe in his innocence—and the only man who's ever gotten under Rook's skin.

www.dreamspinnerpress.com

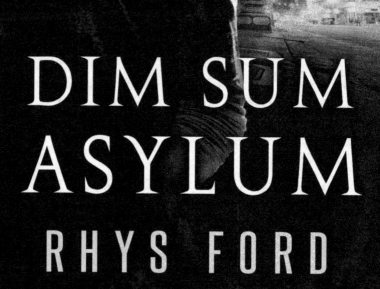

DIM SUM
ASYLUM

RHYS FORD

Welcome to Dim Sum Asylum: a San Francisco where it's a ho-hum kind of case when a cop has to chase down an enchanted two-foot-tall shrine god statue with an impressive Fu Manchu mustache that's running around Chinatown, trolling sex magic and chaos in its wake.

Senior Inspector Roku MacCormick of the Chinatown Arcane Crimes Division faces a pile of challenges far beyond his human-faerie heritage, snarling dragons guarding C-Town's multiple gates, and exploding noodle factories. After a case goes sideways, Roku is saddled with Trent Leonard, a new partner he can't trust, to add to the crime syndicate family he doesn't want and a spell-casting serial killer he desperately needs to find.

While Roku would rather stay home with Bob the Cat and whiskey himself to sleep, he puts on his badge and gun every day, determined to serve and protect the city he loves. When Chinatown's dark mystical underworld makes his life hell and the case turns deadly, Trent guards Roku's back and, if Trent can be believed, his heart... even if from what Roku can see, Trent is as dangerous as the monsters and criminals they're sworn to bring down.

www.dreamspinnerpress.com

THERE'S THIS GUY

Sometimes all a broken man needs is a bit of light and love.

RHYS FORD

How do you save a drowning man when that drowning man is you?

Jake Moore's world fits too tightly around him. Every penny he makes as a welder goes to care for his dying father, an abusive, controlling man who's the only family Jake has left. Because of a promise to his dead mother, Jake resists his desire for other men, but it leaves him consumed by darkness.

It takes all of Dallas Yates's imagination to see the possibilities in the fatigued art deco building on WeHo's outskirts, but what seals the deal is a shy smile from the handsome metal worker across the street. Their friendship deepens while Dallas peels back the hardened layers strangling Jake's soul. It's easy to love the sweet, artistic man hidden behind Jake's shattered exterior, but Dallas knows Jake needs to first learn to love himself.

When Jake's world crumbles, he reaches for Dallas, the man he's learned to lean on. It's only a matter of time before he's left to drift in a life he never wanted to lead and while he wants more, Jake's past haunts him, making him doubt he's worth the love Dallas is so desperate to give him.

www.dreamspinnerpress.com

FISH STICK FRIDAYS

RHYS FORD

Half Moon Bay: Book One

Deacon Reid was born bad to the bone with no intention of changing. A lifetime of law-bending and living on the edge suits him just fine—until his baby sister dies and he finds himself raising her little girl.

Staring down a family history of bad decisions and reaped consequences, Deacon cashes in everything he owns, purchases an auto shop in Half Moon Bay, and takes his niece, Zig, far away from the drug dens and murderous streets they grew up on. Zig deserves a better life than what he had, and Deacon is determined to give it to her.

Lang Harris is stunned when Zig, a little girl in combat boots and a purple tutu, blows into his bookstore, and then he's left speechless when her uncle, Deacon Reid, walks in hot on her heels. Lang always played it safe, but Deacon tempts him to step over the line… just a little bit.

More than a little bit. And Lang is willing to be tempted.

Unfortunately, Zig isn't the only bit of chaos dropped into Half Moon Bay. Violence and death strike, leaving Deacon scrambling to fight off a killer before he loses not only Zig but Lang too.

www.dreamspinnerpress.com